Dutchman's Puzzle

Marte Brengle

LOGAN BOOKS

Dutchman's Puzzle is a work of fiction. Names, characters, places and incidents are either the product of the author's imagination or are used fictitiously. Any resemblance to persons living or dead, actual events or locations is entirely coincidental.

Published in the United States of America
by Logan Books LLC

ISBN 978-0-9829280-4-2

Dutchman's Puzzle

Also by Marte Brengle

Closed Circuit

Author's Note

Several of the characters in *Dutchman's Puzzle* were first introduced in my previous novel *Closed Circuit*. While it's not essential to have read the previous book to figure out what's going on in this one, I think that it would help the reader to understand what motivates some of the people of Lyric. (Plus, I'm just totally impartially saying it's worth reading.)

There are similarities between the fictional town of Lyric and one of my favorite places on earth, Fairfield, Iowa (where a building much like the one Electronic Wizardry inhabits in these books really does stand on the northwest corner of the square). But keep in mind that Lyric is an imaginary place, even if bits and pieces of it resemble something real, and the inhabitants of Lyric are imaginary as well.

Chapter 1
Season's Greetings

January

Dave Van Meer guided the shuddering rattletrap delivery truck slowly down an alley that was almost invisible behind a wall of swirling snow. The journey had been one long wrestling match with the steering wheel and he was exhausted. He inched past a darker area that had to be the entrance to the loading dock he'd come all this way to find, slid to a stop and opened his door in hopes of being able to lean out and see where he was going. A blast of exhaust-smelling icy air and dirty snow-flakes swirled in, killing that idea in no time flat.

He coughed and yanked the door shut again, gritted his teeth and backed carefully toward the building, aiming by instinct since the side mirror was useless. Just as he came within a few feet of the dock, the truck slid sideways on the ice and one rear corner hit with a jolt that almost made him bite his tongue. The engine immediately gave up the ghost. He turned the key and got a rattling wheeze in response. There were only a few choice things to be said about the situation and he said them—but he had to admit that after nearly seven hours of being jolted around and half frozen, the stillness of the truck was actually a relief.

The truck's already anemic heater had failed miles back. He'd covered his legs with a ratty blanket he'd found behind the seat, and about all he could say about it was that it was better than nothing. The long wool scarf wrapped around his head and face and tucked into the collar of his Army-surplus jacket had kept that part of him passably warm in the icy cab. He pulled the blanket out from under him and threw it on the floor on the passenger side. Pushing the door open against the wind, he slid down into a nearly knee-deep snowdrift. They'd just have to do the best they could with the unloading.

With one hand on the side of the truck so he could stay upright, he plowed his way through the drifts to check the damage. The back of the truck wasn't dented too much, and it was such a piece of junk to begin with that he doubted its owners would notice even if large pieces fell off. The doors to the loading dock were closed. The dispatcher had told him to ring the bell and someone from the store would come and help him. Yeah, right. What bell? He nearly had his nose against the wall before he spotted the small button by the door. He did as instructed and waited, stamping his feet. Shit fire, he should have had more sense than to wear worn-out cowboy boots in a blizzard. Now he couldn't feel his toes. He punched the bell again, and again got no response.

Dave stood with his hand on the wall for a moment, thinking. Then he made his way unsteadily back down the alley and from there to the street. At least someone had cleared the sidewalk earlier, so the drifts there were only ankle high. All the lights in the store were out. He put a hand up to the window and peered inside. What the hell, did stores take snow days? Did this armpit town have a pay phone somewhere? Not for the first time, he cursed his stupidity in giving up his cell phone. There were no cars on the road, no houses nearby, not many lights on in what he could see of the town square half a block away. Well, nothing for it but to start walking before he froze his ass off. Surely there had to be a restaurant open somewhere, with a phone he could use. He shoved his hands deep into his pockets, hunched up his shoulders and got moving.

As he neared the corner his feet suddenly flew right out from under him and, unable to break his fall, he crashed down on his tailbone. *Oh, Jesus. Oh, Jesus.* He couldn't move. He'd die on the sidewalk in the middle of nowhere and nobody would know or care till they dug his body out in the spring. He managed to get his hands out of his pockets and tried to stand up, but it was no use. It hurt too much to move his legs and he knew his feet wouldn't stay under him anyway. The pain made tears slide down his face to solidify on the edge of his scarf. He struggled to prop himself up on his elbows so his back wouldn't freeze to the pavement.

"Hello?" It was a woman's voice, from his right. A dark blue Jeep had pulled to the curb. "Are you all right? Can I help?"

"Huh... huh..." He turned toward her as best he could, but he couldn't get the words out. He squeezed his eyes shut and shook his head. Even doing that was painful.

He heard the car door slam, and suddenly she was beside him. "Here, at least let me help you get up."

He shook his head and tried to speak. Finally he managed "Can't."

"Well, you've got to try, or we'll both be frozen to the sidewalk in a minute. Come on, let's give it a try."

He opened his eyes. She stood in front of him, snow boots firmly planted on either side of his cowboy boots. "Come on, grab my hands." Only her eyes were visible in the small space between her thick knitted hat and the scarf wrapped around her neck, nose and mouth. Snow was already sticking to the shoulders of her green wool coat. He struggled to sit up far enough to reach for her mittened hands. She leaned farther over to make it easier for him. He grabbed her hands and hung on.

"I can't... ow, ow, *ow!*" His feet were under him now, but his knees wouldn't straighten up. She pulled him slowly forward and somehow he made it to a more or less standing position. "*Aaaaaah!*" He wobbled and she caught him. She was nearly as tall as he was, so after a moment she was able to steady him on his feet.

"OK," she said, "lean on me and I'll get you into the car. Are you new here?"

"Ow... yeah, tried to deliver... *ow!* Oh crap, that hurts... to that store there, but I guess it's a snow day." He moved one foot and found that he could limp forward slowly. He didn't want to lean on her, but there seemed to be no other way to make his legs move. They inched across the sidewalk together.

"The power was out for over an hour, early this afternoon, so everyone pretty much closed up shop. Who sent you? Didn't they call to let you know the store was closed?"

"No phone." He gritted his teeth against the pain.

"Oh. Here, see if you can slide in." She pulled open the car door. He eased forward, still leaning on her shoulder, and held on to the top of the open door.

"I'll get your seat dirty."

"No more than my dog usually does. Get in, hurry, before all the hot air gets out."

He eased his butt very carefully onto the seat, tensing up with the effort. She helped him pull his feet into the car and closed the door. They hadn't let too much of the warm air out. He leaned back and managed to get settled and get his seat belt fastened. The woman slid into the driver's seat and turned to look at him, pushing down the scarf. She had friendly brown eyes and she looked to be about his age. He unwrapped his scarf too, leaving it draped around his neck.

"Do you need to see a doctor?" she said, sounding concerned. "I can take you to the ER."

"No. Thanks. I'll be all right."

"Are you sure? You took quite a fall."

"What could a doctor do, put my butt in a cast?" he said, irritated, hearing the tone in his voice as he said it. *Come on, it wasn't her fault.* He tried again. "Seriously, I think it'll be OK if I just give it some time. If there was anything really wrong I doubt I could have walked to the car."

"That's true. OK, but if you change your mind about that, let me know."

"I don't have insurance, so I'd just as soon not run up hospital bills if I don't have to."

"Fair enough. Where were you headed?" she asked. "Do you have a place to stay in town?"

"I brought a load of appliances and I just found out the store is closed. It wasn't snowing when I started out, and the radio in that piece of crap truck didn't work. So I had no idea what I was driving into, otherwise I would have stayed home." He shifted position, trying to get comfortable. It was no use. "I figured I'd find someplace to stay when I got here. Is everything else in town closed down too?"

"I don't think the motel would be closed. On a day like today they'll probably be so glad to have one customer they'll roll you out the red carpet." She smiled. "I'm Eleanor Ward."

5

"Dave Van Meer."

"Have you had anything to eat today, Dave?"

"Hit a fast food place a few hours ago." He suddenly realized he was hungry. "If there's anything open in town you can drop me off there. I need to find a phone anyway."

"Nothing open on the square, I don't think, and what passes for fast food places around here are not likely to have the A team on duty today. But we can go look, if you like."

"I don't want to put you to too much trouble."

"I think we can drive past every restaurant in town in about ten minutes even in the snow." She smiled. "It's no trouble. Do you have a suitcase or something in your truck?"

"Oh... yeah, duffel bag behind the seat. The truck's in back of the store. I'll get it."

"No you won't. Give me the keys."

Just turning sideways the amount necessary to get the keys out of his coat pocket was enough to convince him that her way was better. "Behind the passenger seat. Don't look at the other crap that's back there. It's been a long drive."

"Wouldn't dream of it. Don't you look in my back seat either. I've got kids. Hang on, I'll be right back."

Dave shifted on the seat and closed his eyes. He must have dozed off, because the blast of cold air when Eleanor opened the back door of the Jeep and tossed the bag onto the seat made him jump and sent a lightning bolt up his back. "*Shit!*"

She slid back into the driver's seat and handed over his keys. "Interesting key ring you've got there. What is that?"

He'd had that key ring so long he'd forgotten the shape of it. "It's a drafting square. Friend of mine made it for me a long time ago."

"What's it for?"

"Oh, just a memento." He smiled.

Eleanor looked at him for a moment, but he'd explained as much as he'd wanted to. "OK, off we go, then," she said, fastening her seat belt, and started the car. She pulled away from the curb and Dave bit his lip to keep from yelping as the motion made him shift in the wrong direction. She was right, though. It didn't look like any of the businesses on the square were open, since there were no lights visible through the snow. After circumnavigating the square, she turned the Jeep carefully onto the highway leading west out of town, where it was soon apparent that not even the McDonald's had its lights on.

Dave peered through the window, looking for anything that might be open. "Isn't there a restaurant in the motel?"

"We're about a quarter-mile from the motel and this is what there is," she answered. "It's just a mom and pop outfit and neither Mom nor Pop felt like cooking."

"Oh." There seemed little else to say. "Well, just drop me off and I'll manage. I'm not that hungry." She gave him a glance but said nothing.

The motel, clearly a relic of the 40s, was open and its VACANCY sign was glowing cheerfully through the swirling flakes. Eleanor parked right by the door. There were only two other cars in the parking lot and both of them were shrouded in snow. Dave took a deep breath and got out of the Jeep all on his own, declining Eleanor's offer of help to the door, although he did let her open it for him. Once inside he was greeted with delight by the desk clerk, who had been glumly watching the Weather

Channel. Dave leaned on the counter, inched his wallet out of his back pocket, and paid cash for two nights. After accepting his room key he looked at the vending machines in the lobby, which both sported OUT OF ORDER signs.

"Sorry," said the desk clerk. "They're actually working but there's nothing inside because the guy who's supposed to fill them up couldn't get here."

Dave shrugged and headed for the door. Eleanor followed and moved past him to get his bag out of the back seat. "Well, thanks for everything, Eleanor," he said. "Without you I'd have had to wait till they dug me out in the spring." He took the bag from her and slung it over his shoulder, wincing. The room was only a short distance away and he started walking toward it, picking his way through the snow with care.

"You know what?" said Eleanor, from behind him. "Why don't you come to my place for supper? I've got a Crock Pot full of soup that's been simmering all day and I can make some garlic bread to go with it. You're welcome to join us. That is, if you think you can survive 11-year-old twins."

He was speechless for a moment. "Um... well, thanks, Eleanor, but I'd better not."

She'd wrapped the scarf around her face again, but he thought she might be smiling. "We don't dress for dinner at my place, if that's what you're worried about."

"Good Lord. That never crossed my mind," he snapped. "Sorry. Didn't mean to snap at you. I just don't think you should invite a complete stranger into your house. Who knows what kind of lowlife I might turn out to be?"

"I appreciate your concern. When you get right down to it, for all you know I could be a black widow who'll poison your dinner and bury you in the garden as soon as it thaws. So that makes us even, doesn't it? But honestly I don't think you'll be too dangerous for a while at least, with that bruised butt and those boots. I'm pretty sure I can outrun you, and remember, I've got a dog. Come to think of it, I should get that bag away from you right now and search it for weapons."

He stared at her, open-mouthed. And then, for no reason at all, he laughed. "Oh man, you don't want to do that. The bag is full of toxic waste. Been a long time since the last laundromat."

"I can call home and tell my kids to arm themselves with a couple of aluminum bats and their spiked shoes if it'll make you feel better. They're pretty darn athletic and both of them hit home runs all the time." She pulled one mitten off with her teeth, took her phone out of her coat pocket and flipped it open.

He laughed again, shaking his head in disbelief. This small act of kindness after the long wretched day caught up with him all at once, and he had to clench his hands tightly on the bag's strap to keep emotion from over-whelming him. He took a deep breath, held it for a moment and let it out slowly. "OK," he said, finally, "you win. Let me throw the bag in my room and wash up a bit. I would love to join you for supper and do my best to survive the twins and keep them from hitting home runs on my head. After all, I survived this trip. I bet I can survive anything."

Chapter 2
The Comforts of Home

As the Jeep moved slowly through the silent streets, Dave began to fret. He'd never been any good in social situations. In ordinary workplace interactions he was an ace, but casual, social conversation, especially with women—not so much. The day had wiped him out, physically and emotionally, and now he was in completely unfamiliar territory. But what could he do about it? Asking Eleanor to forget it and take him back to the motel would make him look like an oaf. At least the pain from the fall had receded, so he told himself to relax and make the best of it. No sense fretting himself into a panic attack. How long could it take to eat soup and garlic bread, anyway? He leaned back against the seat and was actually starting to doze again when Eleanor spoke.

"Will your truck be OK where you left it?"

"You'd likely know more about that than I would. It's not going anywhere under its own steam."

"One of us can call the store when we get to my place. I think they have voicemail. At the very least you should let them know where to find you."

"Yeah. I guess you can tell I don't have much experience with small towns." He paused. "Don't take that in a bad way. I was just thinking that if I left the truck like that in New Jersey I'd come back five minutes later and it'd be stripped."

Eleanor chuckled. "This is definitely not New Jersey. In this town the truck thieves are smart enough to stay inside when it snows. Are you from New Jersey?"

"I've been living there for a while, is all." Dave smiled. "Oh well, at least this time it wasn't my truck."

"You have your own truck?"

"Not any more."

Eleanor glanced at him and was quiet for a moment, but he didn't want to talk about it. "I work at the real estate office," she said, turning back to watching the road. "Not exactly a hotbed of excitement, but it pays the bills."

"You sell houses?"

"No, I'm the office manager. Much safer paycheck that way."

Dave couldn't imagine what a real estate office in a small town would do, nor why they'd need an office manager. Just his ignorance showing again, he thought wryly. "Yeah, working on commission is the pits. I tried that for a while. Didn't last long."

"You sold houses?"

"Appliances," he said. "Ironic, isn't it?"

"And now you deliver them. I bet that's easier."

"In the springtime it probably will be."

The blowing snow made it difficult to see what kinds of neighborhoods they were passing through and what the architecture looked like. The houses were set farther back from the street than he was used to and the occasional wind-blown gap in the snow showed him only enough to make him think that nothing new had been built on these streets for decades. He liked the way the overhanging canopy of snow-laden trees reflected the streetlights here and there through the sideways-shifting curtains of white. He could see just enough to make him change his original impression. This town might not be quite as close to Armpit Village as he'd thought.

Eleanor eased the Jeep around a corner and pulled into a short gravel driveway, close to the solid wood door of a weatherbeaten old garage that stood about twenty feet from the back of the house. The house itself was painted Federal blue and had gingerbread gables and tall windows.

"Want me to open the garage door for you?" He thought he could manage that much.

"That'd take a miracle. I don't think that door's been opened since about 1965. The springs are all rusted inside and I'm afraid they'd snap and kill someone if we tried. We just use the garage for storing junk. But thanks anyway."

Dave slid out onto the driveway and was glad she'd turned his offer down. He was still not able to walk normally, his butt hurt, and his boots were no more suited to snow over gravel than they had been to snow over concrete. Still, he pulled himself up the worn wooden steps to the back porch without assistance, so he counted that as progress.

Eleanor lifted the back hatch of the Jeep, lowered the tailgate and pulled out a canvas bag full of groceries. She declined his offer of help with a smile. "I need my exercise. This is better than paying for a gym membership. I'm just glad the supermarket stayed open long enough. The kids and I would have been OK, but the dog would never have forgiven me."

They scraped most of the snow off their shoes on the porch and stepped into what Eleanor called the mud

13

room. Dave unwrapped his scarf, took his faded blue baseball cap off, and hung them both on a wooden peg on the wall, next to a rack that held four aluminum bats, two mitts and two caps with a team logo on them. Eleanor handed him a thick wooden hanger for his jacket. Since she had slipped off her boots and left them by the radiator to dry, he did the same. He'd forgotten that one of his socks had a hole in the heel. *Argh.* Well, nothing he could do about it now.

The kitchen was full of delicious smells. His stomach growled, and he hoped she hadn't heard.

If she did, she gave no sign of it. "Go on in the living room and have a seat," she said, pointing the way. "The bathroom is to your left if you need it. I'll call my mom and let her know that I'm home, so she can get rid of the twins. Then we'll see if they make it across the street without stuffing each other's coats full of snow."

The furniture was both well-worn and well-made. Dave could tell by the pile of books beside it that one wing chair, with matching hassock, was someone's favorite place. He eased his way into one corner of the couch, pushing aside two patchwork-covered pillows to make room for himself, and tried to relax. It was no use; all he really wanted was to get this over with and get back to the motel.

To distract himself, he looked around at the room. There was ornately carved crown molding at the top of the light blue walls, and the doors were obviously original, paneled solid wood with brass escutcheons behind the glass doorknobs. A tall hutch made of some kind of dark wood stood against the wall across from him, filled with mementos. An 11 x 14 framed photo of Eleanor hugging her son and daughter sat in the center of the top shelf, along with school pictures from various grades and assorted small oddities. He could see no accompanying photo of their father.

To his left, against the wall, was... what on earth was it? Some kind of large wooden drying rack? Would she hang things to dry in the living room? It looked big enough to hold an entire washer-load. Maybe she didn't have a dryer. Giving up the puzzle, he leaned his head back and admired the plaster rosette around the ceiling light. He'd just close his eyes for a second...

An explosion of sound jarred him awake. Part of it, he realized belatedly, was a door slamming. Voices came from the other room. A dog was yapping.

"She started it!"

"He..."

"I don't care who started it. Either you finish it or I will."

"Not FAIR!"

"Since when have I ever been fair?"

Two young voices spoke at once. "Never." "Never." There was a brief silence and then mother and twins started laughing.

The dog nosed its way around the corner and gave a surprised woof. Dave leaned slowly forward so as not to startle him, and extended a hand, knuckles down. The dog was dubious. "Hello, dog," Dave said gently. The dog, tail not quite wagging but not quite still, edged over to give the hand a wary sniff, then backed away to a safe distance and sat down. Dave was amused, remembering how Eleanor had mentioned him as her protector. This was a medium-sized, multicolored, long-haired mutt who looked like he might possibly be fierce enough to shred a leather bedroom slipper.

"We've got company," said Eleanor from the kitchen, "and if you guys don't settle down he's going to run straight back out in the snow to get away."

"Who?"

"Nobody you've met. Let's go in the living room and say hi."

Oh no, thought Dave. The room seemed very crowded, all of a sudden. The twins, tall for their age, resembled each other not at all, except for their height and the rosy aftereffects of cold winter air on their faces. The boy had his mother's dark brown hair, with hazel eyes and an angular face dusted with freckles. The girl's hair was golden brown, her face was rounder and her eyes were green, and she had braces on her teeth. They both looked as athletic as promised. Dave tried to smile.

"I see you've already met Phydeaux," said Eleanor. The dog looked at her and thumped his tail on the floor. "And this is Andrew and Rachel. Kids, this is Dave Van Meer. I picked him up off the sidewalk downtown."

Various expressions of scorn and ridicule came from the twins while Dave had to laugh at the all-too-apt description. "No, she really did," he assured them. "I definitely should not have worn old cowboy boots on a day like today and I landed flat on my butt. Actually, if I'd had any sense I wouldn't have been driving on a day like today, but I didn't figure that out till I got here."

"Where'd you come from?" asked Andrew

"Joliet, believe it or not."

"Why wouldn't we believe it?" Rachel demanded.

"Kids, that's enough," said their mom, firmly. "Go get washed up and set the table for supper and feed this dratted dog."

The twins issued token protests at this, then did as they were told, having established that they were only doing it because they chose to, not because they'd been asked. The sphere of noise shifted back into the other room, and dishes started clanking. Dave looked at Eleanor for the first time. She had dark brown hair to go with the warm brown eyes, and a lovely, rounded face. She wore a soft, faded yellow turtleneck sweater over equally faded jeans, and an echo of his grandmother saying "Pleasingly plump" with approval went through his mind. He wondered if she'd made the freeform silver-and-stone pendant that hung from a delicate silver chain. He realized he was staring and tried to find something to say.

"Um... Fido?" he asked. "I don't think I've ever actually met a dog named Fido."

She smiled. "It's spelled P-H-Y-D-E-A-U-X. I figured he's a one of a kind dog and needed a one of a kind name."

"Hello, Phydeaux," he said, holding out his hand again, and the dog inched forward and licked him. Dave gave him a pat and Phydeaux gave Dave a wag. Cordial relationships established, the dog departed for the kitchen.

"Supper should be ready in just a few minutes. We're just waiting for the garlic bread to warm up. It's my own recipe—the garlic's baked right into the bread dough."

"Really? I'd never heard of that. Do you make all your own bread?"

"Well, actually, the bread machine does most of the work." She waved a hand. "I bake a lot more now that I've got a machine to take care of everything for me. I did have to find a special container for the garlic loaves, though, because if we used those for sandwiches it might cause a few social problems."

"Yeah," said Dave, "nothing like greeting your teacher with garlic breath."

"Or your boss. Well, let me go check and see if we're ready to eat. How are you feeling?"

"Much better." He smiled, feeling more at ease now that the end was in sight. "Eleanor, thanks for inviting me."

She laughed. "You're welcome, but wait till after you've eaten my cooking and lived to tell the tale and then we'll talk." As she turned around, he noticed that her hair was in a single braid and nearly reached her waist. Long hair. Another check mark on his list of approval.

⊠ ⊠ ⊠

As Dave ate soup and garlic bread and talked with the twins about traveling across country in a truck, Eleanor got a chance to look him over. His well-worn green plaid flannel shirt and the tanned, somewhat weatherbeaten skin on his angular face gave him the look of an outdoorsman. He was a little taller than she was, maybe 5'9". There was a touch of grey in his light brown hair, but despite the lines on his face around his mouth and his startlingly blue eyes, she got the impression he was pretty much the same age she was. He reminded her a bit of a young Kirk Douglas, without the dimple in his chin. Now that he'd had a chance to thaw out and recover, he seemed somewhat more at ease. Well, at least he was at ease with the twins. Somehow, he didn't manage to look her way very much. She conceded that keeping up with the twins did require a good deal of attention.

After supper, the twins were shooed into their rooms to do their homework. "Mom! School was CLOSED today! We didn't HAVE homework" was met with "Then you can do the homework you didn't do last night" and a parental glare that brooked no nonsense. Dave and Eleanor took their coffee cups into the living room and he found that he could walk and sit without wincing. Phydeaux, who'd obviously revised his first opinion of Dave, settled in at his feet, tail wagging. Dave patted him and Phydeaux wagged faster.

Looking up from the dog, Dave asked "Do you have a phone book? I better leave a message for the appliance store so they know why the truck's blocking their loading dock and where they can find me."

"Sure." She handed him the phone book, thin enough to look like a pamphlet, and the cordless phone, then got up and went back into the kitchen to refill her coffee cup.

When she returned, Dave said he had let the phone ring fifteen times and had gotten no answer of any kind. "I'll try them again tomorrow. The truck will have to be OK where it is."

"I'm sure it will be. We don't have much in the way of big-time thieves in Lyric."

"Larrick? What kind of town name is that?"

"It's spelled L-Y-R-I-C but pronounced funny. The first settlers were an extended family who came here from Europe someplace, and the matriarch had read the word somewhere and liked it, but nobody knew how to pronounce it. So she took her best guess and that's what we're stuck with."

"I didn't do much more than look at the map to see what road to take, so to be honest with you I'd forgotten the name of the town. Interesting. Every place has its own peculiarities, I guess."

"Some more so than others." She smiled.

"Speaking of which... If you don't mind my asking, what on earth is that thing over there? A drying rack?"

19

She chuckled. "I guess you haven't seen a quilting frame before?"

"I can't remember the last time I even saw a quilt. How does it work?"

"Oh, once you've got all the pieces made for the quilt, you lay them down, pin them together, and then put them on the frame. It holds everything while you sew the layers together."

"You do that all by hand? Sounds like a lot of work."

"Yes and no. I put the individual squares of the quilt together with a sewing machine, but I like to sew the layers together by hand. I don't have the latest one ready to put on the frame yet..." She stopped for a moment. "Oh, you'll probably laugh, but believe it or not, the pattern I'm working on right now is called Dutchman's Puzzle."

He did laugh. "Must be some complicated piece of work."

"Of course it is," she said. But she smiled. "If you're around long enough, I'll show it to you when it's ready to be quilted."

He smiled back. "I guess you'll have to send me a picture of it."

"That's almost as good. Be sure to let me know your address."

"Have you made a lot of quilts?"

"Oh, not a lot, but it's something I enjoy doing, so I usually make at least one a year."

"Do you make them for sale?"

"No, but I've given a few as gifts. And people have asked me to make them as wedding presents, and they pay for the materials and pick the pattern. But I've never made any specifically for sale."

"You made these pillows, then," he said, pointing to the ones beside him on the couch.

"My first experiments. If they'd turned out badly, that would have been the end of it."

"This one looks complicated. What's it called?"

"Mariner's Compass, and yeah, leave it to me not to know you don't start out with something like that. But since I didn't know it wasn't a beginner piece, I sailed right in. So to speak. After that, everything looked easy."

They sat there in congenial silence for a moment. Finally Dave looked up. "I hate to drag you out of a nice warm house on a night like this, but I've already fallen asleep twice. Would you mind running me back out to the motel?"

"No problem at all." She crossed the room and looked over the top of the cafe curtains in the front window. "Looks like the snow's just about stopped."

"That's good."

As Eleanor went back into the kitchen, Dave stared into his nearly empty coffee cup, suddenly wishing he could stay here in this warm and welcoming world. No, better to get out now before she found out what a total fraud he was. He got up and put the cup on the kitchen counter and went to get wrapped up for the bitter outside, where he belonged.

Chapter 3
Social Calls

By the next morning the city's crews had done a reasonable job of getting the drifts off the streets and the sun was doing its part to get rid of the rest, but no one in Lyric's one real estate office was planning on going anywhere that day. Eleanor worked on the office calendar, checked in with their crew of maintenance workers, and chatted with Ron and Linda, the husband and wife who owned the agency, as they caught up with their own paperwork and did some office cleaning.

The three had been friends since grade school. Ron and Linda had married right out of high school, had gone to college together, had gotten real estate licenses together, and after all this time had come to look a lot like each other—short, round, cheerful, with faces that were nearly always smiling, and showing no signs of age. Ron's eyes were blue and his hair was blonde and carefully combed; Linda's eyes were hazel and her hair was dark brown and artfully mussed. They wore matching maroon blazers and white shirts while on duty in the office.

The coffee maker was burbling out its second pot of the day and Ron had just suggested getting a pizza for lunch when the front door opened, letting in a shaft of brilliant winter sunlight, a small pile of blown snow, and

Dave Van Meer, who was well wrapped against the cold and holding a large plastic bag.

Ron perked up. This was someone he hadn't seen before, and any newcomer might be a prospective buyer. "Hi! Haven't seen you here before. I'm Ron Richardson. What can I do for you?" He stepped forward, hand outstretched.

Dave unwrapped his scarf, took off a glove and shook the offered hand with a smile. "Dave Van Meer. Sorry, I'm just here to see Eleanor."

"Well, there she is. Would you like some coffee, Dave? We just made more. Here, let me get your jacket."

"I'd love some. Thanks." He stuffed his gloves in his pockets and then handed Ron the jacket, his scarf, and his baseball cap and sat down in the chair closest to Eleanor's desk. Linda put a steaming mug with the agency logo on the table beside him. He declined the offer of additives. "Black is fine."

"Dave brought a load of appliances in, and House and Home had no way to tell him the store was closed yesterday," Eleanor explained to her colleagues. "I picked him up off the sidewalk by the store." Ron and Linda gave her startled looks. "No, really," she said. "I was on my way home from the grocery store and happened to see him take a bad fall. He ended up having supper with us and managed to survive the kids and the dog." She turned back to Dave. "Are you feeling better today? What happened with the truck?"

"I'm much better, thanks. And as for the truck, it's good news and bad news. Paul from the motel gave me a lift into town first thing this morning, and the guys at the store didn't mind me leaving the truck there. They had no idea the delivery was coming, because they assumed I'd be smart enough not to keep on driving through a blizzard.

Well, they were polite enough not to put it that way, but that was a given." He smiled. "We got all the appliances unloaded and they were fine, but when I tried to get the truck started to at least get it out of the way it was no go. Had me a fine little old argument with the trucking company about that. It didn't stop till I told them I'd taken pictures of the engine and those tires before I started out and I'd turn them in to the Interstate Commerce Commission if they got on my case any more about it."

"Smart move," said Ron.

"I was just shining them on. Don't even own a camera. But they don't need to know that. Anyway, it's their truck and their problem. Good thing I made them pay me up front. I'm done with that outfit. The appliance store guys just laughed. They said they could get a tow truck to move it out of the way and they'd take the cost off the invoice for the appliances and let the company send someone to come get it. Oh, and then on my way over here I stopped by the surplus store and got some real snow boots." He held up one foot for everyone's approval. "Nobody else is going to have to pick me up off the sidewalk again if I can help it."

Eleanor laughed. "Oh, so that's what's in the bag, those poor old cowboy boots. I'm surprised the surplus store guys didn't offer to throw them out for you in their hazardous-waste bin."

"They did. Funny thing, I turned 'em down on that."

"You might consider getting a real hat, too," said Eleanor with a wink.

"I have a real hat." He pointed at his faded blue baseball cap on the coat rack. "And," he said, rummaging in the bag, "I got some earmuffs to go over it, so I'm all set." He held them up for approval.

"If you say so. Too bad they don't make a baseball cap with ear flaps. So what happens next?"

"Bus out of town, back to where I came from."

The other three laughed. Dave looked around, wondering what was so funny.

"There is no bus service out of this town, Dave," said Ron. "No taxis, no train, no nothing. We used to have all that, but that was years ago. The closest bus station's in the next county."

Dave blinked, momentarily at a loss. "Well, I guess I'll have to figure something else out," he said, "unless I can talk someone into driving me to wherever the bus station is." He concentrated on the coffee mug, not looking at any of the other people in the office.

"Oh, I think we could manage that," said Eleanor, easily, "but I really doubt there's a bus out of there for a couple days. Why don't you stick around at least for the weekend, and I'll drop you off in town on Sunday afternoon? You can stay over there if you need to wait a day or so for the next bus."

"I've imposed on you enough already, Eleanor."

"You can ask these guys—nobody imposes on me, no way no how." She smiled. Her colleagues emphatically agreed.

"She kicks our butts so nobody else gets a chance to," said Linda. "That's why we hired her."

"Got anyplace else you need to go this morning, Dave?" Ron asked. "If not, want to join us for lunch? I was just talking about getting a pizza."

"That sounds great. How about I pay for the pizza to make up for interrupting your office's busy day?"

"Busy day, yeah right. You're on."

After the men had left, Linda turned to Eleanor. "Are you out of your *mind?* Picking a... an *axe murderer* up off the sidewalk and taking him *home* with you?"

"Oh, come on, it's not like that."

"You're kidding, right?"

"No, really. He was wearing those worn-out cowboy boots and fell smack on his tail. I was driving back from the grocery store and saw him walking along, and all of a sudden his feet went right out from under him. He had his hands in his pockets and couldn't break the fall. Couldn't even get up."

"And?"

"And nothing. I fed him some soup, he survived the twins and the dog, I dropped him at the motel, end of story."

"I still can't believe you went and invited him in like that."

Eleanor sighed. "Well, there was more to it than just that. The poor guy had been driving through the snow for hours, had no way to find out the store was closed, and when we drove around looking for a place for him to get something to eat nothing was open. I took him to the motel and I saw him looking at the vending machines and they were all empty and all he did was shrug. It just broke my heart. So I offered to feed him. And you'll be happy to know he raised the same objections you did."

"Really?"

"Yup. He told me I shouldn't be inviting strangers into my house and I didn't know what kind of a lowlife he might be, and I told him we were even because he had no way of knowing if I'd poison his supper and bury him out back. The thing is, we'd been driving around for half an hour by then and... well, it just felt like it was the right thing to do. I liked him. I don't know why."

Linda shook her head, skeptically. "OK, you didn't get Ted Bundy this time. But you really should be more careful."

"You're right, but come on, have you ever known me not to be careful?"

Linda raised her eyebrows for a moment, then shrugged. "All right. You were there and I wasn't. You know, he does seem like a nice guy."

"He is. And the kids like him."

"OK, I'll shut up. You've always been good at reading people, so that means Dave probably isn't an axe murderer."

"No, he's not. I just got the feeling he's a genuinely nice person, and you don't meet one of those every day."

Linda started to say something, thought better of it, and turned her attention to clearing brochures, pens, and other bits of debris off the table at the side of the room so they'd have somewhere to put the pizza box. She put an OUT TO LUNCH sign on the door, not that there were any prospective buyers to turn away.

When the last greasy, fragrant square of pizza had vanished, hands had been washed and the evidence hustled outside to the trash, Dave asked "Can you guys give me directions to the library?"

"Oh, that's one place in town you really can't miss." said Linda. "Go back to the square, walk south on the east side, and look for the castle on your right."

"Castle? Say what?"

"It's one of Lyric's real conversation pieces. Once upon a time, the mayor's brother the architect had some Arthurian fantasies, and wound up with the contract for the library building. You'll see what I mean when you get there. Turrets, arrow slits, the whole nine yards. The front door looks like they just removed the drawbridge."

"Um... OK. A little nepotism goes a long way?"

"Exactly!"

"I'll do my best to appreciate the 'conversation piece,' then. I was thinking of catching up on some newspapers and maybe finding out a bit more about Lyric."

"The library's the place, all right. Ask Debbie at the reference desk. She'll show you where to look."

"I'll walk part of the way with you," said Ron, heading to the back to get his coat and hat. "I have some ad copy to drop off at the newspaper office."

Shrugging into his jacket and taking his scarf and cap off the coat rack by the door, Dave asked, casually, as if it had only just come to mind, "Eleanor? You fed me last night, how about I feed you guys tonight?"

"Oh, thanks, Dave, that's very nice of you, but the kids and I are having supper with a friend tonight."

"Oh. Well, maybe some other time." His shoulders drooped ever so slightly, and then he straightened up, put on the hat and scarf and dug his new earmuffs out of the bag.

As he put his hand against the door to push out, Eleanor said "You know, the supper isn't exactly a formal affair. Why don't I check with my friend and see if she's got room for one more?"

"Eleanor..." he shook his head.

"We went through this last night. If you're an axe murderer, these guys know your name and you'll have to compound the crime by carjacking someone if you want to get out of town. Seriously, though, if you don't want to go, that's not a problem. I just thought you might like to have one more home-cooked meal before you leave."

Dave looked down, shifting slightly from foot to foot. He really did not want to do this, but didn't know a polite way to say so. On the other hand, who in their right mind would agree to having some random stranger dragged in off the street? Figuring the friend would hit the ceiling and he'd be spared, he finally said "I... OK. If you're sure your friend..." He shrugged, letting the sentence trail off.

"Don't worry. I'll make absolutely sure she thinks it's OK." Eleanor smiled. "Tell you what, why don't you stop back here around 4:30, and if we're good to go we can pick up the kids at the after-school program. I'll go home a little early and change into some real clothes." She waved a hand at the white blouse and dark slacks she was wearing. "How does that sound? If it doesn't work out, I can make you some sandwiches and haul you back out to the motel, or just drop you at Mickey D's. Now that you've got some real winter gear the walk from there won't be a hazard to your butt."

"I... all right." He was already kicking himself for not saying no to this harebrained scheme.

"Good. Have fun in the castle."

❇❇❇

After the door swung closed behind the men, Linda rounded on Eleanor. "What on *earth* are you doing? You better hope he's not an axe murderer or Ruth will never forgive you. If she lives."

Eleanor found she had no answer to that.

"Seriously," said Linda, "aren't you being awfully pushy? The guy just wanted to deliver his appliances and get out of town, and you haven't even known him for 24 hours yet, and now you're trying to drag him off to someone else's house uninvited and she doesn't know him from a hole in the wall either."

Eleanor opened her mouth, then closed it again. Linda was right. She thought about it for a moment. "Well, now that you put it that way, yeah, it *is* awfully pushy. I... I

30

don't know why I did it. Do you think I should just tell him that Ruth said no and let it go at that?"

"That's definitely what I would do. But I'm not you."

"Maybe I should... well, let me talk this over with Ruth. Between the two of you maybe someone can beat some sense into my head."

"Good idea. Take your cell phone in the bathroom and I'll crank up the music out here."

"Heck of a way to get some privacy in this place." But she said it with a smile as she took her phone out of her purse.

Ten minutes later, she returned to report that Ruth had been surprised but had said it was all right. "Adam's on his way, which I didn't realize. He'll be there by the time we arrive, and he's a lot bigger than Dave is."

"Well, then, I guess that settles it," said Linda. "I still think you're out of your mind, but if you live, I want to hear all about it on Monday."

"Deal," said Eleanor, putting away the phone.

⊠⊠⊠

When Dave returned at 4:30, Ron was just turning the sign on the door to read CLOSED. "We'd have done this an hour ago if we hadn't thought it'd confuse you," he joked.

"Not many mansions for sale in the winter, huh," said Dave, unbuttoning his jacket. The office was really toasty compared to the outside, where the sun had already gone down behind the buildings on the west side of the square and the wind had picked up.

"Don't mind Mr. Real Estate," said Eleanor, taking her purse out of her desk drawer. "And Ruth says it's fine with her to bring you over. She's making chili and cornbread and there's plenty to go around. I'll need to get the twins into plastic bags first if last time was any indication, but otherwise we're good to go."

"Oh... um.... great," said Dave, trying to sound like he meant it. *Damn!* he thought. "Should I change into something better than this?" He brushed at the front of his red plaid flannel shirt and looked down at the small hole on the left leg of his jeans.

"Did you not notice what I'm wearing?" said Eleanor, standing up to show off a dark blue flannel shirt and faded jeans. "Let's go grab the twins."

Their dinner destination turned out to be on the upper floor of an interesting old two-story building on the northwest corner of the square. To take his mind off the upcoming social minefield, Dave concentrated on the architectural details. He admired the vaguely Palladian trio of high-arched windows facing the square, the well-preserved red brick walls, and the ornamental details around the roof. On the side of the building was a staircase surrounded by what looked like a board-and-batten tunnel leading up to the second floor. The old wooden stairs inside were worn thin in their centers, and the railings had long since lost all their paint on the upper surface. The twins racketed up at top speed, proving beyond all doubt that everything was more sturdy than it looked.

By the time Eleanor and Dave had reached the halfway point, the twins had gained entrance and their hostess was standing on the top landing smiling down at them. She had a heart-shaped face and her honey-blonde hair was pulled back in a scrunchie, and she was wearing a somewhat spotted green apron over a dark green turtle-neck sweater and tan corduroy pants. Dave gave her a quick glance and the briefest of smiles and said hello when she was introduced as Ruth Peyton, then sought out someplace to sit inside the apartment.

The couch was already occupied by a tall man with dark curly hair and a mustache, and the twins had disappeared round the corner into the kitchen and were pulling dishes out of the cupboards to set the table. "Hi Adam!" said Eleanor. "Glad to see you made it through the blizzard."

"I made darn sure it wasn't snowing before I started out," the tall man said with a big grin. "Hi," he said, getting up and extending a hand to Dave. "I'm Adam Talbott. Ruth's boyfriend. I am still your boyfriend, right, Ruth?"

"Not for much longer if you don't settle down, pal," said Ruth with an answering grin.

"Um... hi. Dave Van Meer," said Dave, giving a brief shake and hating the fact that he had to look up at Adam and wishing he'd never been dumb enough to agree to this.

"Come on, take your coat off and sit down," said Adam. "I know from experience that the twins will take up more room than ten people in the kitchen, so we'd better stay out of the way."

Feeling trapped already, Dave handed Ruth his jacket, hat and scarf and pushed himself into the other corner of the couch. His face felt like a mask, trying to smile and respond to Adam's casual conversation-starting questions, but the other man didn't seem to see anything amiss. Yes, Dave was a trucker, delivered a load of appliances and got stuck in the icy parking lot. The truck belonged to the cheap-ass company that had paid him for the trip and it was their problem now. Didn't watch sports much, didn't follow any team in particular... oh, God, would it never be time to eat and get out of here?

But when the twins finally announced that dinner was ready, Dave found that he felt more trapped than ever. He made himself walk to the table and find a place to sit down, and hoped everyone would be busy eating and wouldn't require him to talk much. For a while, the conversation swirled around him, and he began to relax, but then the old familiar feeling of sounds beating against his ears began again. He fought down rising panic. If he made a run for the door, he'd hurt these kind people's feelings, and he'd have no place to go once he was out. He excused himself to go to the bathroom.

Once there, he ran cool water in the sink and rubbed some of it on his face. He made an effort to breathe slowly. It was no use, though. He sighed and dug the small container out of his pocket, looked at it with distaste, and then bowed to the inevitable and swallowed one pill. If he stayed in the bathroom much longer they'd think he fell in. It wouldn't take too long for the pill to start working. He picked up what he hoped was a guest towel, rubbed his face and hands dry and took a couple of deep breaths.

When he rejoined the others at the table he tried to be calm and asked Andrew to pass the cornbread. The problem would go away soon. He could get through this. He realized that Andrew was saying "Adam, you can take Dave with you tomorrow!"

"Sorry, I was paying attention to the cornbread," Dave managed. "Take me where?"

"Andrew said you'd come from Joliet," said Adam. "I'm driving back to Chicago tomorrow afternoon and I'd be happy to drop you off."

Dave shook his head. "I'm not from Joliet. That's just where I picked up the load. But thanks anyway."

"You said you came from there," said Andrew. "Where did you really come from?"

34

"Andrew," said Eleanor, "that's enough. You don't need to be so nosy. I'm sorry, Dave, these two are just endlessly curious."

"It's all right. I... ah, I've actually been moving around the past couple years, trying to figure out where to go next. I was always stuck in one place when I was growing up, so it felt like time to see more of the world."

"So that's why you drive a truck," said Rachel with an air of complete satisfaction.

"Yep, you're right. Best way to see places, figure out which ones look good." He took another bite of cornbread.

"Don't you like Lyric?" Andrew chimed in.

"What did I say about being nosy?" Eleanor said sharply.

Dave chewed and swallowed the cornbread while he considered this. "I hadn't really thought about Lyric. It seems pretty good so far, except for the place where I fell down." He smiled at Andrew. "Do you like Lyric?"

"No, it's stupid. Mom, can we drive around like Dave does, sometime?"

"Maybe when you're older you can drive yourself. For now you'll just have to put up with staying right here."

General grumbling. "Why don't you two clear the table and serve the dessert," said Ruth. The twins got up.

"Nice diversion," said Eleanor, *sotto voce*.

"Experience counts," said Ruth, equally softly. The children were loading the dishwasher and appeared not to hear.

By the time everyone was settled with a plate of brownies the twins had moved on to squabbling about school. This, all the adults cheerfully tuned out. Dave was feeling less trapped now, and even asked a few questions about Ruth's repair shop downstairs, which Eleanor had told him about. They'd only recently started fixing computers, Ruth said, and were getting a lot more business doing that than fixing other things. She wasn't sure why they'd never thought about doing computer repairs till the previous summer, but it hadn't taken her and her assistant Chet long to get up to speed with it. "I don't know a thing about computers," Dave admitted. "But I guess it's inevitable that I'm going to have to learn. The trucking company people were really surprised that I don't have an email address."

"Listen," said Ruth with a smile, "if Chet and I can figure it out I know you can." Not knowing anything about Chet, Dave assumed it was a vote of confidence.

"The twins are getting to be real computer aces too," said Eleanor. "I have to work hard to keep track of what they're up to. Outsmarting smart kids is a full time job."

"I'm glad I don't have to do that. I'd never stand a chance." Dave smiled, settled back, and bit into his brownie, which was spectacularly good. He said so.

"It should be," said Eleanor. "That's one of the few recipes my mom's been willing to share. She's got some other recipes that you'd think were CIA secrets, the way she guards them. But this one she gave up after Ruth pestered her for years."

"Your mom sounds like quite a character," said Dave, politely.

"Like mother, like daughter," laughed Ruth, and ducked as Eleanor took a playful swat at her.

"Ruth?" said Andrew. "When we're done with dessert, can we look at some comic books?"

Ruth looked at Eleanor, who thought it over and said "If you guys get the table all cleaned up first and go wash your hands."

That seemed to be plenty enough motivation for the twins, who immediately started gathering up dishes and debris. Ruth explained to Dave, "My brother Rick was a collector, and he left a couple of boxes of comic books behind when he joined the Navy. I had no idea what to do with them. They'd just been sitting on a shelf in the storage closet downstairs. Last year the kids started getting interested in comic books, so I asked Rick if it would be OK if they looked at some of his collection. He said some of them would be all right, so Eleanor and I went through the boxes and separated them out into twin-friendly and adults-only piles. I think there are enough safe ones to keep them occupied for a while. And they're old enough now to read them without tearing them up."

Ruth went into the bedroom and came back holding what looked like an oversized archival photo box and set it on the table. The twins returned from the kitchen, carefully drying their hands, and took some comic books out of the box. The adults moved to the living room, leaving the unusually quiet twins to their reading. Ruth asked if anyone wanted coffee, and everyone did, so she returned to the kitchen to start the coffee maker.

Things got quieter as everyone drank coffee and relaxed, not needing to keep the conversation going. Eleanor noticed that Dave was finally beginning to lose the tense, almost hunched, slant of his shoulders, but still didn't look entirely at ease. She considered this, and after the coffee was all gone and Ruth had taken the cups back to the kitchen, Eleanor politely suggested that maybe Dave had had enough noise for one day, and he admitted that this was true.

"I'm sorry, everyone," said Dave. "I have really enjoyed this and it was kind of you to include me, Ruth. But I spend so much time alone in that truck that I'm not used to being sociable. I hope I haven't been too much of a drag."

Amidst general protestations that he'd been nothing of the kind, Adam said he'd be happy to run Dave back out to the motel and firmly declined the twins' request to ride along. "Dave doesn't need any more twins right now," he said firmly, staring down the protests.

"More like Adam doesn't need any more twins right now," said their mother.

"No comment." Everyone, including the twins, laughed.

⊠⊠⊠

With Andrew and Rachel settled with more comic books in the living room, Eleanor and Ruth sat down at the table with more coffee. "Thanks for letting me bring Dave along, Ruth."

"Now, how could I turn you down? It's been how long since you went out with anyone?"

Nettled, Eleanor snapped back with "I am *not* going out with him!" She put a hand over her mouth and glanced at her children, who were fully focused on their reading, thank goodness. "Sorry. It's not you. Linda gave me a lot of grief about it today. Dave's just a nice guy I happened to help up off the sidewalk, nothing more. And he's leaving on Monday. End of story."

"I was kind of surprised, that's all. I mean, here's a perfect stranger and you seem to have taken to him."

Eleanor thought about that for a moment. "Everyone's been saying that, and I suppose everyone's right. I don't know why I did it, myself—maybe it's just because he's someone I *haven't* known all my life. Something out of the ordinary." She shrugged. "We all seem to have survived it."

"Funny, though," mused Ruth. "For a while there he almost looked like he was frightened. I wonder what that was all about?"

"Yeah, I noticed that too. I have no idea. He wouldn't tell me much about himself, and I'm not nosy like those two are." She looked at the twins, lost in their own comic-book world.

"Too bad he's not sticking around. He seems like someone it'd be good to get to know."

Eleanor eyed her friend suspiciously, but it appeared Ruth was speaking for herself. "I suppose so," she said, easily, "but he's not sticking around, so that's that."

Chapter 4
Red Tide

In the end, after treating everyone to Sunday brunch at a restaurant, it was Adam who drove Dave to the neighboring town where he could catch the bus. Everyone said goodbye in the restaurant parking lot, telling Dave quite truthfully that they'd love to see him again someday. Ruth called Eleanor on Monday to pass along Adam's report that Dave had not been forthcoming about where he was going or when the bus was leaving and had politely evaded all Adam's attempts to get more information.

Adam had also on the spur of the moment offered Dave a job. Property manager in Lyric, with the apartment over the Caldwell & Talbott offices thrown into the deal rent free. Dave had turned that down politely as well, with the comment that he wasn't done traveling yet. And that's where things stood.

The following Thursday morning, Eleanor found a square blue envelope addressed to her in the pile of mail at the office, with a return address in a New Jersey city she'd never heard of. Happy that her colleagues were out somewhere doing something else, she slit open the envelope to find a thank-you card. In neat, legible handwriting Dave had written *I'm sorry I forgot to get your home address. I hope sending this to the office is OK. I just wanted to thank you again for everything. Dave.* Down below he'd added *The address is one of those mailbox places. I check it as often as I can. You can reach me there if you need to.* After that, he'd started to write something else and had firmly scribbled it out. Eleanor smiled and slipped the envelope into her purse.

Two weeks later, on a sunny, surprisingly mild Saturday afternoon, Eleanor dropped the twins off at the movies and climbed the stairs to Ruth's apartment, musing that this was more visits in one month than she'd managed in heaven knows how long.

Ruth was thinking the same thing, she discovered. "I hate to be the one to say this, but we really should do this more often," she said with a grin, as she put a plate of cookies on the table and got out the coffee mugs.

"I'm not ossified yet. It just looks that way."

"Heard anything from Dave?"

"He sent me a thank-you card. That's it. Why would I hear from him?"

Ruth opened her mouth and closed it again, apparently thinking better of what she'd been about to say.

"Look," said Eleanor, "I know you and Adam and my mother and the guys at the office and probably the whole damn town had us married off already in your minds. But you're all going to have to just suck it up and think of something else for a change." She didn't really know why she was so annoyed, and tried to change her tone of voice. "Why don't you and Adam get married? That's a better question."

"Ha. No mystery there. There's nothing on this earth that could persuade me to move to Chicago. And the internet connection here isn't anywhere near good enough for Adam to run the business from Lyric, not to mention our miserable excuse for an airport. End of story. Now, back to you and Dave."

"There's nothing to get back to—I just told you that," Eleanor fumed. "You know what? If Dave ever gets in touch again, I will definitely think twice before I tell anyone."

"And spoil our fun?" Ruth laughed. "Come on, El. If people didn't care about you they wouldn't give a crap who you picked up off the sidewalk. Dave just seemed like a nice guy, that's all."

"He was a nice guy. I wish people wouldn't read more into it than there was, though. Seems like being a Good Samaritan isn't all it's cracked up to be."

"I bet the original Good Samaritan caught hell from the neighbors, too."

Eleanor had to laugh. "Yeah, there is that. I hope Dave's happy wherever it was he went. You could tell the poor guy wasn't very good at socializing."

"Your kinda man for sure. How often have you socialized in the last geological age?"

"I did more than enough of that," Eleanor snapped. "That's how..." She stopped. Took a breath. Let it out. "Never mind."

How she got the twins, Ruth thought, but said nothing.

No one, not even Eleanor's mother, knew who the twins' father was, and no one had been nosy enough to find out in all this time. When Eleanor wanted to talk about it, she would. In the meantime, Ruth thought, it was enough that her friend had actually gotten out of the house and come to visit her today, even for the all-too-short time the twins would be occupied elsewhere.

Ruth knew that Paula, Eleanor's mother, was happy to babysit, and that Eleanor didn't want to lose that goodwill, so she didn't take advantage of the offer very often. And, if Ruth was honest with herself, she didn't go visit Eleanor nearly often enough either. They were lucky if they managed the occasional lunch hour together on a weekday. She silently promised herself to change that.

Up till very recently she'd worked six days a week, because she couldn't afford to hire more employees, and that meant her weekends were filled with personal errands. But now that they were fixing computers she had more money coming in and more leeway with her scheduling, and had hired a community-college student to come in and do computer work after class on weekdays and on Saturday mornings. High time to take some weekends off.

❌❌❌

Naturally, it didn't work out that way. On Wednesday, a customer brought in a computer with a strange problem. When the computer was started, the monitor displayed a pulsing red screen and nothing else. They were ready to chalk it up as a bizarre hardware malfunction and start testing the video card when someone else called to describe the same problem. And on Thursday, eight more people called. On Friday, there were ten, plus some of the earlier callers tried again, wondering if anyone knew how to fix it yet.

By that time it was quite apparent that some kind of computer virus was at work, but neither Chet nor Brad, their part-time worker, could find any information on anything like it on the internet, and none of the tools they had on hand could clear it up. Brad sent in queries to several antivirus-software providers and then they all had little to do but wait. It didn't help that their internet connection, never world class to begin with, was flakier than usual. Or was it just impatience that made everything seem so slow?

None of the companies had an immediate answer, but all promised to get right to work on it. Computer users all over town were getting upset, and there seemed to be nothing besides the red screen that tied them all together. Ruth, Chet, and Brad worked out a list of questions to ask each person, hoping to find a pattern, but the answers were all over the map—except that none of the affected computers was a Mac. Of course, it didn't help that most of the callers had no clue whether they had any kind of protection installed.

"How can you not know whether you've got an antivirus program?" Brad asked someone who'd been quacking at him on the phone on Saturday morning. "Just because your brother set it up for you doesn't mean you don't have to know what you've got. Well, fine, ask your brother and call us back." He managed to hang up the phone without slamming it down. "Idiot," he muttered under his breath. He ran a hand over his hair, which was dark brown streaked with light blonde, already receding in front, and gathered into a mid-back-length ponytail. Ruth always thought Brad looked rather like a stork—tall, bony, sharp-faced, with round wire-framed glasses that were always just slightly askew. Brad sat down and folded his legs under the table in the back and scowled at the computer in front of him.

"They must be doing something the same, some-where," said Ruth, after making no progress with the fourth customer that day. "But I can't figure it out. There don't seem to be any web sites in common except Google and I doubt they got a virus from that. We must be asking the wrong questions. Or is it just lack of protection that's doing them all in? It's not affecting Macs, so is it the Win-dows built-in security that's not catching this thing?"

"It's possible," said Brad, "but if it's a virus, it might be sneaky enough to get past some of the other software as well. I've talked with too many people whose system was set up by someone else and they have no clue what's on the computer or what isn't. I don't see how anyone could live like that, myself."

"Well, this time last year I didn't even own a computer, so I can sympathize," said Ruth. "If I hadn't taken those classes I'm sure I wouldn't have known what an antivirus program even was."

"I'll talk with my professors and see if maybe they can set up some kind of free or low cost basic computer skills classes," said Brad, looking at a laptop with a pulsing red screen. "If they can do that, we could spread the word when someone brings one of these things in."

"That's a great idea," said Ruth, "but ye gods I hope this is a one-time thing. It'd definitely be worth teaching people basic security, though. It just seems like we're going round in circles at the moment."

"Yeah," said Brad, sighing. "Like I said, all we can do is wait till someone gets back to us."

"Fine help that is," groused Chet.

"You got any better ideas?" said Ruth. "We've asked every question we could think of, so far."

"Beside the point," Chet fumed. "Gettin' darn sick of this stupid color." He stabbed a finger into the power button of the computer on his bench and eventually the red went away. "I give up on it, Ruthie. You're right, we just have to wait and let those anti-virus boys do the job. Doesn't mean I have to like it, though." Chet's grey hair was standing straight up again, a sure indication that he'd been running his hands through it in frustration.

Short, wiry and pugnacious, Chet had joined Ruth's brother Rick at Electronic Wizardry after retiring from a job as an electrician with the city years ago. He wore wire-rimmed bifocals and was partial to well-worn jeans, chambray shirts that looked like thrift-store rejects, and shop aprons splashed with... well, probably better not to ask. Ruth's best guess was that Chet was pushing 70, but she didn't know from which direction. She'd never asked. He certainly had made no concessions to his age, whatever it was. And she'd be the first to say that Chet was probably the smartest person in the shop. It had been his detective work both in and out of the shop that had located some well-hidden drug dealers only a few months past.

The phone rang again. Ruth debated not answering, then gingerly picked it up. It turned out to be a representative from Horemheb, one of the anti-virus software companies, saying that one of their techs would be attending a meeting not terribly far away (Ruth thought that a matter of 350 miles must mean something a bit different where they were from, but said nothing) and asking if it would be all right if she stopped by to take a look at the problem on Monday. "That'd be fantastic. We're not making any headway ourselves," said Ruth, gratefully. They made arrangements for the tech to come on Monday morning. "That was a guy from Horemheb," she said, hanging up the phone.

"Horem what?"

"You must not be as old as I thought you were, Chet. Ancient Egyptian guy, I figured you knew him personally."

"Very funny, whippersnapper."

Brad smothered a snicker and moved smartly out of range to put the laptop on a shelf in the far reaches in the back. But the mood in the shop was decidedly brighter all around.

Before they closed the store at noon, Ruth put a message on the answering machine telling the world (or the people in it who hadn't already given them an earful) that the computer problem was almost certainly a virus, they didn't have a fix, it wouldn't do any good to bring the computer in yet, and that a technician was on the way. She debated asking everyone to wait to call back till Tuesday but realized the utter futility of that idea. And then for the first time ever she shut off the ringer on the phone.

The technician, who arrived just after 10:30 Monday morning, turned out to be a short, stocky, fortysomething woman named Maria, who moved one of the infected computers to the table in the back, sat down, did something complicated-looking with her laptop and an interface box of some kind, and then sat watching a cryptic display scroll down her screen for what seemed like ages. Ruth and Chet watched her for a few minutes and then tried their best to keep busy at their benches. There were a few non-computer gadgets to be fixed, that had languished on shelves while they'd tried to deal with the red tide. Ruth was still answering a steady stream of phone calls. "I swear I'm turning on the machine and turning off the bell," she groused.

"How's your internet connection here?" called Maria from the back.

"Terrible, especially considering what you're used to," said Ruth. "It's a local ISP that's mostly powered by squirrels. We're just too far from the big city to have any big company think we're worth their while to wire in."

"Oh no, don't tell me it's dialup."

"We have DSL, but it's more like Don't Start Laughing. I'm sorry."

"Well, never mind, I'll just tether the laptop to my phone."

Ruth and Chet looked at each other. This had gone out of the realm of the known and into the theoretically known but never tried. Whatever it was Maria was doing didn't take long. "I sent the data back to the lab and they'll pound on it for a while. Can I treat you guys to lunch somewhere?"

Chet had one of his usual gloppy tuna sandwiches in a lunch bag, and declined the offer with thanks, but Ruth accepted it as a great opportunity to get the heck away from her bench and the phone for a while. She made a few suggestions and they decided to try the lunch specials at La Cocina Mexicana across the square.

As they sat eating fresh tortilla chips and salsa, Maria said "You've definitely got a virus of some kind. But it's not one we've seen before, and nobody outside of this area has reported it. That's what's so strange, that it hasn't spread anywhere else."

"Maybe our terrible internet connection is protecting us because it's too darn flaky," said Ruth, thoughtfully.

"You might have something there, actually. I'll mention that." She pulled out her smartphone and made a quick note.

They had just left the restaurant when Maria's phone rang. She answered, said hello to one of her colleagues and then put her hand over her open ear, pressing the phone a bit more firmly against her face. Ruth walked away a bit to window shop and give Maria some privacy. Once again, it didn't take long. "You were on the right track," said Maria. "The virus appears to be local and it might be possible that your ISP has something to do with the fact that it seems to be staying local. We're still not exactly sure how it works, but the guys should have a patch for our software to get rid of it by later today."

"That's wonderful! I'm telling everyone to buy your software from now on. None of the other companies have even called us back yet."

"All of us love solving puzzles. The more impossible, the better. I don't see how the ISP could be part of it, though—surely they wouldn't want to sabotage them-selves."

"No, I don't think they're involved either," said Ruth, thoughtfully. "A couple of my friends work there and I know they'd never go along with anything like that."

"That's good to know. Helps us focus on where else we should look."

⌗ ⌗ ⌗

Rick Peyton slid his key into the lock on his apartment's front door, wiggled it, then pulled firmly up on the doorknob and kicked the bottom of the door in just the right spot. The door snapped open. He'd gone through that routine so many times to get his door open that it had become just part of the background, but today he couldn't help noticing what he was doing.

And today he noticed how sad the entire inside of his apartment was, too. The furniture it had come with all sagged, and no two pieces leaned in the same direction. The wall around every light switch was three shades darker. The Indiana Jones poster taped to his living room wall had come loose at the lower left corner again, and two days' dishes littered the coffee table. His neighbors were chain smokers and he himself hadn't ever been any too energetic about taking out the garbage in the kitchen or taking his clothes to the building's laundry area, so the general *Eau de P.U.* was depressing. Why hadn't he paid attention to any of this before? He started to sigh and thought better of it.

His commanding officer had been crystal clear. He'd maxed his leave for the year again, already, and it was use it or lose it and now hear this, sailor. What was he sup-posed to do, sit around in this dump and contemplate his... navel? Still irritated, he threw his jacket over the back of the couch and hit bottom when he dropped into the cushions. Dust blew up all around him and yesterday's sports page slithered to the floor. A headline caught his eye. Iowa in the playoffs?

Iowa.

Huh, he thought. *That'd do it.* If he had to take so damn much leave, why shouldn't he go home? Hop on his Harley and head cross country and forget this fucking base and this shitty jacked-up apartment and by-god TAKE a vacation for once.

Iowa. Yeah. It was time.

He shoved the newspapers into the recycle bin and took a good look around at the slum he lived in. *Time enough,* he thought, *to take the trash out to the dumpster and maybe do a couple loads of wash before bedtime. Yeah.*

Chapter 5
Odd Jobs

February

Dave wiped sweat off his face with the corner of his apron and started scraping down the grill. Only half an hour before he could get out of there, and that half hour couldn't possibly go fast enough to suit him. The timer on the deep fryer went off. Mechanically, he picked up the baskets of chicken pieces, shook them and dropped them into their racks to drain, and he then went grimly back to finish the job on the grill. *If the customers could see where their food came from,* he thought, *they'd never set foot in this ptomaine palace again.*

His boss came through the doorway to the hall that led to the restroom, scrubbing at the front of his shirt with a wadded paper towel. His multi-chinned face was already blotchy red from the effort. "Dave? Need you to stay a little extra. Bill just called to say he'd be late." He balled up the paper towel, flung it toward the wastebasket and missed by about three feet.

"Can't do it, Mr. Edwards," said Dave, still scraping away. "I've got plans tonight." The plans involved a couple cans of beer and a game he'd recorded, but they were still plans.

"I mean it, Dave. Just till Bill comes in."

"I mean it too. Last time Bill called in late he never showed up and you still owe me for the overtime."

"Overtime, my ass. You must not care too much about keeping this job," said his boss. Dave had heard that one way too many times before. The honest answer was "You got THAT right," but he said nothing. "The cook can't leave the kitchen," said his boss, a little more loudly, as if the volume level would carry the day, "so you're staying here till Bill gets his ass in the door".

Dave shoved the last of the greasy crud off the edge of the grill into the trap and tossed the scraper aside. "Fat chance." He gave the boss a smirk.

"What did you say?"

"You heard me." He wiped most of the grease off his hands on his apron, knowing what was coming.

"You giving me lip, boy?"

"Would I do that?"

His boss huffed and took on a more belligerent stance, which was wasted on a body that was five and a half feet tall and nearly as wide. "Either you do as I tell you or you get your ass out for good."

"You got a deal." Dave took off the grubby apron and tossed it on top of the overflowing trash can. "Pay up."

"You... you... You're not doing this," Edwards sputtered, his face turning from blotchy to solid red.

"Yeah? Wanna bet? I'll meet you by the register. It's payday." He turned away to wash his hands.

"If you think I'm paying you for quitting, you've got another think coming."

"Really?" Dave turned around. Since the dented, spattered towel dispenser had been empty for days, he dried his hands on someone else's fairly clean apron that had been left lying on the counter. "I can see five code violations from right here where I'm standing. I think I'll go report you to the health department the minute I walk out the door, get them to shut this flytrap down." The two men glared at each other. Dave won the glare-down. His employer spat on the floor and turned away. "That's another violation," said Dave, cheerfully, but his former boss gave no indication he'd heard a thing.

Five minutes later Dave was out on the street, walking away unemployed once again but feeling surprisingly good. He still had the beer and the game, and time and money enough to figure out what to do next. Louisville was a nice place. Maybe he'd take some of his "severance pay" and go to the track tomorrow. He walked off toward his apartment, cheerfully whistling "Dixie." After the first chorus he burst out laughing. It took him half a very pleasant hour to reach his apartment, look in his empty mailbox and get set to watch the game.

The next morning, reading the newspaper at the library, he noted that one of the horses running at Churchill Downs that afternoon was called Sweetly Lyrical. He smiled. Maybe he should check the schedule for the bus. He'd never gone to the racetrack before, and now that he thought about it, that would be fun—an inexpensive adventure. In the time he'd been living in Louisville he hadn't actually seen much of the city. He'd gotten here by flipping a coin at the bus station in New Jersey, picking a destination, riding away and not looking back. He'd done that so many times over the years that he didn't even think much about the process any more. All he needed, no matter where he ended up, was a cheap furnished apartment and a reasonable job. The fact that some of the jobs turned out to be less than reasonable was just the luck of the draw. His Louisville apartment was a dump, but just about everything he needed was within easy walking or bus distance, so he hadn't felt the need to explore farther afield. Time to fix that. No sense being in a city with a world class racetrack and never setting foot in the place, right?

Sweetly Lyrical, a long shot, paid 15 to 1. Dave, having risked a whole $20, was not exactly rolling in money, but still entirely satisfied. He pocketed his win-nings and then strolled around, sightseeing, till he reached the bus stop near the track. He had never been the kind of guy who'd gamble again once he'd won. He'd won so seldom that he never pushed his luck.

⋈ ⋈ ⋈

The airless little room had an olfactory overlay of dirty socks and old garbage, and was lit only by three large computer monitor screens, but its occupant didn't notice or care. Neither the curtains nor the window had been opened for weeks. You never knew who might recognize what was going on if they happened to be walking past on the sidewalk, that was the theory. Given what was going on, and the fact that the only way to arrange such a large desk in that cramped, oddly-shaped space meant putting the screens facing the window, a little paranoia seemed entirely reasonable. He typed a few more lines of code, made a backup, and then ported it over to the next computer for compiling and testing. The third computer, the only one running Windows, displayed a screen saver that faded photos from the Hubble telescope in and out.

This edition of the virus was taking a bit longer than the first one, but the results, he thought, would definitely be worth it. He wondered if those suckers at Mintaka Iowa even had a clue. He'd heard nothing to indicate anyone had gotten suspicious the last time, and the fact that that crew of amateurs at the repair shop had been clueless and helpless made him happy. Nobody expected a first attempt at a custom-written virus to be golden, but his first try had definitely been good enough.

The compile looked to be going smoothly. Time to take a break, get something to eat, play some games, whatever. Tomorrow or the next day it was going to be bombs away again. He got to his feet, stretched his hands to the ceiling and laughed out loud. He already had plans for the money he'd get for this. Turning off all three monitors, he picked up his phone and his keys and headed out to the pizza place.

⊠⊠⊠

Whenever the weather changed, Eleanor had learned to expect a huge increase in the number of phone calls, and this spring was no exception. The real estate office also served as property managers for three apartment buildings and quite a number of rental houses. What with leaky roofs, clogged toilets, flaky furnaces, moribund water heaters, drippy faucets and all the other residential catastrophes major and minor, Eleanor had hardly been able to turn around twice for days and her small crew of repair people barely had time to eat lunch on the way from one job to another. Still, by Thursday the tide seemed to be turning, and they'd had sunshine for long enough that people's attitudes were changing as well. What would have looked like an outrage on a dreary Monday was just an inconvenience while the sun was shining today. She hoped, though, that the noises in that one house's attic came from squirrels and not bats. The exterminators would let her know.

Ron came in with a bag of sandwiches from the deli and put the OUT TO LUNCH sign on the door. "Turn on the answering machine for a while, you need a break," he announced. Linda was treating a prospective client to lunch at the steak house.

"You're the boss," Eleanor smiled, and pushed buttons on the phone. "What kind of sandwiches did you get today?"

"Peanut butter, Miracle Whip and pepperoncini, your favorite."

Eleanor made gagging noises, which is what Ron had been angling for, and took her turkey-avocado sandwich on sourdough with thanks. "I think the Burtons have squirrels in their attic. Everyone in the family is convinced it's bats."

"Sure am glad we're paying someone else to deal with that one," said Ron, shaking his head. He sat down at his desk and unwrapped a real Dagwood style club sandwich. "Jeez, I asked them for a little extra bacon and they gave me three of everything, looks like. I'm going to have to attack this thing with a chain saw." He went to the staff room in the back and returned with a plastic knife and fork. After a few minutes where nothing but munching was to be heard, Ron took a sip out of his can of Dr. Pepper and asked, oh so casually, "So, heard anything from Dave lately?"

Eleanor choked, coughed, and managed to spit out a small soggy wad of bread. "NO!" she finally managed. Then she coughed some more, cleared her throat loudly and took a swig out of her water bottle. "Would you please give it a rest? Even if there were something going on, which there IS NOT, it would be none of your business!"

Ron pulled his head back. He was apparently talking to an alien being who only looked like Eleanor. In all the years they'd worked together he'd only heard her raise her voice when she was dealing with hard-of-hearing clients.

"Wow, I'm sorry, I had no idea it was such a touchy subject. Now I know. I won't bring it up again!"

Eleanor gave one more small cough, took another drink of water and wiped her mouth on a paper napkin. She took a deep breath through her nose and let it out slowly. "I'm sorry. I shouldn't have done that. You're just getting yelled at because my mom won't quit bugging me. And she never even met Dave. I'm getting sorrier I ever met him all the time."

You don't really mean that, thought Ron, but wisely concentrated on his lunch and said nothing.

The twins were literally jumping up and down and waving papers when she arrived at the school building after work. "Mom! Mom! Look what they handed out in math class today! A two week computer camp! Can we go? Can we go?"

"I can't tell you right this minute, I don't know anything about it. Let's get home and I can read over the flyers and we can talk, OK?"

At the kitchen table the twins pointed to the activities and the classes. Eleanor, however, turned the flyer over and looked at the price. *Yipe!* Oh man, there was just no way, and especially not times two. But the kids were so excited that she couldn't bring herself to say no, at least not that minute. The deadline for applications was in mid-May, so who knew, maybe there'd be some miracle and the money would come from somewhere by then. The twins would be fine with being away for the two weeks, and she would definitely be fine with the twinless time span. So she smiled. "It's really expensive, so don't get your hopes up, please. Let's see what we can work out between now and the deadline. But I'm not promising anything, OK?"

Rachel and Andrew were well acquainted with household economics, but still, Mom hadn't flat-out said no, so they were hopeful. They took the flyers into their rooms along with their school supplies. The table got set, supper got eaten, and the dishes got dealt with afterwards in unusual harmony as the twins talked about what they thought the classes would be like, and what the camp buildings would be like, and who else from school might get to go. Eleanor finally asked them to go get started on their homework, hoping she hadn't just set them up for a horrible disappointment. She sank into her chair in the living room and tried to read, but half an hour later the magazine slid off her lap, unnoticed. When the phone rang, she was so startled that she could have sworn she levitated six inches off the chair. "Hi Ruth! What's up?"

"I've been promising myself a day off, but then that stupid virus hit, so I'm way overdue. Want to take the twins to the lake on Saturday?"

"You know what? My mom's yard needs work, and I know just the two kids to get the job done. I'll call Mom first thing tomorrow and then you and I can go laze around the lake together. We can both use a day off."

"Whoo, sounds like a plan!"

"Yeah, time Chet and Brad did some actual work around that place, right?"

They both laughed. Then Ruth said "You know, I have to remind myself of that now and again. I've been so wrapped up in that shop for so long that it's hard to admit that someone else can actually handle things without my breathing down their necks all day."

"Yeah, I know how that feels. That's why I send the kids across the street sometimes when I don't actually have anything to do over here. Although I usually feel so guilty about it that I don't have much fun while they're out of my hair."

"Thus conscience doth make cowards of us all, or some such nonsense," laughed Ruth.

"Wait till YOU have kids," said Eleanor, trying to sound stern and failing.

"That'll be the day," said Ruth.

⛒⛒⛒

Rick scowled at the row of fat government-issue three-ring binders lined up on the table. And he scowled at the cartons full of pages that were going to have to be sorted out and inserted into the binders, one by one, replacing the pages that were now out of date and needed to be removed and shredded. This was the kind of ridiculously tedious busywork he hated more than anything. But he couldn't blame anyone but himself for having gotten stuck with it.

He'd put in for his 90 days leave, expecting the commanding officer to turn him down, since the time he'd asked for overlapped most of a short training exercise. Instead, the CO had just said "About fuckin' time, Peyton," and approved it. And then, since Rick would be on leave during the exercise, the CO set him to work on the manuals so his shipmates could concentrate on getting the sub ready to go. As an Information Technology Specialist, ordinarily he'd have been working with the onboard computer system instead of shuffling papers. Not for the first time, he cursed his stupidity in not finishing college. If he'd been an Information Warfare Officer he'd be too important to get stuck with this kind of crap work. Or so he told himself. In any case, what he was right now was a guy who needed to get these damn binders done by the end of the day. He took a shrink-wrapped pile of pages out of a box and got busy.

Four hours later, he shoved the last of a stack of old papers into the shredder and stretched. He'd been sitting at that table way too long. And he still had four more dreary hours ahead. Time to go get some lunch and some fresh air, not necessarily in that order. As he lined up for chow, a couple of his shipmates gave him some grief about the timing of his leave. "Can't help it. Captain made me," he said with a straight face.

"Oh yeah, captain who? Mary? Jennie? Susan? Caroline?"

"All of 'em," said Rick. "Think anything else would get me off this miserable fuckin' base?"

"Now that you mention it, no!"

The men all laughed and moved on down the line. But Rick wasn't really paying attention to what landed on his tray.

Chapter 6
All Secure

March

Dave finished walking his second circuit of the outer perimeter of the mall at 2:15 AM and radioed in to the dispatcher to tell her he'd done so. She confirmed that it was time for him to take his break. There was still a stream of cars moving steadily up and down the main drag on the east side of the mall. Dave shook his head. Everything he'd heard about California seemed to be mostly true. The weather was the same almost every day, the cars never stopped coming and there were just too many people with attitudes too big for their own good.

This place he was guarding didn't even look like a mall. It was a cluster of storefronts and apartment buildings around a central plaza equipped with an elaborate fountain and a mini-playground. He'd spent most of his first three weeks on the job asking people to put out cigarettes, calm down their children and get their hands and feet out of the fountain. And for that, he'd gotten shouted at, cursed and threatened by people who thought they owned the place—most of whom were half his age.

He didn't take any of it personally. Attitude never bothered him, and he was good at standing his ground, which was usually all it took. He'd started on the afternoon shift and it hadn't taken him long to end up on very good terms with his supervisors. They'd called him to handle tricky situations a time or two—but still, when an opening on the graveyard shift had come up, he'd immediately applied, and he'd appreciated the quiet environment ever since.

Now, at this hour of the morning, the only people he could see inside the mall were members of the late night cleanup crew, moving around at medium speed to get the last of the trash picked up, wastebaskets emptied and glass de-fingerprinted for the next day. Dave strolled down the central sidewalk and said hello to the two men with the dumpster on wheels as he passed them on his way in to the office.

After the dimness of the lamps on the mall's sidewalks, the security center's outer office's lighting hurt his eyes. Squinting, he went through to the staff room at the back, tossed his jacket and hat on a chair and poured himself a cup of coffee. He had never been one to adulterate coffee before, but he'd quickly learned that the only way he could swallow the swill that came out of the guards' coffee maker was to hit it up with a big slug of creamer and hope for the best. You'd think in a place with this much money floating around they'd at least have drinkable coffee. But it wasn't the rich people filling that pot. Or cleaning it.

He slid onto the well-worn plastic-leather cushion of one of the chairs and leaned back. At least his feet didn't hurt any more. The first week on the job he'd been sure he'd never be able to make it the four blocks to his room at the Y at the end of his work day—in fact, he'd even idly wondered if he should rent an electric scooter just so he could manage the journey. The transition came about so gradually that he hadn't really been aware of it, till one day he realized that he'd gotten home in half the usual time and was able to run up the front stairs. After that, he'd moved right along. But tonight for some reason he was slowing down. He'd been sneezing earlier, so maybe he was just coming down with a cold. The hot pseudo-coffee seemed to be helping light a bit of a fire under him. His shift was half over. He'd make it OK.

Next on the schedule was a survey of the parking garage, a part of his daily duties which he had hated from Day One. There were always odd noises and echoes, and someone always seemed to leave a car or two in the garage after closing time. Inevitably, the cars had darkly tinted windows so he couldn't tell from a safe distance if some-one was inside lying in wait for an unsuspecting guard to approach. His co-workers told stories of drug deals, people passed out in the back seat, cars with puddles of unidentifiable glop underneath and people jumping out and running for the stairs without warning. The story about the kids popping out of the car with air horns that had made a guard pee his pants seemed pretty tame in comparison. So far, though, the vehicles had been verifiably empty and the only thing out of the ordinary he'd seen was the occasional feral cat skittering along the wall down by the valet's station. He still couldn't under-stand why the mall owners had been so stingy with the security cameras in the garage. There was a lot of territory that could not be properly watched from the safety of the dispatcher's station, so regular foot patrols were essential.

Oh well, time to drink the last of the swill and get moving again. He rinsed out his mug and put it back on the shelf and then shrugged into his jacket and re-settled his hat. *Once more into the breach, dear friends...*

The stairwell's lowest point always smelled faintly of urine, but he couldn't decide if it was feline or human. He trudged up a floor, pushed the heavy metal door open and looked cautiously around—nothing there to be concerned about. He walked the perimeter as he'd been instructed to do, then went up a floor. Back in the far corner, a dark green late-70s Monte Carlo sat with the passenger side door partly open and no lights inside. He radioed the dispatcher. That was an area where there actually was a camera, so she could have someone quickly review the recordings to see if they could tell what was up with the car, and keep an eye on the guards when they checked it out. She advised him not to approach till she sent backup.

Five minutes later, Marco, the biggest guard on the shift, showed up. He was an ex-Marine and built like a tank. Dave had been sent this kind of support by dispatch before and he couldn't decide whether to feel good about having backup or get pissed because they thought he needed a way bigger guy watching over him. Good thing he and Marco were buddies and worked well as a team.

He greeted Marco and checked in with dispatch, who cleared them to take a closer look. The two guards moved slowly and carefully toward the car, circling around and trying to see through the windows. "Damn," said Marco, softly. "Why the hell don't they let us carry guns?"

"Because half the numb-nuts on our shift would shoot themselves in the ass in five minutes flat and you know it."

"Eff that, man, at least let us have pepper spray."

"Yeah right, let's just pepper spray that heap and get out." They were getting closer to the back of the car. It looked empty, but that open door was definitely cause for concern. "Dispatch, be advised we are approaching the suspect vehicle," said Dave into the radio.

"10-4" came crackling back.

Marco got close enough to penetrate the interior with the beam from the monster flashlight he'd brought. Nothing. The two moved cautiously closer. Still nothing. Finally they were close enough to be sure that the car was empty. "Dispatch, be advised that the vehicle is empty," said Dave into his radio.

"10-4," said the dispatcher. "We'll keep an eye on it. The two of you patrol the rest of the garage together."

The next two floors were quiet and empty, but they dutifully circled them anyway. The next floor up was one used by employees and there were several cars parked there. They had walked halfway around when something clanged on the concrete floor by the elevators. Both guards spun around, instantly alert. But there was nothing to be seen. "Should we go check that out?" asked Marco.

Dave considered. "No, doesn't look like there's anything there, let's finish the circuit."

They'd gone about a quarter of the way along the third wall when there was another clatter, this time near the door to the stairs. The two men looked at each other. They were on their way in that direction without thinking twice. Dave clicked the radio just long enough to say "Dispatch, be advised we are checking out suspicious noise." They passed the last few cars, all senses on the alert. Marco motioned to Dave to check by the stairs while he looked along the one wall they had not checked, to see if someone or something was hiding behind the cars there. Dave looked behind the wastebaskets and along the wall and saw nothing. Cautiously, he opened the door to the stairwell to check inside. He'd gotten maybe two feet onto the landing when he heard a thud behind him in the garage. Whirling around, he'd just gotten the door open again when someone hit him full in the chest and he went flying off into space. He felt the metal stairs the first time he landed on them, and the second, and the third.

⌗ ⌗ ⌗

Lights that seemed brighter than the sun pierced his eyes. Something warm pressed on his face. He tried to lift a hand and couldn't. "Dave?" said a female voice.

"Eleanor?" *Wait, why did I say that? Eleanor who?*

"Lucy. I'm your nurse. You're in the hospital and it looks like you may have a concussion. I'll call the doctor. Try not to move."

Try not to move? I'm where? I'm... ohhhh God....

He rolled onto his side and heaved. What was around his neck? He could barely move his head. He was up against some kind of metal bars. Wait, he'd been in the stairwell. But the stairwell didn't have bright lights... he gagged, retched, tried to bring up something that wasn't there, and oh God his chest hurt. Someone was talking to him but the words made no sense. Something pressed firmly on his shoulder and rolled him onto his back. He was too weak to resist it. There was a bright white spike through his head—he could feel it pinning him to whatever it was he lay on.

Something rubbed his face gently, leaving it damp. He got one hand part way up and had to drop it again.

Someone else spoke—another woman's voice. Why had he said Eleanor?

"I'm Dr. Frederick. Can you hear me? Can you tell me your name?"

"Mmf. Dave."

"Dave what?"

"... Van Meer."

"Do you know where you are?"

"Uh... nurse... hospital..."

"OK, that's good, I won't have you talk any more than necessary, but I do need to ask you a few things. Do you remember what happened?"

Happened? He tried to think. "Fell."

"Yes, you fell. Someone apparently pushed you down the stairs in a parking garage. You hit your head and it looks like you have a concussion and you may have cracked ribs and a broken wrist. Your neck is in a brace, that's why you can't move it. We're going to check you over for other injuries. I will be as gentle as I can, but we can't give you painkillers till we've checked you out, because we don't want you falling asleep before you can answer us. Do you understand?"

"Mmmf."

"We had to cut your clothes off to see your injuries. I'm sorry."

"Uni... form. No... cut."

"I'm sorry, but we had no choice. There was no way to remove it without moving your head, and we definitely didn't want to do that."

The effort of keeping up the conversation was too much. He tried to shrug a shoulder and the white spike lanced back through his head. He yelped and rolled over to heave again, which wrapped the pain clear around his chest. He heard the doctor talking with the nurse but it might as well have been Martian. Nothing made sense. Again he was eased onto his back. Someone picked up his left hand and did something with the back of it. He cried out again as a ribbon of cold fire spread out from where the hand was held. "This is just something for the nausea," said Lucy.

"Shit," he managed.

"Yes, I know, this stuff burns. I'm sorry. But it will make you feel better fast."

Tears of pain trickled toward his ears. Couldn't help it. Gentle hands wiped his face, moved his legs, rotated his feet, picked up his right hand. He let out a whimper. Couldn't help that either. The hand was gently put back, on some kind of hard surface that hadn't been there before.

"All right, we're going to do some x-rays to see for sure what's happened. You won't have to go anywhere, we have the machine right here."

He'd just go to sleep while whatever they were doing was being done. He drifted off.

"Dave, no, don't go to sleep. You can't sleep till this is done, we may need to ask you some more questions."

"Go 'way."

"We will. Soon. But right now you need to stay with us."

They were making him angry. He tried to sit up, but knew immediately that was a mistake. Tried to roll over and heave again, but this time he just coughed and was eased quickly back into position. He tried to push them away. No go. Exhausted, defeated, he lay where they wanted him and waited for the world to end.

They did something else to his right hand that made him yelp. It was laid gently back beside him. Then they rolled him on his side and slid something underneath him. Machinery clicked and whirred, and then whatever was under him slid back out and his hand was gently lifted and replaced again. "All right, Dave, the worst is over. We'll give you some painkillers and leave you to rest. But we're going to have to wake you up about once an hour to make sure there's nothing serious going on with your brain. Do you understand?"

All he could manage was a sigh, but that appeared to be enough.

⌘ ⌘ ⌘

Two days later, he remembered none of it. The doctors had explained his injuries and he understood that he'd had a concussion, but a huge chunk of time had simply vanished. The doctor told him that there was no way of knowing whether he'd get it back, but not to wear himself out worrying or trying to remember.

He could now navigate to the bathroom and back on his own and he'd been walked down the hallways several times by the staff, so it was looking good for going home. He'd figured out how to take care of most of life's necessities with his left hand, although the lightweight brace on his right wrist didn't get in the way nearly as much as he'd feared it would. His ribs had been badly bruised but not broken.

The director of security had made a point of stopping by and telling him not to worry, he should take all the time off he needed to get well and not to rush back to work too soon. Dave had been concerned that he hadn't built up enough sick leave, and he sank back onto the pillows with great relief. At least one thing was going right.

Marco came to see him, looking not too much the worse for wear, other than a bandaged hand and a scrape on his cheek. "Yeah, two guys jumped me, but they were both p..." he glanced at the nurse... "um, wimps. I could whup guys like that when I was in grade school. They've got both of them locked up in the jail ward upstairs and they won't be out any time soon. I just wish I'd gotten a better look at the guy who jumped you. He got away."

"I guess you were pretty busy at the time," said Dave. "I don't remember any of it."

"Not much to remember other than you got pushed down the stairs. Good thing the dispatcher had already called the cops, they got the ambulance there real quick. One of the officers told me yesterday that the Monte Carlo belonged to one of those jackasses and that they had tools to get car doors open and steal stereos, but apparently we surprised them before they did any actual damage. The guy who pushed you was the one who owned the car, so they'll dig him up eventually."

"That's good," said Dave, whose head was starting to ache again.

"Hey, the guy at the desk said he thought they were letting you out today. I'll give you a ride back to your place."

"Oh, that's OK, I..."

"Do you even know where you are? You think you're walking to your place from here?"

"Actually, I was going to call a cab."

Marco gave that notion all the scorn it deserved. Then he said "Listen, if you'll trust me with your keys I'll go get you some food for your fridge, and maybe by the time I get back they'll be ready to spring you loose. Don't you dare try getting home without me or I'll hunt you down." He was smiling as he said it.

"If you could whup two guys and go looking for a third one... I'm not that crazy. Besides, you'll have my keys." He tried to laugh, even though it hurt.

"That's good. I'll be back."

Two hours later, Dave was safely back in his room at the Y and thinking of nothing more than a nice long nap. Marco shoved a large bag of grilled chicken and containers of rice and salad from the nearby Mexican chain restaurant into the fridge. "That'll keep you for a couple days. This stuff tastes just as good cold." He checked the other contents of the fridge, pushing containers to and fro. "Anything else I could get you? Some cereal or coffee or whatever?"

"No, thanks Marco, you're a lifesaver."

"Yeah. Just don't give me any more opportunities to do it, OK?"

"You got it."

All Secure

Dave lay back on his bed. Eyes closed, he saw images of the bandstand in a small town square.

Chapter 7
Flowers on the Wall

The next computer virus struck three weeks after the first one. This time, a wave of red pulsed back and forth across the screen, dark to light and back again. Like its predecessor, the virus did no actual damage to the computer—it just made it impossible to use it until the infection was eradicated. Despite having spread the word around town as emphatically as they could about using firewalls and antivirus software, Ruth and Chet and Brad were inundated again. One of the infected computers was indignantly marched up to their counter by a repeat offender, a guy who had already claimed to know everything he needed to know about how to keep it from happening again and had rudely declined Brad's offer of protective software. Brad took the computer in without comment, but it was a real battle to keep a straight face while he asked if the owner would like antivirus software installed this time.

"Now you've seen what happens when a human slinks away with his tail between his legs and tries not to show it," said Ruth as Brad carried the computer back to his workbench.

"Too bad I'm not a gambler, because I could have made book on that guy coming back," laughed Brad. "At least he didn't slam the door on the way out."

"Didn't you notice? I had a big hydraulic door closer installed," said Ruth. "It'd take Superman to slam it now."

"Wise move," said Brad.

They'd put in a call to Horemheb, figuring that the company that had done so well the last go-round deserved first crack at this one. Maria would come as soon as she could. Ruth emailed the other companies on her list and got assurances they'd take a look right away.

Ruth printed out some short instruction sheets, explaining what was going on and offering practical suggestions to keep it from happening again. For the next two days, when infected computers came in, all the staff could do was put them in the back and do their best to deal with customers who swore (sometimes with actual cuss words) that they could NOT be without their precious machines for that long. "Look, buster, if you needed it that bad you'd have taken better care of it," snapped Chet. "I can't help it you don't know what you're doing." The man grabbed his computer back across the counter, made some rather violent suggestions as to what Chet could do, and stormed out. Brad, who'd come quickly out of the back just in case, looked at the still quivering bell on the front door and said "Bet he can't stand being without his porn stash that long."

Chet snorted with amusement. "No kidding. That's the first thing I learned—the more X-rated stuff they got, the more they get the heebie jeebies. Dunno if it's an addiction or if they think one of us is going to get our jollies looking at it. Get sick, more likely."

"So far," said Ruth, "not one of them has had anything even vaguely interesting."

Brad slapped a hand over his heart in mock shock. "Ruth! Oh my God, you *looked?*"

Ruth snorted. "Just long enough to see that none of these guys have even a shred of imagination."

Brad and Chet looked at each other, eyebrows raised, but wisely let the subject drop.

The phone, which had been mercifully silent for nearly half an hour, started ringing again. Ruth made some suggestions about what it could do to itself, making the men gasp in mock horror, and then answered it. "Electronic Wizardry, if you're calling about the virus..."

"No virus here, Ruthie," said Eleanor.

"Well, thank goodness for that! What's up?"

"Just wanted to ask if you'd like to have lunch with me. I wanted to talk with you about something."

"Now, why would I ever want to get out of virus central here? Surely you jest."

"I'll be over in ten minutes, and don't call me Shirley."

They stepped out of the shop into a surprisingly breezy day. "Sometimes I forget it's supposed to be spring around here," said Ruth. "I need to get out more."

"No comment."

"Hmf. So what's so mysteriously up? You almost never head this way for lunch any more."

"Someone sent me flowers."

Ruth stopped short, hand reaching for the coffee shop door. "Really? Who?"

Eleanor pushed past her. "I have no idea. Just a small arrangement in a coffee mug. It showed up at the door about ten minutes before I called you."

"No card?"

"No, and the flower shop said they got the order from one of those internet services so there was no way to trace who bought them."

"Did you check the calendar to see if it's Office Manager's Appreciation Day or something?"

"Very funny. Any time Ron wants to do something nice for me he's darn sure to stick around and make sure I notice it."

"Must be nice to have a secret admirer, then."

"VERY funny, har de har har har. Let's eat."

⊠⊠⊠

Ruth pushed her plate and the remains of her lunch to the side and leaned back against the well worn dark green vinyl of the booth. "You have no idea how nice it is to sit here and talk with someone who's got nothing to do with computer viruses."

"Fat chance any of our computers would get one. Ron's so paranoid about his precious files, I doubt the CIA could get in there. And I had him set up my home computer and my mom's, too. I must admit I don't know a lot about it, but ye gods, it can't be that hard to take precautions."

"It's easy, which is why people undervalue it. If it's too easy they figure it's not worth doing, and if it's too hard... same story."

"That same company coming out again?"

"They're sending someone as soon as they can. I've talked with a couple other companies and have emailed them the information they asked for. The problem is that this thing seems to be extremely localized, so they can't allot much in the way of resources. If it was a nationwide problem they'd be on it in a flash."

"Oh, the joys of small town life."

"Yeah, but it's still weird that it seems to be only around here. Usually those things get spread far and wide, but this one doesn't seem to be showing up anywhere else. The programmer must be really good."

"Or really bad. I thought the whole idea of those things was to infect everyone?"

"You'd think so, judging by what's been in the news in the past—but this red screen thing seems to be sticking close to home. What really gets me is how many people have gotten hit twice. They just don't seem to learn."

"I know—same thing with real bugs. We've had to have the exterminators go to some people's houses day in and day out because they won't quit leaving old food and dirty dishes lying around. There was this one couple who didn't get the idea till Ron talked with the property owner and got her to agree to tell the idiots that the cost of any further exterminator visits would be added on to the next month's rent."

"Maybe we should double bill for the second infestation, triple bill for the third... hmm, that has possibilities," laughed Ruth.

"Just send Chet out there to casually mention the porn he found the first time around," said Eleanor, giggling. "That'd keep them from EVER coming back."

"That's what YOU think," said Ruth.

⛋⛋⛋

"Hey, nice flowers," said Linda, as Eleanor pushed the door shut against the wind. "Anyone we know?"

Eleanor ground her teeth together, briefly, remin-ding herself that it was just a friendly question. "No, there was no card with it and the flower shop said it was ordered through the internet. Guess whoever sent it doesn't want me to know who they are." She frowned at the flowers. "I wish they'd at least have had the decency to add some kind of note."

"That's too bad. Well, even if you don't know where they came from, they look nice. What's my calendar look like for the afternoon?" Linda always took her calendar with her everywhere, in her head and on her smartphone, so Eleanor recognized a subject changer when she heard one and accepted the gesture as it was meant. She sat down and checked her computer. "Someone coming to look at the Reynolds house at 2:30 and I think that's it."

"Good thing we didn't get that virus. I don't know how people kept track of their lives without computers."

"A virus wouldn't dare come near this place," laughed Eleanor. "Ron would shoot it on sight."

"Your computer at home is still OK too?"

"Of course."

"Are the kids going to that computer camp? My nephew's all excited about going."

"I don't know yet. It's awfully expensive."

"You know, we'd be happy to chip in on that. I love those kids and I'd hate to see them miss out."

"I... well, I'll let you know about that. It's nice of you to offer. There's still time for me to figure out how to pay for it all. The registration deadline isn't for a while yet."

"I want you to take at least a week of vacation while the twins are gone," said Linda. "Or two weeks. You deserve a little time to yourself."

Eleanor was touched. "That's the best idea I've heard in ages. Thanks, Linda."

"You're welcome. Now get back to work," Linda said, laughing. "I want everything taken care of before some dumb temp comes in here and screws it all up again."

⚃⚃⚃

After nearly a week of forced inactivity, doing little more than staring at his walls and his TV, eating his meals in the small nearby coffee shop after he polished off most of Marco's supplies, Dave decided it was now or never and ventured out the six-block distance to the library. He had books to return and newspapers to catch up on, and let's face it, any more time cooped up in that room and he'd go nuts. His first stop was the upstairs area where the newspapers were kept, which was next to the room that housed the public computers.

As usual, someone was arguing with the person behind the desk about computer access time. It hadn't taken Dave long to figure out that the internet computers were prime attractants for every jerk and grubby loser in the building—and then some. He'd signed up to use a computer a time or two, but between the crowded tables and the decidedly unsanitary surroundings, he didn't need internet access that badly. He didn't know what to do with the internet once he was connected, anyway, other than to read news stories and look at some of the sites that played clips from comedy shows. He'd browsed some of the online stores he'd heard about, but had quickly lost interest.

Dave wished he could take the newspapers downstairs to the main reading room where the sounds of internet access combat would be less noticeable, but that was against the rules. *Whatever happened to being quiet in the library?* For that matter, whatever happened to using libraries for actual book reading? He shook his head and concentrated on the editorial page.

Maybe he'd walk over to one of those electronics places downtown and buy a small music player... no, wait, you had to have a computer for those. Well, a portable radio, then. Anything so he could put on headphones and read in peace. They let you do that here if the headphones weren't cranked up too loud. Too bad this wasn't that funny library castle in Lyric. There didn't seem to be any computer combat there. He'd actually seen people reading books. But maybe he'd been there on an off day.

Was he just thinking about small towns because he'd had such a hard time in cities lately? Cities were pretty much all he knew. He'd been getting tired of California before the accident, and getting shoved down the stairs had just accelerated his feeling of distaste. But, he reminded himself, at least this job had benefits. What kind of benefits would a small town job pay? Another unknown. But still...

He pulled out his wallet and took out Adam Talbott's business card. What the hell would be involved in being a property manager? How much property was there in Lyric to manage? Eleanor would know, working at the real estate office and all... He shook his head sharply and put the card away. *Lyric, indeed.*

That night, though, the local independent TV station seemed to be having a slow news day. After playing a lot of filler and fluff and dog manicure stories, the anchorman introduced the next segment by saying "Did you know that there's a town in Iowa that grows computer viruses instead of corn? You'll want to hear about this. Stay tuned for the story of Lyric."

"Larrick," said Dave, automatically, then caught himself. "Hey!"

And sure enough, after a barrage of ads, a reporter stood in Lyric's town square, introducing the story. After a repeat of the "grows viruses instead of corn" line, the camera crew zoomed in on the front of Ruth's building from across the street. Then they played an obviously pre-recorded interview with Chet Walker, looking ruffled, standing outside the store. Chet was introduced as the town's main computer technician, a title he immediately denied. "Three of us here, missy, you keep that in mind or back in that door I go." The camera cut to the "Electronic Wizardry" sign on the door.

Dave, who hadn't even met Chet, could easily tell that the interview had been carefully edited to make him considerably more... well, colorful. But the idea that someone had somehow produced a virus that affected only a small geographical area was intriguing. Dave knew very little about computers, and even less about the things that could go wrong with them, but the reporter pointed out that it took sophisticated skills to limit the spread of the virus that way. And someone had already programmed two of them that worked like that. When asked if there could be more in the future, Chet said "Your guess is as good as mine. I think whoever's doing this is just playing games with us. I wish they'd go play in heavy traffic instead."

The reporter came back after the pre-recorded segment, and the camera panned around the square as she spoke. "Most people in Lyric (Dave noted that she pronounced it correctly) and the surrounding area get their internet service from a small local provider, Mintaka Iowa, rather than a large nationwide carrier. There's been speculation that this is what's helped prevent the spread of the virus to other areas. Mintaka spokeswoman Amy Kim," and here the background changed to an image of a somewhat harassed-looking Asian woman, "told us that the company was working with investigators to try to determine the cause of the problem, but had no further comment on the matter." Back to the live shot of the square. "We'll bring you further developments as they happen."

Dave laughed and muted the sound as the station went into yet another ad break. Oh sure, that was such a major story that the big news networks would be hot on its trail, all right. But wasn't it funny, seeing Lyric again? Was the cosmos trying to tell him something? He didn't believe in that kind of thing for a minute, but it was nice to be reminded that not every place in the world was crowded, dirty, and full of thugs. He pulled out the business card again and looked at it for a long time.

On his way to get breakfast the next morning, he took a short detour, to stop by a chain drugstore and buy another long distance calling card.

Chapter 8
Catch a Shooting Star

T his time, the third computer's screen showed a slow whirl of multicolored stars. It was almost like one of the Windows screen savers, except that it rotated and the stars appeared in rainbow colors. "Like an acid trip," said the programmer, whose only personal experience with intoxication had been strictly via overindulgence in other people's alcohol supply. "Far out, man."

Laughing at his own stellar wit, he started the instant-messaging software on his main computer and sent a coded text to three people, then quickly shut the software down without waiting for replies. He didn't know nor care if the message recipients were online. His job looked to be done for this week, but he'd give it another day of testing just to be sure. Maybe he'd see if he could shoot it right into the city's servers for a laugh. He'd been warned not to deviate from the plan, but he was getting very tired of just cranking out this stuff for nothing, and he'd just about had enough of those airheads trying to tell him how to do his job. He'd been doing this job since grade school, one way or another. Aaah, the hell with it, let this thing stew for a while. Time to get some food and fire up World of Warcraft.

Dutchman's Puzzle

⊠ ⊠ ⊠

Three days later the first "shooting star" infected computers started showing up. "Jeez Louise!" said Chet, in frustration. "Ain't you numb-nuts got the message yet? Get some damn anti-virus software and for pity's sake learn how to use it!"

"You got that kind of attitude? Then I'll take this piece of crap computer someplace else where the guy behind the counter ain't a smartmouth old geezer can barely tie his shoes!"

"Better'n havin' to have your mom snap your shorts to your shirt every day, sonny!" Chet shouted as the man tried and failed to slam the door on his way out. Chet smacked the counter. Where the hell was Ruth, leaving him out front here forever instead of safe working in the back!

As if she'd read his mind, Ruth came through the front door holding a bag from the drugstore and a box from the bakery. "Oh, don't you think you can buy me off, missy," said Chet, scowling at the bakery box. "Ain't a cookie in this world good enough to make up for dealing with these dipwads. Another damn virus and he says this time it's got stars. Stars! *This* time! If he had it before he should at least've had a damn clue!"

Ruth just blinked. What on earth could you say after being greeted by something like that?

"Aw, the hell with it," said Chet. "Come on in the back and feed me. I've had it up to the eyeballs with this. Then you can go out there and poke those guys in the teevee truck and tell 'em to steer clear. If they try asking me to talk again the FCC will have them and their truck for lunch."

"The truck's been gone for days, Chet. I think your interview gave them everything they wanted." Ruth was trying very hard to keep a straight face. "Here, chocolate macadamia nut. Put it on a paper towel or you'll get grease all over your bench."

"Better cookie grease than some of the other things on that bench," he growled.

"I was just about to say that too. So put the paper towel down so you're not eating dirt or heat sink compound, OK?"

Chet harrumphed, but pulled a disreputable-looking roll of paper towels out from under the bench and ostentatiously laid a reasonably clean square on one of the few spaces clear of junk. He made quite a show of picking just the right cookie and sat down again.

Ruth set the box on the table in the back. With any luck there'd still be a few cookies left in it when Brad came in. Then she restocked the bathroom's supply of pain-killers and bandages from the drugstore bag. They'd been going through a lot of both, lately. And Ruth was thinking seriously about getting her eyes checked. Working on computers had never given her headaches before.

Fortunately, what faced her on her bench was a portable music player that just needed a new battery. Piece of cake. She pulled her magnifying lamp down and started the slow and careful process of prying it apart. Sounds of muttering and munching came from the other side of the room. Ruth smiled and tuned it out. Maria from Horemheb was due in late that afternoon, and the shooting stars would then be someone else's problem.

⊠ ⊠ ⊠

"Hi, Ms. Ward, it's Carole from the school office."

Eleanor blanched. What had the twins done now? "Hi Carole, what can I do for you?"

"I'm just calling the parents of the kids who said they'd be interested in the computer camp. We found out that we can get a small state grant to help with everyone's fees, but that won't come through for a bit, so we talked with the camp people and they agreed to let us extend the deadline to apply. We can give you another two weeks past the original deadline."

"Oh, that's great, thanks for letting me know."

"Are the twins still planning to go? I haven't seen their applications yet."

"We haven't made a decision yet. They may be... spending time with family friends this summer," she improvised. "I'll let you know as soon as I can."

"Great, I'll look forward to hearing from you."

Eleanor set down the receiver and closed her eyes. Everyone assumed her kids would be going. How on earth was she going to manage this? She couldn't bear to think of disappointing the twins, but even with a small reduction she just couldn't see being able to afford it. She'd have to hope some miracle happened between now and the time she'd have to explain why they couldn't go. They were remarkably mature for their ages, but this would be a serious blow to anyone, any age, who'd set their heart on something wonderful. She knew exactly how that felt.

She pulled up her calendar and changed the deadline date for the application. As she typed, she thought wryly about setting herself up a few reminders to pray for a miracle. But she didn't really believe in miracles. Well, nevertheless, something still might make it possible—and there was no sense fretting about it now. By the time Ron walked in with a prospective buyer in tow, Eleanor had put the matter of camps and miracles firmly out of her mind.

⊠⊠⊠

When Dave returned to work, they first assigned him to take over as the dispatcher. He managed that for one night, but he'd go nuts if he had to sit inside for his whole shift night after night. So he made up a story about all the monitors giving him a headache, and persuaded his sergeant to reassign him to patrolling outside again. "All right, if you insist. But you stay the hell out of that garage," the sergeant groused.

"The garage is part of my job. How about I just stay the hell away from the stairs," Dave countered. And that's where they left it.

The first night he walked onto the employees' parking floor he was jumpier than he'd ever been before, hearing noises everywhere and turning around to look behind him, constantly. He'd turned down Marco's offer to go with him and wished he hadn't. After that first night, though, it quickly got easier. He was soon back into the rhythm of the nights. Too much so, in fact. Night after night went by without impinging much on his consciousness. He'd make his rounds, take his breaks, chat with his colleagues just as he always had, but it felt like he was on autopilot.

About the only change in the routine was that the brace came off his wrist two weeks after he went back to work. He didn't dislike the job, he just couldn't connect with it any more. And he knew that could be dangerous, if he was supposed to be paying attention and was flying on autopilot instead. He tried to give his full attention to what he was doing, but he kept thinking about packing up and moving on. Not till he was healed, though. He hadn't had a job with benefits since he couldn't remember when, and as long as he had to keep seeing the doctor for follow-ups he couldn't quit.

How could anyone stand California, year after year? He wanted real weather, for one thing. Give him a good honest broiling hot humid summer and give it to him soon. He'd taken the bus to the beach a few times, and spent the day walking around. It was still too chilly for sunbathing or swimming, but at least he'd had the sound of the waves and the smell of the sea, and he'd waded into the surf a few times. It had been too long.

When a co-worker offered a ticket to Disneyland, he surprised himself by agreeing to take it, and was told to make the trip in the middle of the week so the tourists wouldn't run him over. That suited Dave, since his days off were Wednesday and Thursday. Getting there was complicated without a car, but he used a computer at the library and discovered that public transportation was available. Amazing.

And so, bright and early one Wednesday morning, Dave set off. Traffic crawled along for most of the trip, but once the bus got closer to the park the streets expanded to many more lanes and the last part of the trip went much faster. Dave got off the bus and found himself in a huge plaza. No one had mentioned the shopping mall, or that there were two parks, not one. He walked into one souvenir shop out of curiosity, looked at the doodads, looked at the prices, and went on his way. And as for that second park, he'd had plenty enough California adventures already. He got in line for one of the ticket kiosks.

Disneyland itself was nothing like what he had expected—of course, nothing in this crazy state was anything like what he had expected. At least it wasn't wall to wall people, so his co-worker had been right about the proper choice of days. He spent the first two hours walking around, checking his location on the park map, looking at the rides and restaurants. He decided to do the Pirates of the Caribbean ride, since he'd liked the movies. The plunge caught him by surprise, which made him laugh. He laughed again when he saw Jack Sparrow hiding among the robots.

He didn't think as much of the Haunted Mansion nearby—seemed to be trying too hard and it wasn't remotely scary. *What the hell happened to the guys who made Pinocchio?* he wondered, remembering having the crap scared out of him by the whale as a boy. Oh well, now he could say he'd seen it.

And then he found himself outside in New Orleans Square wondering what to do next. Lunch? It was still early, but the restaurants were beginning to fill up. He chose a nearby place that didn't look as outrageously expensive as some of the other eateries he'd passed earlier. As he ate, watching families stream by, he decided that Disneyland was actually designed, not for children, but for the people who'd wanted to go there when they were kids.

He set off again, but there wasn't much else to see and none of the other rides looked appealing. Not long afterwards, Disneylanded out, he sat down on a bench in the central plaza and checked his watch to see when he could catch the bus back to the train station and head for home. He looked toward Main Street, and he could see that it was a pretty good imitation of a small town, but not as good as the real thing—now that he'd had a chance to see the real thing. Still, he could understand why it was so appealing. He couldn't be the only one whose experience with real small towns was limited or nonexistent. Maybe it was an indication that people had a natural place in small towns? Something to think about, at any rate. He got up, dusted off the seat of his jeans, and strolled toward the gate. On impulse he went into one of the souvenir stores and bought a key ring with an enameled figure of Donald Duck.

At the Anaheim train station he made up his mind. Checking his watch again, he figured out what time it was in Chicago and dialed. Adam Talbott's assistant caught him just as he was leaving for the day. "Hi," said Dave. "About that job? I'll take it. Any chance I could get a ride?"

"You want it? That's great! Where are you?"

"Disneyland, believe it or not. I didn't mean a ride from here. Can you pick me up where you dropped me off, in a couple weeks?"

"You got it. This is great news. I'm glad you're coming. I can really use your help."

"I need benefits."

"Oh? What kind of benefits?" Adam sounded faintly amused.

"Health insurance, dental, vacation time, that kind of thing."

"Oh, that goes without saying. I was thinking maybe you wanted a Jacuzzi and a corporate jet."

Dave burst out laughing, feeling lighter than air. "Maybe after I've been there a while we'll talk about that, OK?"

"Sure. Although, come to think of it, I should look into getting you a company car if you're going to be my on-site manager. That way you won't have to hitch a ride when it comes time to inspect the tenants."

"Anything that's got a good engine and good tires will be fine as far as I'm concerned."

"No more beat-up trucks, I guarantee. OK, great! I'll call Ruth right now and have her tell Eleanor you're on your way."

"No! I mean... no, let's make that a surprise for both of them, OK?"

"Oh... sure, if that's what you want, no problem. Call me back and let me know your timetable and if you have a preference on the health insurance and so forth. You can call collect if you want."

Dave was mildly insulted by that, but shrugged it off. "Thanks, Adam. See you in a couple weeks."

He hung up the phone, still not able to believe he'd just done what he'd done.

⛝⛝⛝

Late on a Friday afternoon, Dave followed Adam up the rickety back stairs to the apartment. Adam opened the door and then turned to hand Dave the keys. "It's not much, but it's all yours. If you want to change the furniture, let me know. We have quite a few odds and ends from other properties in storage, and if nothing appeals to you we can go shopping. I didn't furnish this place for long-term occupation and it shows, so don't be shy. Kick back this weekend and I'll get you going on the job on Monday."

Dave dropped his bag on the floor and looked around. He was in a vintage, but spotlessly clean, kitchen that had been updated with modern appliances, including a stacked washer and dryer in an alcove to his left. Adam opened the cupboards and the refrigerator to point out that there were enough provisions to see him through a few days. "There's a Mom and Pop grocery store a couple blocks off the square on the east side, and the big one is near the city limits on the west."

"Doesn't sound too hard to find when the time comes."

"There's a drugstore on the west side of the square, a hardware store three blocks from the northwest corner and a really good pizza place half a block from the square on the other end of this block."

"What more could a man want?"

They walked through to the living room and Dave was delighted to see that the library's red brick castle facade was right across the street. They'd come into town by a back road he hadn't seen before, and then through the alley in the back to park, and he'd had no clue where in town he was, other than that it was somewhere near the square. He checked his watch.

"Adam, would you mind..."He cleared his throat. "Would you mind dropping me off at the real estate office? I'd walk it, but..."

"But you wouldn't get there before she goes to pick up the twins?" Adam grinned.

"Yeah." Dave grinned back.

⊠ ⊠ ⊠

Eleanor was gathering up the debris on her desk to put it all away for the night when the door opened. She looked up from her file drawer and dropped a folder full of papers on the floor. Dave stood just inside the door, not making any move to help pick them up. She solved the problem by asking him to please just come sit down.

Face bright red, Eleanor hastily scooped up the papers, shoved them in their folder any old way and shut the folder in the file drawer. "Um... so, you're back?" *Oh damn, what a dumb thing to say! Just let me crawl under the desk and die right now!*

"Yeah. Sorry to barge in this late in the day, but I just now got here."

"Oh... well, that's OK. Are you settled in? Want to come with me to pick up the twins now? They'll be thrilled to see you again."

"Yes, and yes. I took Adam Talbott up on his job offer."

Eleanor, of course, knew all about the job offer but wasn't sure it would be wise to say so. "Oh?"

"Property manager. I got the apartment upstairs, too."

"Well," she said with a smile, "you can visit the castle any time you want, then."

"A regular knight in shining armor, that's what I'll be."

"OK, come on, Sir Galahad, let's go get the twins. You'll probably wish you were just slaying dragons before they get done with you."

"As you wish, Maid Marian."

That caught her by surprise, but after a moment's hesitation she smiled and gracefully extended a hand toward the door. "Can't wait to hear who you think is Robin Hood in this town," she said.

"How would I know? I just got here." He laughed and held the door open for her, gallantly.

Chapter 9
Hearts and Minds

There followed a period of time where, Eleanor reflected, it was rather like being back in junior high and discovering that you "liked" each other. She'd forgotten that lovely thrill at seeing someone, the planning to just casually happen to meet. Of course, when you were way past the junior high stage and both working full time, the opportunities to casually meet were slim to none. It wasn't like they'd run into each other just passing in the hall.

For her part, she had to admit that she was too far out of practice with the dating game. She had no idea what Dave's social life had been before he got here, and she wasn't about to ask. He seemed OK with taking things at her pace, and he always included the kids in invitations to go out to eat or see a movie. Both of them found that they felt most at ease spending a lazy Saturday afternoon doing yard work or housework or just talking quietly while the kids made all the noise with their video games.

Dave said he was surprised to hear that Rachel and Andrew didn't usually watch TV. "Too much garbage on TV these days," Eleanor explained. "I try to set a good example by not watching much either. I record stuff from the History Channel and the Discovery Channel we can all watch together on weekends—we all love Mike Rowe and the Mythbusters. We go to garage sales and the thrift store to buy DVDs, and some of my friends who have older kids give us the ones they've outgrown. When we get tired of the ones we've got we donate them to the library. And check them out from there too."

"That sounds like a great idea," said Dave. "I didn't know you could get DVDs at the library. I'll have to see what they've got. I could use some better quality enterainment myself."

Eleanor and her children quickly found out that Dave was a good cook. "I ought to be," he said. "Spent enough time working in places where you'd get your butt kicked if someone didn't like what you served them."

"So you weren't always a truck driver?"

"Oh, he... heck no. Jack of all trades, that's me. Chief cook and bottle washer, too."

"You know, I do think I may have heard the word 'hell' a time or two outside of a sermon. You won't burn my ears by saying it."

He laughed, sounding slightly embarrassed. "Yeah, but I'm not used to cussing in front of ladies and children. Just the way I was raised. My parents were really strict about that."

"I'm glad you think I'm a lady. And it would do these two some good to hear a grown man think about what he says." She looked at the twins, who put on an air of bafflement that fooled no one. She waited for Dave to coninue with what he'd been saying, but he didn't elaborate beyond that. She let it go. But now she knew just a little bit more about him than before. She smiled.

Dave was already in Paula's good graces, having walked across the street, introduced himself, and helped her re-plant the flower bed in front of the porch. She sent him home with a plate of cookies and an invitation to come back and get his hands dirty any old time.

The weather was getting warmer, the spring foliage had arrived, and life seemed improved beyond measure. It became their routine that Dave would cook dinner on Friday night at Eleanor's house, and they'd rent a movie or pick a TV show that they could all watch together. The twins did a lot of giggling and elbow-poking and whispering, and the adults ignored this as thoroughly as they could. They both knew perfectly well what the twins thought they ought to be up to, but they weren't going to do any of it in front of an audience.

"You know, I'd be happy to keep the kids overnight some weekend," said Paula, oh so casually, one day.

Eleanor looked at her mother, momentarily speechless. "Oh?"

"For pity's sake, don't get your feathers fluffed. I just figured you could use a break, that's all, and I could definitely use those two doing a few chores around my place."

"Right. That'll be the day. I can't even get them to do their own laundry."

"It's different when it's not your mom."

Recognizing the absolute truth of that, Eleanor laughed. "You can keep them for a weekend sometime, Mom, but if you think I'll be swinging from the chandeliers once they're out the door, think again." *We've never even kissed,* she thought, but took care not to let any whisper of that show on her face.

Still, the prospect of a twin-free weekend made for pleasant daydreams, when she had time for such things. Mostly she thought about work, and grocery shopping, and keeping track of the kids and the dog, and wondering if she'd ever get enough money put by for that computer camp. So far, that last part wasn't looking good.

⊠ ⊠ ⊠

Eleanor shooed Rachel and Andrew over to their grandmother's house one Saturday morning, to free up the time and floor space for the final work on the Dutchman's Puzzle quilt. Paula was thinking of dropping them off downtown, since there was a good Pixar movie playing.

When Dave arrived, Eleanor was running the vacuum cleaner over the living room floor. He sat down on the couch and pulled his feet up to give her room. Then Eleanor laid down an old sheet. On top of that went the quilt's backing, then the batting, and then finally the finished quilt top with its pattern of pinwheels, which covered quite a bit of the floor. Dave, who had not even the vaguest notion of quiltmaking, was just going to sit on the couch and watch, but "Oh no, you get down here and help me with this," said Eleanor, smoothing out the top to its edges and setting a big plastic container of oddly shaped safety pins in the middle. "Take your shoes off. Look, you start in the middle and smooth everything out to the edges and put these pins in about every six inches. You go that way and I'll go this way. Don't pin the quilt to the sheet."

"This quilt ain't big enough for the two of us," he joked, slipping a shoe off.

"All right, then, pardner, one at a time. Quilt. Very dangerous. You go first."

"So who do you think would win, John Wayne up against Indiana Jones?" He took off the other shoe and put them both under the couch, stalling for time.

100

"Depends on who gets the whip. Come on, let's get this over with."

He knelt on the quilt top and took a pin out of the box. The part that went through the fabric was curved. *Oh, so it could hold all those layers together,* he realized. *Interesting. Whoever invented them must have pinned a lot of quilts.* He pushed the pin through the fabric, fastened it, and sat back to admire his handiwork. "That's one down and 657 billion to go," said Eleanor, from her side. "Git a move on, cowboy."

Working together, they slowly filled the quilt with pins, not talking much. Leaning over to put the last row in, Dave asked "This is probably the world's dumbest question, but why do you go to this much work instead of just buying a quilt at the store?"

Eleanor sat back on her heels and looked at him, finally deciding he wasn't being snarky. "Well," she said, "besides the fact that I've always liked doing this kind of sewing, if I were to buy a handmade quilt of this quality at the store it'd likely cost me an arm and a leg. And that's if I could find one, these days. Mostly what's in the store is cheap imports."

"Oh," he said. "Why don't you sell these for an arm and a leg, then?"

She smiled. "Never crossed my mind. Like I said before, I don't do this to make money. I've given a few away as gifts, but I keep the best ones for myself, always."

"Like the Dutchman's Puzzle," he said.

She looked at him and smiled. "Exactly like that," she said softly.

Dave blinked. He opened his mouth to say something, but nothing came out. He sat back on his heels. The room was quiet. And then, without a sound, they both got to their feet. Dave held out his arms and Eleanor stepped across the quilt and was enfolded.

He was a talented kisser, too. *Oh*, she thought, presently, *how I've missed this.*

She pulled gently away, suddenly shy. "Let's... um... let's get this all rolled up before we... before we hurt ourselves on the pins."

He smiled, and gently brushed a strand of hair off her face. "Of course." They both moved to one side of the quilt and carefully rolled it up. Eleanor took it and set it on the rack. And then, there was a bit of lost time to be made up for.

⊠ ⊠ ⊠

When the twins came racketing in half an hour later, they found their mother and her boyfriend peacefully drinking coffee in the kitchen and the quilt all full of pins, draped over the frame, waiting to be attached.

Rachel and Andrew had talked about the situation, privately. The whole idea of their mom having a boyfriend was weird. Their mom had never had a boyfriend before, at least not that they could remember. They knew that their parents hadn't been married and their dad wasn't around, so there was nothing wrong with their mom having a boyfriend, exactly... but it was still weird. The twins had manners; they knew they weren't supposed to ask nosy questions, but they had their own notions of what boyfriends and girlfriends did—and to think that their mom might be doing that... Well, it gave them both the fidgets, that's what it did, so they looked at each other and without a word quickly headed for the video game console.

Eleanor called after them, "Why don't you guys go outside and play for a change? You've been inside all afternoon."

Dual noises of scorn and derision came from the living room, followed by the opening chords of the video game theme. Eleanor laughed. "You can see how well I rule the roost around here."

Dave patted her hand. "Want me to take them outside and play catch or something?"

"Good luck with that. You can always try."

Ten minutes later she was sitting on the back porch steps, finishing her coffee, watching Dave skillfully throw the ball so that the twins did ten times more running around than he did. *There's no end to that man's talents,* she mused. *Maybe I should mention Mom's offer.*

But there was no chance to do that, not that night, not with the twins right there. There was no way she wanted them to get ideas. So Eleanor decided to let it go for the moment, and figure out how—and when—best to bring up the subject. There was plenty of time. Neither of them was going anywhere, and waiting for the right moment would just make it all the better.

Two days later, the handset on the office phone dropped right out of her hand as Rick Peyton walked through the door.

⊠⊠⊠

Rick had started his journey with the best intentions. He'd duly headed west on the freeway, intending to go from Norfolk to Cincinnati, then diagonally across Indiana and Illinois. The weather was perfect for riding, and he'd poured enough money into his Harley over the years that it purred. But somehow, the farther west he went, the harder it was to get going again in the morning. He'd take long lunch breaks, and get off the freeway for any local attraction that had any kind of amusement value, and stop earlier and earlier for the night. By the time he got to Indianapolis he'd convinced himself that what he really wanted to do all along was check out his old stomping grounds in Chicago, which he hadn't seen since he'd left Great Lakes Naval Training Station years ago. Sure, that's what it was, he needed to go see how things looked around there, see if any of his local acquaintances were still around, do a little catching up on friendships.

He did his level best to maintain that illusion through two days in Chicago, during which he managed to connect with only one old friend and say hi to one former instructor on the base. On the third day, he stared at his reflection in the motel bathroom mirror and said "You're a chickenshit, and you know it." The tall, muscular man in the mirror with the very short light brown hair and green eyes looked back at him and agreed. And with that, he got on the bike again and headed west.

Ruth had just started the virus scan on yet another computer when the bell over the shop door jangled. Before she could even get up from the bench someone out front shouted "How the hell can I get some service in this dump!" Chet was up and moving, a pipe wrench in his hand, and Ruth wasn't far behind, hoping to catch Chet before he took out his frustrations on yet another virus-riddled computer—or its owner.

A tall man, wearing a full-length black leather motorcycle suit, gloves, and boots, stood grinning at them. "Well?" he said.

Ruth gasped. "RICK!" And two seconds later she was hugging her brother with all her strength. "Oh my God! Why didn't you tell us you were coming!"

"Eep! Can't talk, you're squashing my lungs!" he said in a mock-strangled voice.

She let go. "Oh, yeah, big tough sailor, sure, I'll believe that."

Chet moved in for a vigorous handshake. "Damn, it's good to see you, boy. I thought you were another one of those numb-nuts with a virus."

"How do you know I'm not?" Rick laughed.

"Aw, come on in the back. Tell us all about it." Chet pushed past Ruth and flipped the sign on the door to read OUT TO LUNCH, then locked the door for good measure.

Rick pushed through the curtain and stopped, looking at what had once been his shop. The basic layout remained the same—Ruth's bench on the left, relatively tidy, Chet's bench on the right, looking like a bomb had gone off beneath it, dusty brick walls lined with beat-up wooden shelves—but there had definitely been some changes made. The floor was cleaner than he'd ever seen it, there was a Masonite-topped folding table in the back equipped as a third workbench, and the antique paddle-bladed fan that hung from the center of the high ceiling was now surrounded by ductwork that had been painted in an attempt to make it blend in with its surroundings. He turned to his sister. "Did someone finally air condition this dump?"

She looked up at the ductwork. "That's the general idea. I'm waiting to see how it works when it's actually hot outside. We had to close down for a couple days back in November so they could put it all in and we haven't had a chance to put it to the test yet."

"Huh, must have cost a fortune. What happened, did Old Man Shapiro win the lottery, or what?"

Ruth flushed and looked down. "Something like that," she said. "It's a long story. I'll tell you all about it when we've got time to talk."

"Fair enough," said Rick. "The place looks pretty darn good, Sis. You're a better shopkeeper than I ever was."

Ruth laughed. "I had help. I'll tell you about that later, too."

Chet sat down at his bench. "Take a load off, son, and tell us what you've been up to."

Rick pulled off the leather jacket and gloves and dropped them on the table in the back, then liberated one of the two chairs and sat down by Ruth's bench. "Well, what can I tell you? Rode here on my Harley, took me a week. Hey, Ruthie, come to think of it, what the hell were all those letters from Old Man Shapiro last year about selling the building? Did he completely forget about you? By the time I got them I figured it was taken care of, otherwise you would have written me or left me a message."

"The letters... Oh, yeah." said Ruth. "It'll take a while to explain it all. I don't know where to begin. The building got sold all right, I'll tell you about that in a bit. I've been waiting to talk with you instead of trying to sort it all out back and forth in letters, and I had no idea when you'd be on dry land so we could talk. What made you decide to come back here after all this time?"

"Oh, I hadn't been using up anywhere near the leave I was earning and they finally just kicked me right off the base and said not to come back for a while." He smiled, but Ruth knew her brother too well. That wasn't all there was to that story, either. They'd have to spend a good long time catching up.

"Did you bring a lot of stuff with you? How much can you carry on a motorcycle?"

"A lot more than you think, but no, I traveled pretty light. Let me go unload my bags and take them upstairs and then let's get some lunch." He held out his hand and Ruth tossed him her keys.

He came back down in a World of Warcraft t-shirt and jeans and lighter weight boots than he'd worn for riding. "Any new places to eat around here? Come on, Chet, I'm buying."

"Whoa, wait a minute, what's that?" Ruth pushed her brother's right sleeve up to reveal the rest of an intricate tattoo of two red, orange and golden jewel-colored fish curved around each other in a field of stylized blue and white waves that covered most of his bicep. Chet came over to take a look too.

"I thought I told you about that. I got it done in a Japanese tattoo parlor in Hawaii ages ago. Koi for good luck."

Ruth ran her fingers over the finely done ink. "No, I don't think you mentioned it before. It's beautiful. A real work of art. Almost a yin-yang symbol, too."

"I'm glad you like it. I've had it so long I'd almost forgotten it's there."

Ruth rolled the sleeve back down and patted her brother on the arm. "Koi and tattoos and sailors, a match made in heaven."

"Looks more like a match made in a fish pond to me," said Chet. "Shoulda got an anchor on your butt."

"How do you know I didn't?" said Rick, turning around as if to drop his pants.

"One full moon's enough. I'll take your word for it on that one, sonny." Chet hastily turned away.

"Chicken." But Rick was grinning from ear to ear. "I bet you got a hoochie coochie girl hidden away somewhere yourself."

"Ha. I was in the Army. We got more brains than that." Chet went back to his bench.

"There's a tattoo parlor on the east side of the square next to the music store," said Ruth, in a very loud whisper. "Maybe you should treat Chet to some ink."

"I heard that, missy. If I ain't been in that place in all these years you ain't about to get me in there now."

"I still say you got decorations you're not showing," said Rick, with a laugh. "Don't you want to come have lunch with us, you cranky old coot?"

"Not this time. But you better be ready to treat me some other day."

"You got it. So, Ruth, any new places to eat?"

"Oh, a couple, but let's go hit the coffee shop," said Ruth. "I know everyone in there will flip when they see you."

"That's what I was afraid of." He said it lightly, but Ruth could tell there was an element of truth in that, too.

The siblings found a booth at the back of the coffee shop, and as predicted, people swarmed around Rick for a while. When the food arrived, though, everyone backed off and let them eat in peace. "Damn, it's good to be back here," said Rick, around a bite of club sandwich.

"It's good to have you back. I wish you could stay. I've missed you."

"I've missed you too, Ruthie. I can stay a couple months this time. There's a few things I want to take care of here before I go back."

Ruth set down her glass of iced tea. "Speaking of which..." She took a deep breath. "Adam Talbott's the one who bought the building."

Rick scowled. He'd had absolutely no use for Adam Talbott since the day the dirtbag had dumped his sister with a crude Dear Jane letter years ago. "I'll get you a new place for the shop as fast as I can, then."

"No, believe it or not, it's fine. There was a whole lot more to that story, too, and Adam's apologized ten ways from Sunday. He's doing his best to make up for the past, so if you see him, cut him some slack."

"See him? Is he living in town too?"

"No, he's got an office here, and they're mostly doing property management, but he's only here a few days a month. Eleanor's friend Dave is running the office full time."

Rick took another bite of his sandwich and turned to look out the window for a moment. After he finished chewing, he asked "Dave? Do I know him?"

"No, you wouldn't know him. He just came back here himself not long ago. Got involved with Eleanor over the winter when he fell on the ice trying to make a delivery to the appliance store and she rescued him, and then he left for a while and now he's back. He doesn't seem to be the kind of guy who stays long anywhere, though, so who knows what will happen with that."

"Ah," said Rick, and took another bite of sandwich. "Well, I hope he doesn't run out on her. Poor Eleanor's had enough of that already."

Ruth shot him a puzzled look, but he was concentrating on the sandwich. She let it go.

As they stepped outside after lunch, Rick said, "Speaking of Eleanor, is she still at the real estate office?"

"As much as she runs that place, I doubt she'll ever leave it."

"I'll go stop by there and say hi to her, then. I'll be back in a bit and we can talk about dinner."

⌗⌗⌗

Eleanor was speechless for a moment, and then finally managed "Is this where I get to say I always knew someday you'd come walking back through my door?"

Rick did his best to smile. "Do I look like Indiana Jones to you... Marian?"

"Not without the hat. Come on in and sit down. How long have you been back?"

"Got here right before lunch. Sorry for the surprise. I wasn't sure I'd make it across the city limits till I actually got here."

He sat. They looked at each other.

"Yeah. Well," said Eleanor, finally, "are you back for good or just visiting?"

"Just visiting. Got a lot of leave time to use up. Used up a bit of it getting here. Took the scenic route."

"Oh."

Silence. Rick was just about to reach for Eleanor's hand when Ron and Linda came through the door. And if they noticed any awkwardness in the office, they gave no sign of it. They'd both known Rick since high school and greeted him with delight. Eleanor pretended she had a lot of computer work to do.

"You staying with Ruth?" Linda asked.

"For a while. Got to get used to the place again. Speaking of which, I better get back there, I told her I was just coming over to say hi and she'll think you guys shanghaied me into buying an apartment building or something."

"Or something. When you come back for good, we'll talk."

"We will." He looked at Eleanor, tried to think of something to say. She wasn't coming up with anything either. They smiled at each other and Rick walked out.

"Don't ask," she warned her office mates. "Just don't ask." And she meant it.

Chapter 10
Periods of Adjustment

April

D ave set down his copy of *Database for Dummies* and rubbed his weary eyes. He was just never going to figure this thing out. When Adam had gone over it, it had seemed so straightforward, but now it was all Martian as far as he was concerned. The phone rang and he glared at it. No getting around it, though, he'd have to answer.

"Caldwell & Talbott property management, this is Dave speaking."

"Hi Dave, it's Ruth. What's wrong?"

"Just trying to figure out this damn software. Again."

"Yeah, I thought it had to be something like that. You sounded a bit PO'd."

"I am! Adam made it look easy when he showed me, but now I am just totally lost. I'm hopeless with computers." He sighed. "I didn't realize I sounded that bad. Guess I better stop and take a deep breath—don't want to scare the tenants." He closed the book with a snap and set it aside. "So what can I do for you?"

"I just wanted to ask if you were busy Saturday afternoon. I don't know if you heard, but my brother's back in town for a while. I thought it'd be nice to have a get-together. I called Eleanor to invite her just now, but she was tied up with something and Linda asked if she could call me back. I'm going to assume she can come, though."

"What time, and where, and do you want me to bring anything?"

"Oh, around one at my place, and I haven't even decided what we'll do yet so there's nothing to bring. So far."

"Well, let me know if you do want me to bring something. I'm a good cook."

"So I hear," she said with a smile. "Believe me, I will let you know. Hey, changing the subject back, why don't you hire an assistant to pound that computer into submission for you?"

Dave blinked. That had never occurred to him. "That's a fantastic idea. I bet Adam would go for it in a red hot minute, after watching me pecking at that keyboard. Do you know anyone who might want the job?"

"Not offhand, but I'll ask around. Maybe one of Brad's friends would be interested."

Now that he thought about it... "You know, if I hire someone I wouldn't just want computer work done. They'd need to answer the phone and deal with the people who come in the office—be a regular office assistant. I think the job would be part time to start, but we could make it full time later if we need to."

"Ah. Well, the people-skills part, when it comes to Brad's friends, I don't know about. You could put an ad in the paper, though; there are a lot of good people in town."

"I'll do that. Thanks for everything, Ruth."

He was about to sling the book in the direction of the wastebasket when he remembered it belonged to the library. And he'd still need to function somehow till he could hire someone. OK, reprieve for the book. But he'd definitely studied enough for one morning. He switched the phone over to voicemail and went out, whistling happily, to buy a newspaper.

Ruth set down her phone. The easy part was done. Next, she had to play lion tamer, and she wasn't looking forward to it. She'd given Brad some extra hours and had taken the morning off so she'd have time free from distractions to build up her courage. When Rick walked in ten minutes later with a bag of groceries, she waited till everything had been put away and then ever so casually said "Rick? We need to talk."

"That sounds pretty damn serious, Ruthie." He was smiling as he sat down on the couch facing his sister.

"Well, it is and it isn't. I was thinking of having a get-together here this weekend."

"And we need to talk about it? What do you want to do, throw an orgy?"

"Um..." Well, there was no way to say it but to say it. "Adam will be here."

Rick gritted his teeth. "There damn well better not be an orgy, then. Why is that asshole invited?"

"Because..." She took a deep breath. "Because he and I are seeing each other again."

Rick opened his mouth and then shut it again, shook his head violently. "Are you fucking *kidding* me? No way! Not after..." he stopped and cleared his throat loudly. "Not after what he put you through."

"No, Rick, listen to me. I..." She took a deep breath and let it out. "Believe it or not, things are different now. I know how you feel about him, and you've got good reasons—and I felt the same way too, especially after he came back here last summer and nobody could figure out why, and it was obvious to just about everyone that he was hiding all kinds of slimy stuff. He was a total ass, no two ways about it. But you know what happened? He went through absolute hell in this town, trying to make it up to me and everyone else for what he'd tried to do. It's hard not to at least try to forgive someone who goes down on his knees in the middle of the Veterans' Club floor with a hundred people staring at him, you know? He still hasn't told me everything that was going on with him and his parents when we knew him before, but what he told me was bad enough."

"*His* parents? What the hell? Our parents pulled enough crap on us and we didn't..." He stopped. Looked away. Sighed. "Well, OK, maybe we did. Or I did, anyway." He straightened his shoulders and looked his sister in the eye. "OK, if you're fine with it I'm fine with it, but you better not expect me to get all kissy-kissy with him."

"Of course not." She smiled. "I love you for being my brother and my defender and I couldn't have gotten through all those years without you. Just go into this with an open mind now, please?"

"I love you too, Ruthie, and I'm never going to stop being your big brother. I'll give Talbott the benefit of the doubt. Just for you."

"I can't ask for more than that. Thank you." Ruth was finally able to relax for the first time that morning. Charlie, her long-haired black-and-white cat, sensed an opportunity and hopped up in her lap. She skritched him behind the ears and was rewarded with a purr. "I've invited Eleanor and Dave, too."

Rick was silent for a moment, looking down. He clenched his hands. Then he came to a decision and looked up with a smile. "That's good. I'd like to meet Dave. If he gets Eleanor's seal of approval he must be one of the good guys."

"He is. Now let's figure out something fun we can all do." She got up. "Come on, you dumb cat. Don't think I don't know why you're so friendly all of a sudden." She had just finished pouring out cat food when the phone rang. It was Eleanor, calling from the office. Told about the get-together and its purpose, she was silent for a moment.

"El? You still there?"

"Still here. Um, someone just came in. Let me see if my mom can handle the twins all afternoon, but I'm pretty sure I can make it."

"You could bring the twins."

"No, I couldn't," she said, firmly. And that's where they left it.

⌗ ⌗ ⌗

Late on a Thursday afternoon, the programmer looked at the latest instant message. *What the...!* They had to be fuckin' kidding. **BIG ANTIVIR CO IN NOW, 2 BIG RISK**, he typed quickly back.

-JUST DO IT.

He gave the screen the finger and typed **MORE $$$$**.

There was no reply. Just as he was about to type it again, **-DO IT THEN TALK $$$$.**

$$$$ 1ST.

Back came **-WORK 1ST / WE TALK / OR TURN U IN**

He stared at the screen. Did they really think they could turn him in without cutting their own throats? They must have no idea how much he knew and how much he'd saved. He patted the stainless-steel-cased USB flash drive that hung from a ball chain around his neck, down inside his shirt. *We'll just see about that, assholes.* He waited.

-GOT THAT?

He waited till they typed it again. Gave the screen both middle fingers this time. Then **GOT IT**, he typed, and slipped the USB drive into the computer to save yet another log file to blow those fuckers to kingdom come someday.

⊠ ⊠ ⊠

At 9:25 Thursday morning, Mintaka Iowa's customers found that their internet connection was down. Nobody flew off the handle about it when it started. Every other time there had been an outage—and there had been plenty—the company had fixed the problem in less than half an hour. It had long since become clear to anyone with even a few functioning brain cells that berating Mintaka didn't help. When they said they were working on it, they were working on it. Besides, chances were pretty good you'd be yelling at someone you knew, and the next time you ran into them at the grocery store or in church it could get pretty awkward. Still, there were a few people in Lyric whose internet connection was so vital that they couldn't help getting frantic when it wasn't working.

By 4:30 pm that day, with no connection and no news other than "we are working on it," more tempers began to flare. And, of course, the less people understood about what the problem was, the more likely they were to try to do an end run around the internet provider—as Ruth, Chet, and Brad quickly found out. How many ways did they have to tell people "I'm sorry, we can't fix your internet" before anyone would listen?

Rick had been working in the back, installing a new hard drive and operating system for a customer, when the deluge of phone calls started. Being without the internet connection was a pain, but they all knew from experience that this was something way out of the ordinary and all anyone could do was wait. Mintaka didn't exactly have an army of techs. "Maybe I should go over there and offer to help them," Rick said. "Computer security's my specialty."

"We need you right here, boy," said Chet. "I don't give two hoots about computer security..." The door bell jangled its head off and an angry voice was heard from the outer room. "What we need is in-person security. Go on out there and give 'em the bum's rush. They won't argue with you."

That, of course, proved to be wildly optimistic on Chet's part, and even Rick's physically impressive presence wasn't quite enough to cut off the portly, red-faced man's heated argument that a computer repair shop ought to by damn be able to fix the goddamn internet. "Listen, pal," said Rick, trying to be patient, "we can't fix it. But *you're* going to need fixing if you don't settle down."

"Don't you threaten me! I know my rights!"

"That wasn't a threat and it's got nothing to do with rights. It was an observation. You're about to blow a gasket all on your own. Want me to call the paramedics for you? No? OK, then I'll just go ahead and call the cops, right now, and you can explain your little problem to them. How's that?" Rick pulled out his cell phone and flipped it open.

"Yeah, well, up yours. I'm taking my business to a real repair shop."

"Be my guest," said Rick, chuckling as the man tried and failed to slam the door.

Ruth came through from the back and leaned wearily against the counter. "I am so glad I had that door closer installed. It was like this when the virus thing was going on, too. They just don't get it."

"What virus thing?"

"Oh, I thought I told you about that. It was all over the news—CNN even sent a truck out here to do a story. I'm sure they wouldn't have bothered showing it if there'd been anything else worth talking about. A while back we had problems with viruses that turned people's screens weird colors and wouldn't let them onto their computers. They didn't do any harm to anything as far as we can tell. We got an antivirus company to come out and find us a way to fix it. We showed up on the news as Virus Town."

"Really? Just here in Lyric? That's bizarre."

"No, it was all around this area, not just in Lyric, but yeah, that's what they told us, a geographically limited virus is something out of the ordinary."

"Huh," said Rick. He scratched his head. "Well, listen, Ruthie, tomorrow I'm going to ride to Cedar Rapids and buy you a better telephone system, at least. I'll get one that lets you screen calls and put up specific messages for people with specific problems."

"That's overkill, really. We wouldn't need that kind of system more than once a year, if that."

"Just let me pretend I still own this place, OK? If I want to upgrade the phone system for you and pay for it, you should just let me do it."

Ruth shook her head. "Whatever you say... boss."

⌗⌗⌗

Dave got the first responses to his advertisement on Friday morning. Two were from high school students who wanted to work after school. He turned them down because school ended at three and the office closed at 5:30. The next two were more promising, though. One was a recently retired teacher, and the other had been laid off from the local farm-machinery manufacturers' office. He called both of them and thanked them for applying, and let them know that he'd wait a few days and give people a chance to send in their applications before interviewing anyone, since the internet connection was out.

He had found some free "How good are you with office software" tests online and had downloaded them before the crash, but there were a few more things that Adam had suggested he ask people to try to do, and he'd need the connection for that. He'd tried one of the tests himself and hadn't felt so completely inept in years. "Good thing I'm the boss."

Friday at lunchtime Ruth called and let him know that the get-together was being postponed because she was so worn out by all the irate computer users that she hadn't even had time to turn around, much less shop. Dave, who hadn't had any trouble doing without the internet connection, was surprised that people had gotten so upset about it. Then he remembered all those pumped-up *I-want-a-computer-now* library warriors back in California. "The internet should be regulated like an addictive drug," he said. "I've seen people get pretty unreasonable about it at the library, so I have an idea what you guys are going through. Not at our library, though. Thank goodness."

"People sure do get addicted to it," said Ruth, wearily. "But treatment for that kind of addiction, that'll be the day. I'll let you know when we can reschedule."

"No problem, Ruth. Take care of yourself, though, you don't want to get wiped out like the connection."

"No chance of that," she said with a smile. "Thanks, Dave. I'll talk to you later."

That, of course, left Saturday open. What would be something fun to do with Eleanor and the twins? *Oh, wait...* Eleanor's mom had already made plans to take the twins to the indoor swimming pool in the next town. He *knew* that. *Duh!* he thought. *Double duh!*

So what could they do that would take advantage of a twin-free afternoon, but not look like all he had on his mind was seeing how well one of her quilts would cover the two of them on the bed? How the hell would he know? Shit, he couldn't even remember his last real date. Lunch and a movie? Fat chance. Lunch, sure, but the two movies currently playing were teen-angst stinkers. Shopping? Oh, please. Just sit at his place or hers and talk or watch a video? They could do that with the kids around any time, and why waste a nice spring day indoors?

Hmmm... they could take a walk in the big park by the edge of town. He hadn't taken a really long walk in ages— well, not for fun, anyway, since he did a lot of walking in Lyric for the necessities of life, even though Adam had come through with a Toyota Tacoma truck—but would Eleanor think he was too cheap to pay for better enter-tainment or too dumb to figure something else out?

He debated for a long time but came to no conclusion. He didn't want to interrupt Eleanor in the middle of a work day, and he needed to get some estimates for roof repairs on one of the apartment buildings and deal with the stupid database. First things first.

About an hour later, the phone rang. "Did Ruth call you about the weekend?" Eleanor asked.

"Yeah, I was sorry to hear about that. I hope the computer stuff doesn't run her into the ground."

"I hope so too, but look on the bright side—that gives us some twin-free time."

"Um... yeah, I was actually thinking about that after she called."

"Were you? So what did you think about?" she asked in a teasing tone.

"No comment."

"Right."

"Actually," he said, clearing his throat, "I've never done more than drive past the gates of the big park out east of town and I thought it'd be a nice place to go walking. Now you can laugh."

"Our first real date, a walk in the park. Actually, I like the sound of that."

"You do?"

"Sure. I'll pack a picnic lunch. I can't remember the last time I went on a picnic."

"Me either."

"I'll come pick you up as soon as my mom hauls the twins away. Or you can come get me."

"I'm looking forward to it."

And for the first time since he couldn't remember when, Dave felt like he was on top of the world.

Chapter 11
A Measure of Understanding

At 8:30 on Saturday morning, the internet connection came back. There was a brief announcement on the Mintaka Iowa home page, something about "denial of service," couched in terms that were opaque enough that only a few people could really understand what had gone wrong. The company announced that it was crediting everyone for the lost time and said they had new security measures in place to prevent such a thing from happening again. The same information was repeated as the initial message on their phone system, just for good measure.

Nobody was particularly pleased, but there wasn't much they could do about it—and they weren't getting charged for service they hadn't gotten. That helped the grumbling die down quickly, and soon enough everyone went back to their usual online haunts. Well, almost everyone.

Chet shoved a laptop across the counter and said "See? Told you it wasn't the computer's fault. Didn't I tell you?"

"Don't expect me to pay you, then," snapped the customer.

"You'd likely give me Confederate money anyway," said Chet, who was having a good time. "Next time listen to the man."

"If you think there will be a next time, you got another think coming!"

As the door closed behind her, Chet burst out laughing. Brad came through from the back. "What's so funny?"

"Oh, nothing. Just enjoying being right for a change. And getting to give an old biddy what-for when she can't smack me one. Some days it does pay to get out of bed." He chuckled. "You should come this side of the curtain more often."

"Oh hell no, I'd rather stay in back out of the way of flying laptops," said Brad.

"Aw. Give it a try. Put hair on your chest."

"It doesn't seem to have worked for Ruth yet."

"Y'got me there. Good thing I'm here. Guess we should get back to work."

"I can't understand why these people don't know the difference between 'the internet' and their computers," said Brad, pushing through the curtain. "Man, that's frustrating. I really need to get those classes set up."

"It sure couldn't hurt. In this case a little knowledge would be a very good thing."

Brad pulled out his smartphone and made a note. "I'll make sure I go see someone first chance I get on Monday."

"Hope they give you extra credit for coming up with the idea," said Chet with a laugh.

"That'll be the day. Good thing I don't need any help with my grades."

"Sounds better'n me when I was in school."

Brad looked at Chet, opened his mouth, shut it, and finally said "Let's get back to work so we look busy when the boss gets back."

"Good idea," said Chet, heading for his bench.

Ruth came in a little later with the usual box from the bakery, and there were still a few cookies left when Rick arrived carrying three plastic bags and a big spool of wire, all of which he shoved under the table in the back of the shop. "Cookie! Me eat cookie! Nomnomnomnom," he said, grabbing the bakery box from Chet's bench and carrying it off in triumph over his head.

Ruth got up and went to look at the stuff Rick had brought in. "What's this?" she said, poking at the wire spool with her toes.

"Your new phone system, m'lady," said Rick, through a mouthful of cookie.

"I hope you didn't pay too much for the phones," said Ruth, returning to her bench. "You notice the one we've got isn't ringing today."

"Nah. Consider it an investment in the business. Did things settle down with the internet?"

"Yeah, it's back up this morning. There's some kind of technobabble explaining it on their web page."

"Yeah? Let me see that. I want to find out what they think happened." He sat and looked thoughtfully at the screen for a long time. "I don't think this means what they want us to think it means," he finally said.

"Really? How so?" said Brad, walking over to look at the screen.

"Well, maybe I'm just used to military terminology. It's probably nothing."

"It was all technobabble to me," Ruth said.

"Yeah, sounds like they got it from Star Trek or something," Brad chimed in.

"I think it was worded like that so it sounded like they knew what was going on, but most people still wouldn't get the idea they screwed up," said Rick. "Whatever, it's working again." He turned away from the screen. "Hey, listen, after you guys close up I'll get to work on installing the phones, how's that?"

Ruth looked at her brother with mock amazement. "If you really want to spend a beautiful Saturday afternoon like that, sure."

"It won't take me that long."

"Heard that one before a time or two, sonny," said Chet.

"Never," said Rick. "You're getting senile and you're imagining things."

"Not too senile to whup your butt, boy, you remember that." Both men laughed.

Running the new phone wires did take longer than he'd expected, but that was because he had to move so much junk out of the way and do some excavating in the basement, and he took time to sweep the floor by the baseboards while he was at it, so he wouldn't sneeze himself right out of his shirt. The phone by the front counter was an ancient pay phone he'd scrounged from someplace years before, and had decorated with a photo of William Shatner as Captain Kirk and the legend *Iowa Bill*. He decided to leave that as it was, since it was a part of the décor, but he attached a Caller ID box to the wall next to it so whoever was out front would know who was calling. The new phones went beside Ruth's bench and on the wall by the table in the back.

After everything was in place and he'd checked to make sure there was a dial tone, he called the local phone company and made arrangements to pay for voicemail, Caller ID, call forwarding and call screening for a year, and asked them to send a full set of instructions for the add-ons. The new services wouldn't be fully connected till Tuesday, but as long as the phones were working as they always had been in the meantime, that would be fine.

He plugged a headset on a long cord into the phone by Ruth's bench, then hung the headset up on a hook to keep it out of the way. It would make it easier for Ruth to talk on the phone and work at her bench or walk around at the same time. As long as nobody tripped over the cord or got clotheslined by it, he realized. Maybe he'd better see about getting a phone and headset for Chet's bench too, although he doubted the cranky old coot would answer it. He could buy another phone and some more wire in town and run the wire through the basement. Later.

He stood looking at the nice new phone, flicking imaginary dust off the top of it. Then he put the headset on and dialed another number from memory. Just to see if the phone worked, of course. Of course. After four rings, Eleanor's answering machine picked up and Rick hung up on it. What the hell was he doing calling her anyway, when he couldn't even think of what to say?

▨ ▨ ▨

At first, Dave had been scrupulous about not using the company truck for personal errands, which meant that it sat in its parking space behind the office most of the time. Adam took a look at it one day and said "That thing's gathering dust."

"I have a cheap-ass landlord who hasn't installed an outdoor spigot so I can wash it," countered Dave, with a grin.

129

"Point taken," Adam said, grinning back, "and I'll get right on that, but I didn't mean it literally. You've only put eight miles on it since you got it."

"I figured a company truck was for company business. And I can actually walk most places I need to go for the company."

"Yeah, small towns are great that way, aren't they? But seriously, I meant for the truck to be used. Sorry I didn't make that clear. Explore. Take Eleanor for a drive. Whatever. Just because the company owns it doesn't mean you don't get to drive around in it."

"Thanks. It'll make grocery shopping easier."

"Don't tell me you've been hauling everything home on foot?"

"Well, not everything. But I've generally just been buying stuff I can carry home."

"Ye gods," said Adam. "Ruth's the same way, hauls everything home in a little wheeled cart and drags the whole kit and caboodle up the stairs. I can't talk her into letting me buy her a car, even though her last one croaked ages ago, before I came back here. I can't figure that out."

I can, thought Dave, but said nothing.

So it was that on Saturday, Dave tied down a newly-purchased cooler full of ice, soda and bottled water in the back of the company truck, threw a couple of blankets he'd bought at the thrift store behind the seats, and headed off to pick up Eleanor for their walk-in-the-park picnic date. It was a glorious day—warm, breezy, full of flying clouds and blooming flowers. Eleanor was waiting on her front porch with a cooler of her own and a canvas tote full of assorted condiments and supplies. She secured those in the back. "I'm glad to see you're finally driving this thing," she said, after kissing him hello.

"Adam said he'd kick my butt if I didn't," he laughed.

A Measure of Understanding

As they drove through town, Eleanor pointed out a few places of interest, like the enormous mansion on the east side of town that was still owned and occupied by the descendants of the family who had built it in the 1870s. Dave wondered what it would be like to be part of a family that had never had any desire or reason to move anywhere else in all those years. The house was a glorious example of Victorian overkill, with a bulb-topped turret in front, gingerbread details all over it, and what looked to be the original slate roof and a copper rooster weathervane, long since turned green and surrounded by green streaks on the slate. "Kinda looks like Rhett and Scarlett's place," said Dave.

"Exactly that kind of idea," Eleanor agreed, with a smile. "Those folks were rich and wanted to make sure everyone in town remembered it."

"These other houses out here don't look much simpler," Dave said, looking around as best he could without driving over the curb in the process.

"Well, yeah. I've often thought of it as the Victorian era of monkey-see-monkey-do."

"Lyric is amazing," said Dave, meaning it sincerely. "I'm glad I came back."

"I'm glad you came back, too," said Eleanor.

They drove very slowly through Chautauqua Park, so Eleanor could point out the sights. "Chautauqua?" said Dave. "Local Indian tribe?"

Eleanor laughed. "You're not from around these parts, are you, stranger? Seems like just about every little midwestern town has a Chautauqua something-or-other in it. It was named after a bunch of people who gave educational lectures, if I remember right. There used to be a fairly large building where they had community meetings and so forth, but it burned down before I was born. The park kept the name, though. It's been here almost as long as the town."

Dave pulled into a small gravel parking area surrounded by tall trees and looked around. "They sure picked a nice area for the park. I always thought Iowa was just another flat place on the map, but this reminds me of places I've been in the Adirondacks."

"I've never been that far east," said Eleanor, as they unloaded their picnic supplies. "I suppose one day I'll get the urge to go traveling and see all these places I've never seen."

"Traveling's not all it's cracked up to be," said Dave, settling down on the blanket they'd spread on the grass.

"Have you done a lot of traveling?" She took plastic plates and silverware out of the tote and containers of sandwiches and potato salad out of her cooler.

Dave busied himself for a moment shifting drink containers around inside the other cooler. "I... well, yeah, I've done a lot of traveling," he said, finally. "Driving a truck, mostly. You don't get to see a lot of the tourist traps that way. Mostly just truck stops, and they're all pretty much the same. I got to see more of the scenery on the way here."

"You mean this time, or the time before?"

"This time. The first time, about all I saw was snow. This time I rode the bus here all the way from California."

She looked at him. This was more than he'd talked about himself since he'd been back. "Really? What was in California?"

"Nothing, as it turned out. Just wanted to see it, never been there before. I didn't stay there all that long. You know, it was while I was wandering around Disneyland that I made up my mind to come back here." It slipped out without conscious thought.

Fortunately, Eleanor burst out laughing. "From one Mickey Mouse place to another, right?"

He grinned, relieved she'd taken it the right way. "Of course! No, actually, I was thinking that Walt Disney's imitation small town wasn't as good as a real one."

"Interesting. I guess someday I'll have to go to Disneyland and check that out for myself."

"Everyone should go to Disneyland at least once. I figured that out after I'd been there."

They ate their lunch, talking about this and that and nothing in particular. After a while, the conversation petered out and they both lay back to look up at the canopy of trees. Dave couldn't remember the last time he'd had a day so peaceful and utterly free of everyday cares, so he was surprised when Eleanor sighed. He turned on his side to look at her. "Sigh? Sigh what?"

"That was a contented sigh," she said.

"Oh. Me too." And he gave an exaggerated sigh. "Very contented." He held out his arms and she snuggled on his shoulder. "I could stay like this forever," he whispered. The small glade was very quiet after that.

He awoke with a start, momentarily disoriented. Eleanor looked up from where she had been quietly putting the picnic supplies away. "I've only been awake a few minutes myself," she said. "I had to make a trip to the restrooms. I'm glad you didn't wake up till after I got back."

"Me too," he said, stretching and sitting up. "I'd never be able to find my way home if you dumped me here."

"Not a chance in the world that would happen, Dave. I want you to know that." She bit her lower lip and paused for a moment. "Believe me, I know how it feels to get dumped."

"The... the twins' father? Is that being too nosy?"

"No, it's not, really. It's... I don't know if you've heard about it from anyone else, but I've never said much about their father. Even to my own family." She looked down. "It wouldn't take Einstein to figure out that the twins were a surprise package. He didn't want to be a father. He said he didn't have any way of knowing what he was supposed to do so his own kids wouldn't get hurt and messed up the way he was. And before we could work it out, he left. But you know what? I got the twins, and that made up for a lot."

"I'm sorry," said Dave. "But I do know how it feels. I was engaged once, paid for the rings and everything, had the wedding all planned, and she dumped me too."

Eleanor smiled. "What a pair of dump-ees we are, huh?"

"Yeah, but those dumpers have no idea what they're missing." He held out his arms. They clung to each other for a moment.

"When you feel like it, I'd like to know a lot more about you, Dave Van Meer."

"Same to you, Eleanor Ward."

"You know, my mother's offered to take the twins for a whole weekend sometime."

He looked at her. "Oh? And what did you tell her?"

"Nothing... yet."

"Well then, one of these days we'll have a weekend to talk about ourselves. And I'm sure that's all we'll do with it." He burst out laughing, pulled her close and kissed her. "Just talk."

⚏⚏⚏

Later that night, work done for the day, the programmer typed **MORE $ 25K** into his instant message client.

He watched the screen for half an hour, but there was no response.

Chapter 12
Varmints of All Kinds

H i Ruth! It's Maria from Horemheb. How are things with you?"

"Fine, everything's pretty much back to normal, whatever passes for normal around here."

"Did you get my email, by any chance? There were a couple of things I wanted to ask you about and I wondered if you'd had time to think about them."

"No, but it most likely got lost in the outage last week. When did you send it?" There was silence on the other end of the line. "Maria? Are you still there?"

"Oh, of course, Ruth, I'm sorry... um, you had an outage last week?"

"Yeah, the internet connection was down for days, and we were going crazy trying to explain to people that it wasn't something we could fix. Some of them just weren't going to take no for an answer from anyone."

"My gosh, that must have been insane. I had no idea you didn't have a connection or I would have called instead of sending email."

"The way our phones were ringing, that might not have worked either. What did you want to ask about?"

"Oh, I just wanted to know if our software was still working for you and if the people in Lyric are still using it and if you had any suggestions for improvement. Since we're such a small company, we want to make sure our customers stay satisfied."

"As far as I can tell, your software's still working fine. The software's not the problem. Some people just don't get this virus business no matter how you explain it. I've learned that the hard way. We got a lot of grousing about the outage from the people who don't know the difference between a virus and an outage. I pity the poor people at Mintaka who had to deal with everyone screaming at them for days. Usually that doesn't happen because they're right here in town and everyone knows everyone who works there, but they've never disconnected for more than a short time before now. Tempers were getting pretty frayed."

"Yeah, I'll bet! I know how that goes, believe me. Our techs always have their hands full, or maybe I should say their ears full, explaining how to get rid of viruses, and I don't think half the people who call understand half of what they're told. Oh well. I'm glad things are working OK now so you have a chance to breathe. Do you need any more retail boxes from us?"

"No, but thanks. I think we have enough to last for a little while longer. I'll put in an order for more when we get down to our last two or three boxes here. We don't usually sell software, so people don't think to come here to find it. With sales that slow, we won't run out before you ship more."

"We're thinking of adding a few more titles to our line, so when we do I'll send you an email."

"Thanks, Maria. You guys have really done a good job here. Now if someone could just catch whoever wrote the virus."

"No kidding. I'm sure they will. Those guys always make mistakes, sooner or later."

Ruth put the headset back on its hook and sighed. Rick looked up from his computer screen in the back. "Something to do with the virus again?"

"Yeah, that was the technician who came out here when the first one hit, just touching base with us. She was able to send the right information to the company so they could get rid of it first, and they were able to nail the second one pretty quickly too. She left me instructions on what to send her if another one came around."

"No response from other companies?"

"Oh, yeah, they all were able to put out patches for their programs too. It just took them a little longer than Horemheb, that's all."

"Horemheb? Where on earth did they get that name?"

"Ancient Egyptian guy, something to do with King Tut, but that's about all I remember. You could look it up."

"Ehh," said Rick, dismissing that. "That virus sure sounds interesting, though. Wish I'd been here to see it. The fact that it was local is interesting, too. I wonder if the ISP is involved?"

"There was some speculation about that after the first virus but I haven't heard anything more since then."

"Well, if they are, it'd be downright crazy—they've got the monopoly in this area and they'd be putting a gun to their own heads if they tried something like that. People would be calling the big name ISPs in droves."

"Not much chance of that. We're so far out in the sticks we can barely get cell phone service, and you'll notice it's not from any of the biggies."

"Really? No, I hadn't noticed that. I guess I'd better check my bill for roaming charges."

"Might be a good idea. I think not being able to set up with the big guys is why cell phones are not such a hot item around here. No way we can take advantage of all those special deals we keep seeing in their ads, and heaven help anyone who wants an iPhone."

"Just out of curiosity, are you planning on expanding into selling software?"

"No. You know there's no way we could compete when people can buy stuff for peanuts on the internet. I just agreed to carry Horemheb's antivirus because Maria was the first one to find the answer. We did sell quite a few at the beginning, because a lot of people around here don't know a lot about computers and just wanted software that's brain-dead simple when something goes wrong. They don't need much more than what comes on the computer to begin with, otherwise."

"That's not unique to Lyric. You should hear some of the guys I work with, especially after they've been browsing the porn sites." Rick thought for a moment. "Somebody around here has gone far beyond that, though," he said. "There's obviously at least one person in town with some pretty high powered equipment and programming skills to match. But I have no idea how you'd catch someone like that. They're not likely to be bringing anything in here to be fixed."

"You really think it's someone local?"

"It has to be. I'm sure of it. But that's the only thing I'm sure of in this sorry mess."

Chet walked through the screen door with a bulky bag from the hardware store. "You two sittin' around flappin' your yaps again? Ain't there anyone in this place who does any work?"

Rick gave him the fish eye. "And just how long does it take to walk over to the hardware store and buy some wire? Even an old geezer shouldn't take an hour. How big a detour did you take and what was on the TV at the tavern?"

"The bookstore, sonny, and I got me a book called *Whupping Whippersnappers*, so you better watch your step."

⁂

Dave was getting a real baptism by fire. Starting on Monday, his phone never stopped ringing. Either it was people who'd applied for the office assistant job and wanted progress reports, or it was people interested in the job, or it was tenants calling for repairs. The repairs were usually the easiest problem to solve—the company had a list of local people who did contract work for Caldwell & Talbott—but who on earth would he call to get a seven-year-old's hamster out of a mouse hole in the wall?

"There shouldn't even BE a mouse hole in this god-forsaken place!" shouted the tenant. "I want my rent money back! You rented it to me under false pretenses!"

"Ma'am, I'm sorry, I'll send someone right out, but I wasn't even here when you rented that place, so I have no idea what you were told about it. I will definitely look into that..."

"Look into it my ass. That's what you people always say when you're not going to do one damn thing. I want my rent money back."

Dave gritted his teeth. "I'm not authorized to do that, ma'am, but I will call the main office in Chicago as soon as we end this call."

"Damn right you will. I'm coming in this afternoon to get my money."

Dave had a flash of inspiration. "You do understand that if I give you the rent money back, that nullifies the rental agreement and you have to move out today, too?"

"What? That's not in the agreement."

"You have your copy of the agreement there?"

"Yes!" she said, much too loudly. "And I'll be shoving it in your fat face this afternoon! Count on it!" *click*

Wearily, Dave put down the phone and rubbed his ear. "Get a damn cat, lady, that'd take care of the problem for you." He consulted his list, picked the phone up again and called the exterminators. They could definitely check the place for mice that afternoon, he was told, but they could make no promises about the missing hamster. "That's all we can ask of you, thank you," said Dave.

He went back to looking over applications. His first thought about the office-assistant position, which was to get someone in from a temp agency till he picked the right person to take the job permanently, had been torpedoed by the simple fact that there were no temp agencies in Lyric. There was a job center run by the community college, but all they could do was post an announcement for him and let people who came into their office know about it. Of course the problem really was that he'd never hired anyone before, didn't know what the job requirements ought to be, and was spending so much time on the phone and on the computer himself that he hardly had time to think.

He pushed all the papers aside, switched the phone to voicemail and went out to take a brisk walk around the square. If any of his tenants or applicants came looking for him, tough luck. He needed a break. After circumnavigating the sidewalks twice, he sat on a bench in the center, shaded his eyes with one hand and looked at the sky. It looked like they were going to get a thunderstorm in an hour or so, given the mass of dark clouds to the southwest, but that didn't bother him. He liked thunderstorms, even if they did tend to knock the power out. That was just another one of the joys of small town life, he'd decided, and he could live with it.

That thought led him to wonder if the machinery and wiring inside the power station were as antique as its exterior. The power company's building was a lovely example of WPA-era architecture, tan brick with sculpted stone accents. He'd noticed it on one of his long exploratory walks around town during his first week in residence. The town was full of a wonderful conglomeration of architectural styles, from the huge Victorian gingerbread mansions on the east side and the mismatched facades that ringed the square, to the plain old farmhouses like Eleanor's and her mother's. Oh, there were plenty of newer buildings in town—Caldwell & Talbott's apartment buildings were mostly of fairly recent vintage, and there were houses that definitely did not reflect 19th-century notions—but they didn't overwhelm the charming older ones. Somehow it all came together in a harmonious whole that made Dave happy.

Happy. Yes, he was. For the first time in years his restless, wounded soul seemed to have lost its constant need to move on. He'd always thought he was a big-city kind of guy, and could easily think of a lot more things Lyric lacked besides a temp agency if he wanted to, but when he got right down to it, who cared? He had everything he needed. This job was like nothing he'd done before, and he still hadn't lost the feeling of scrambling endlessly just trying to catch up, but the fact that Adam had trusted him and had simply assumed he could handle it meant more to him than he could say.

He looked at his watch and decided that he'd better go eat some lunch before the storms hit, either the one that would shortly be provided by Mother Nature or the one that was going to invade the office later, waving a rental agreement. He looked around the corner by the bank and saw no one in front of his building, but decided that discretion was the better part of not having his digestion ruined and took the back way down the alley and up the stairs to his apartment.

A plate of leftovers from the previous night's dinner (chicken breast with jarred marinara sauce tasted even better the second day) and a leisurely cup of coffee while he read another chapter in his latest library book had him feeling ready to go slay dragons in no time. As expected, the message light was flashing on the office phone. He pressed the button. "Hey, Dave, it's Mark from BugOff. Have I got some news for you!" He listened to the message and his face lit up with a big grin.

Twenty minutes later his irate tenant stormed through the door, papers clutched in hand. She proved to be a scrawny thirtysomething with dark roots and a lot of fruitless investments in cosmetics. "There's nothing in this agreement like what you said!" she shouted, rattling papers. "I want my rent money back."

"Please sit down, Mrs. Baker. There's no need to shout. Let's talk about this." Dave gestured to the chair in front of his desk.

She remained standing, belligerent. "You've talked enough. I want my money. You sent the damn exterminators! What were they supposed to do, kill my son's hamster?"

"Sit, please." He waited. Finally she sat, fuming, lip-sticked mouth pressed together in a tight mauve line.

"Yes, I sent the exterminators," Dave told her, quietly. "And the nice gentleman who inspected your house gave me some very interesting news about it."

"Oh, I bet he did. He probably found roaches, too. I want my money back."

"Did you know that an exterminator can tell a mouse hole from a hole someone's drilled in the baseboards?"

"Someone... someone drilled a hole? That... proves it! That place is unsafe! I want my money back!"

"Yes indeed, they drilled a hole so recently, in fact, that there was still fresh sawdust inside it. Did you notice that nice fiber optic device he put in there? He took pictures. I don't know what you had in mind, Mrs. Baker, but deliberate damage to our property most certainly is covered by your rental agreement, and if I find that you've done any more serious damage than that I can have you evicted and charge you for the repairs."

"You... you..." she spluttered.

"I'm sorry about the hamster, of course, but if you drilled a hole for it then I guess it just went where you wanted it to go. You'd best get back so you can explain it to your son when he gets home from school."

Her face under its coat of paint and powder was bright red. As she marched to the door Dave said, mildly, "I'll have the handyman come over in a couple days to patch the hole. Put some food down, maybe the hamster will come out before then."

Good thing the door was on a hydraulic closer and couldn't slam.

The sky was darkening, and he knew the first patter of rain couldn't be far off, but suddenly everything seemed rather bright in the office. He grinned, patted himself on the back and went back to looking over the applications. Twenty minutes later the thunderstorm rolled in, and he turned on his desk lamp, then shut down the computer and unplugged its surge protector from the wall. Maybe it was overkill, but with the way the computers in town had been acting up lately he wasn't taking chances. By the time the power flickered out an hour later he'd winnowed the job applications down to just three, and he'd call those people in the morning.

⌗ ⌗ ⌗

Across town, the programmer reluctantly shut down his three computers as well. They were protected by a huge uninterruptable power supply, but he couldn't afford to take chances either. He wished, not for the first time, that he could get away with putting in a generator. He might as well wish for a Mr. Fusion unit while he was at it. He got up and stretched.

Oh well, time to go get something to eat before the fast food place got knocked off the grid. Then again, if their registers went out again his friend behind the counter could slip him his food for free. This had possibilities.

Chapter 13
Bytes and Pieces

E leanor, sitting at her quilt frame, had completely lost track of the passage of time. When she was sewing a complicated pattern into a quilt top she had to pay close attention, but she was doing just the simplest of outlines on the Dutchman's Puzzle quilt, working her way around each triangular pinwheel segment on its own. So while her needle went up and down, she could let her mind drift if she wanted to, and this evening she was drifting.

The kids were sitting on the couch at the other end of the room, watching a video, and they knew better than to bother their mother while she was working. So the squabbling had been minimal, at low volume, and settled by the parties involved, if not to everyone's entire satisfaction at least to a workable equilibrium. Eleanor didn't notice when the first video ended and they put another one in the player. She did notice when they made themselves a bag of microwave popcorn—kind of hard not to notice that—but popcorn was on the approved-snacks list, even during this after-dinner, before-bed span, so she didn't have to issue a verdict. She sewed on, the needle moving up and down on autopilot.

She had never been a big believer in Coincidence, or Fate, or Karma, or whatever the proper term might be, but she had wondered in recent weeks why she should have instantly chosen the Dutchman's Puzzle pattern out of a huge book of assorted quilt blocks. She'd seen it on the page and had known right then and there that it was the one she wanted to make, and she'd gone out and bought the fabric and that was that. And that, in retrospect, surprised her.

Her other large-scale quilts had come about as the result of careful research and long consideration, and by winnowing down the list of possibilities over time. This one, she'd just picked. It was an easier pattern to piece than some of her previous efforts, to be sure, but was that all there was to it? She had a Winding Ways quilt that she'd worked on for nearly a year, and that she'd never actually put on her bed thereafter, lest the dog damage it. The dog had never damaged a quilt in his life and knew perfectly well he wasn't allowed on the bed, but you just couldn't be too careful after spending all that time forcing all those curved pieces to play nice. Or so she had reasoned. Maybe she should hang it on the wall. There wasn't much pride in the accomplishment if the quit stayed carefully packed away in the antique trunk in her bedroom.

She'd picked the Dutchman's Puzzle pattern for no reason she could explain, and then she had picked up an enigmatic man with a Dutch last name and she couldn't say why. A man whose life might form a pinwheel pattern too, should he ever want to talk about it. She smiled. The needle went up and down, touching one leather thimble and then the other, forming neat stitches around the blue-green calico triangles. She had drifted off into a memory of their afternoon in the park when the phone rang and she jumped and dropped the needle. Fortunately it landed on the quilt top and didn't un-thread itself. She poked it into the fabric for safekeeping.

"Mom," said Andrew, who had paused the video, "it's Ruth."

"You should have told her Mom's busy," said Rachel, in righteous indignation.

"For most people who call here you'd be absolutely right, Rachel, but Ruth's not most people, OK?" said Eleanor.

She heard a sulky assent from her daughter, who dug in a basket beside the couch and picked up a book to read while her mother was on the phone. Andrew got up to take the popcorn bowl back to the kitchen. Phydeaux trailed behind, tail wagging, hoping to get at least a few licks of the fake butter in the bottom. "Fat chance, you dumb dog," said Andrew, over his shoulder, but that deterred Phydeaux not in the least.

"Hi Ruthie, what's up?"

"How about we reschedule the get-together for this weekend?"

"Oh, can't—Mom's got friends visiting from out of town."

"You know, you really can bring the twins," Ruth laughed.

"And you and I both know why that's just flaming nuts," said Eleanor, grinning. "How about the weekend after?"

"I'll check with Adam. At least Rick is going to be in town for a while longer—he decided he'd use up all his leave time so his commanding officer can't get on his case about it again for a while."

"That's good. I bet after all this time he needs to just kick back and not have to stand at attention."

"Yeah, that's how I feel about it, too. And it's so good to have him around without... well, you know, all the fighting and problems we had before he enlisted. Getting away from that has been good for him, too."

"I haven't seen much of him in all the time he's been in town. I guess he's been keeping pretty busy."

"He's been working in the shop, and taking long rides out in the country, mostly. I think he just needs to see all the old familiar places and adapt to life in Lyric again. It's only been a few weeks and it must be quite a change from where he's been since he left."

"Nothing like a submarine around here, that's for sure. But I'm glad he's getting some time to himself. They must keep his days pretty well structured when he's at work."

"He hasn't talked about it much, but I would think so. And I think it's good he's spending time just settling back in here, even if he has to leave again. It gives me hope he might eventually come back here for good."

Eleanor thought about that for a moment before answering. "Speaking of which," she said, "I think Dave's finally getting settled in. From what little he's told me, Lyric is nothing like any place he's ever been before."

"Is he? That's good. Adam wasn't at all sure Dave would like it here."

"He does."

"Yes, and I know why." Ruth's amusement came clearly down the line.

"I have no idea what you're talking about," said Eleanor with mock innocence.

"If you're that clueless, can you be trusted not to sew your pants to the quilt?"

"Well, if you can keep from soldering your shirt buttons to the bench I guess I can manage!"

The two friends laughed, exchanged a few more pleasantries, and hung up. "OK, I'm done," said Eleanor to the twins, sitting back down at her place. "You can finish watching that video, but then it's bedtime for sure."

The twins consulted the clock, noticed that they were getting a half-hour extension on bedtime, elbowed each other with delight and happily settled in. Phydeaux, deprived of all hope of greasy treats, walked over to Eleanor with as much doggie dignity as he could manage, curled up with his tail on his nose and closed his eyes. Eleanor stroked his fur gently with one foot, brushed dog hair off her sock and got back to work. If she kept going, she could have the quilting nearly half done by bedtime.

⊠ ⊠ ⊠

Dave reached across the desk to shake hands with his new office assistant, Peter. Although the eager, freckled, red-haired young man hadn't had much work experience yet, he had aced all the tests Dave had given him, and was clearly very much at ease with both computers and phones. "Welcome to the office, Peter. You can get started tomorrow morning, if you like."

"Sure thing, Mr. Van Meer."

"That's not gonna fly. Call me Dave. I feel old enough already without being Mr. Van Meer on top of everything else."

Peter laughed. "You got it, Dave. Hey, is there just going to be the one computer in here after I start work?"

Dave blinked. "You know, I hadn't even thought about that. I'll have to get another desk and another computer so you'll have your own space."

"You'll probably need to go to one of the bigger cities to get a decent choice of desks. If you rent a folding table from the party store, I can bring in one of my spare computers and work on that till you buy another one and get a desk. I can just run the internet connection over there temporarily till we figure out how to rearrange things."

"The thought of having a spare computer just boggles my mind," Dave admitted. "I barely use this one as it is. I wouldn't have thought of having two in the office, but yeah, I'll get right on that. I'll check with the party store and call the Chicago office about the computer and the desk. The big boss has better resources than we could find around here. Do you have any preferences on the computer?"

"I get a choice?"

"You know a lot more about what would work here than I do."

"Fantastic! Yeah, I'll write that stuff down for you. Wish we had a better internet connection here."

"I don't use the internet often enough to notice any problems. Maybe you can teach me a few tricks when business is slow."

"Sure, I'd like that." Peter got a piece of paper from Dave's desk and made some notes about the computer he wanted. "If this looks too much like Martian when you go to read it to the boss, let me know and I'll translate."

"Adam's good with computers, I'm sure he'll understand it even if I don't." They shook hands again, and Peter gathered up his papers and his laptop bag, saying he looked forward to getting right to work the next day. "Me too," said Dave, and he meant it, even though he now had another man in the office to look up at. *Well, they can't all be my size,* he told himself firmly. He picked up the phone to call Adam.

⊠⊠⊠

This was the programmer's second face-to-face meeting with the others and naturally he'd gotten there late because their directions were totally screwed. He therefore swaggered in as though he owned the place and assumed an air of supreme confidence that he definitely did not feel.

The discussion, needless to say, did not start well. "All right, what the fuck were you trying to pull?"

"Me? Not my fault, buddy. Your directions to this place suck donkey balls."

"That wasn't what I meant, and you know it. A denial of service attack?"

"Yeah. Why the fuck not! I'm tired of your juvenile asswipe viruses. I wanted to show you guys what else I could do."

"You just don't get it, do you? There's a plan, dickwad, even if you don't understand it, and it's not going to work if you keep pulling this crap on your own."

"Yeah, well, at least now you know I can code a lot more than what you ask for."

"We knew that already or we wouldn't have taken you on, did you even realize that?"

He hadn't.

"What we need most of all is for nobody, and I mean NOBODY, to figure out what this is all about till we decide it's time for them to know, and if you screw that up for us you know what will happen."

He did.

"Yeah yeah," he said, hoping he sounded as if he really freakin' didn't care. "But I still want more money."

"Screw up again and you'll get squat. Got that?"

153

He scowled at them.

"*Got that?*" Somewhat louder and with an edge of hostility.

"Got it," he said in a sulky tone.

He accepted the stuffed envelope that was slid across the table and got up to leave.

"No more Lone Ranger shit," one of the others said, in a tone that brooked no argument.

"Yeah yeah, sure sure." But whether he meant it or not depended on what he would find in the envelope. He sauntered to the door as if he hadn't a care in the world. As he went out he considered flipping them the bird, but decided against it. If that kind of gesture turned out to be really necessary he had far better ways to do it.

He managed not to look at the envelope's contents till he was safely back in his lair. Then he stared at the contents in disbelief. It was less than even the original agreed-upon amount.

"Fuckers. Code the plan, my ass. You just wait till the next bomb goes off. You think you can screw with me? Your threats don't mean jack."

He booted up the main computer, thought for a while and then started to type. They'd never know what hit them.

In the room he'd left behind, there was laughter. "You know what he's going to do now."

"Just what we want him to. That's one little turd who's going to get flushed down the can real soon now."

⊠ ⊠ ⊠

Two new desks and one new desk chair were deliv-ered to the Caldwell & Talbott office by a truck from a national office-supply chain midmorning, three days later. Dave had had little trouble getting his few papers and possessions out of the old desk and putting the phone and his computer safely on the floor out of the way. Someone from the thrift store had come by to look at the desk and had agreed to take it. It was stashed out back under the fire escape awaiting their pickup later that day.

Peter's new computer system was still sitting in the boxes in which it had arrived by overnight delivery from Dell, along with some other gadgets Dave had never heard of. From what Adam had told him, the computer Peter had asked for matched up with one of Dell's standard models closely enough that Adam had just told them to ship it on out, along with the necessary software, plus the hardware for networking. Peter had seemed satisfied with it all, and that was what mattered.

"Where do you want these?" asked one of the delivery men.

"Here," said Dave, indicating more or less where the old desk had stood.

"No," said Peter, "you want to put one here, and one over here." He indicated a space about ten feet from the door and off to one side, and another one a bit farther back from where Dave was standing and off to the other side.

"Do what he says, guys," said Dave, moving back to get out of the way. The men hauled the desks in and set them where indicated. Peter asked that the desks be angled a bit, rather than straight-on to the door. That was no problem. Dave signed the paperwork, thanked the delivery men, and stood back to look somewhat critically at the new arrangement. "Why did you want the desks angled like that?"

"Oh, I just thought it would be less like a solid wall of desk facing the door, more welcoming. Plus, this way, each computer screen has a little privacy, since they're facing more toward the side wall. And now we'll have room to put out some better chairs for visitors."

"Oh," said Dave, considering this. "Yeah, that makes sense. Good job, Peter. I'll go see what Adam has in storage and pick out a couple more chairs. Now, what do you want to do about the internet connection?"

"Let me get the computer set up first. I'll probably want to run the wires through the basement, if that's all right with you."

"OK, I think I have enough tools in the cabinet in the back to handle that. I know there's a power drill, but we may have to go get you a longer drill bit. I'm getting to be a regular over at the hardware store. They'll know what we need."

Peter pulled his new chair up to the desk, slid the computer boxes over beside it and started unpacking. Dave was surprised to see that Peter opened the computer and monitor box flaps and then carefully turned the boxes over on the floor. "I've never seen it done that way before," said Dave. "What gave you that idea?"

"Oh, my brother used to work at a big appliance store, and he showed me. This saves you a lot of work, because you're only picking up the box." He lifted the box off the monitor to show Dave how it was done.

"That does work better. Is there anything else you'll need?"

Peter looked around. "Yeah, a ten-foot heavy-duty extension cord. That outlet is too far away. Maybe someday the big boss can get this place rewired for the 21st century," he said with a smile.

"Let's not push our luck." Dave grinned. "I'll go over to the hardware store right now and get the cord and ask them about drill bits, how's that? You can lock the door if you don't want to be bothered while I'm gone, but do please answer the phone if it rings. We've been amazingly lucky this morning, not getting any calls."

Peter looked at the phone. "Likely because the receiver's off the hook."

"It is? Oh crap. Must have happened when I set it on the floor." Dave righted the phone, and it promptly rang. "Here, you deal with that and I'm outta here," he said.

"I'll just blame all the busy signals on you," laughed Peter.

"Might as well, it's true!" And Dave scurried out the door before anything else could go wrong.

Chapter 14
Together and Apart

After his second semi-folded night on Ruth's couch, Rick had pulled up the website of a big camping-supply chain and ordered a lightweight folding cot, next day delivery. He'd packed a good sleeping bag with the rest of the gear on the Harley, but inside the apartment the nights were just a little too warm to sleep in it. The local surplus store had a pretty pathetic selection, but he found a summer weight bag that was in passable shape. After that, his nights were comfortable enough. Physically, anyway.

It was just that he was having such a hard time getting to sleep. And no matter how he tried to convince himself that it was only because he hadn't quite made the transition from shipboard or base living to being home again with no bells, no time clock and no shifts, he still spent many nights reading or watching Ruth's small TV with the sound turned down to the point where he could barely hear it, waiting to get worn out enough that it would pay to close his eyes. He went to the library every two or three days, emphatically ignoring Adam Talbott's building across the street, even when he knew Talbott wasn't in it.

Restless, he took long rides, having no particular destination in mind. When Ruth asked him about it, he told her that there were a lot of dirt roads he'd never seen in the daytime before and he figured he'd better go find out what they looked like while he had the chance. And that was mostly true. In a town like Lyric, there were a lot of interesting activities that were better suited to a dirt road after dark than to someplace in town where half the population would take notice and most of them promptly call your parents.

On the occasional weekends when Adam Talbott was in town, Rick deliberately was not. He knew that eventually he'd have to quit ducking out, but no matter how much he had tried, he still wasn't ready to start being nice to the guy—even for his sister's sake. And there were other issues that he needed to gather up courage to deal with. But not yet.

On those long late nights he sometimes wondered what was wrong with him. Were all his connections with people to be a matter of either love or hate and nothing in between? He had no answer to that. He was going to have to figure something out, though, because Ruth's get-together was fast approaching and she'd made it quite clear that the time for finding oh-so-important things to do elsewhere was over. He'd better brace himself and rip the figurative bandage off his figurative skin. He could do it. It was just that he didn't want to.

One afternoon, poking around the shop, looking for something to do, he noticed a computer that had been sitting on a shelf so long it had gathered a light coating of dust. Chet told him that it was one that had come in with the second edition virus. Its owner, having gotten the previous edition, had told Chet to take the damn thing off his hands and do what he wanted with it, up to and including shooting it. Rick set it up on the table in the back, went upstairs to fetch a flash drive out of his backpack, and got to work.

When Ruth closed the shop for the day, he was still looking at the screen and taking notes.

⊠ ⊠ ⊠

"Mom, why do we have to go to Granny's house? Why can't we go with you to Ruth's?" Andrew was putting dishes away, trying to make the job take as long as possible, while at the same time trying to convince himself that just this one time his mother wouldn't be wise to that ploy.

"Quit piddling around," said his mother, as she always did.

"I'm not piddling!"

"Right. You just like taking one spoon at a time out of the basket. Less efficient that way."

"Come on, Andrew, Mom's not going to fall for it," said his sister, as she dried off the dog dish and poured in the kibble. "Besides, Granny said we could bake brownies." Phydeaux nosed her aside and started munching.

Andrew said something bad, just softly enough that his mother wouldn't hear it. Rachel, who was closer, gave him the fish eye. Andrew gave his sister a *"Who, me?"* look in return. Then he took up the parent-friendly version of the discussion again. "But why can't we go to Ruth's?"

"Sorry, this is a grownup gathering."

"Oh, rated for mature audiences only," he giggled.

"More like PG-13, and you hustle up with those dish-es or your video game privileges are going to be toast."

"Not fair."

"You're right. Get a move on."

Twins safely shooed across the street and admitted to their grandmother's house, Eleanor looked at herself in the bathroom mirror. She picked up a tube of lipstick and put it back down again. The others at the gathering might not notice her wearing lipstick on a Saturday afternoon, but Ruth certainly would. There might not be comments today, but there'd be comments tomorrow. She settled for unbraiding her hair, brushing it and rebraiding it, and putting on some turquoise earrings.

Rick's Harley occupied one of the two parking spaces behind Ruth's building. Eleanor stopped for a moment and looked at it. Then she took a deep breath, squared her shoulders, and walked as briskly up the stairs as she could with a canvas bag containing four two-liter bottles of soda. They were her contribution to the afternoon, all Ruth would allow her to bring. She pulled open the screen door and pushed Charlie the cat away from it with one foot. Charlie knew perfectly well what was likely to happen if he tried to make a break for the great outdoors, but that never stopped him. He was, after all, a cat.

"Hi, El!" Ruth called from the kitchen. "Put those in the cooler, OK? There's no more room in the fridge."

"Am I the first one here?"

"Adam went to the store to pick up some more chips and Rick's in the bathroom."

"Well, good, then I get first dibs on the good end of the couch." She deposited the bottles as ordered, then got herself comfortably wedged into the cushions and patted her lap for the cat. Who, being a cat, made it quite clear he might or might not deign to sit on her lap when he got around to it. And, being a cat, after a few waves of the tail and licks of the front paw, he decided that lap sitting was just what he wanted to do. She skritched his ears and he rewarded her with a purr.

Rick came out of the bathroom, barefoot, clad in jeans and a white t-shirt, scrubbing his hair with a towel. "Hi," he said.

"Hi back," she said.

He stood there for a moment and then took the towel back to the bathroom.

"Rick, want something to drink?" Ruth called from the kitchen. "Eleanor filled the cooler." When Ruth was busy in the kitchen, the others knew from long experience not to bother her in there nor try to offer help.

Rick padded through to the dining area and dug a bottle of beer out of the ice. "You want some beer, El? I can see you're not getting up any time soon."

"I'd rather have soda, thanks. Not too much ice."

He handed her a large plastic cup with some ice in it, and an open can of soda, and settled into one of the chairs. Eleanor poured soda, then looked at him as she set the can on the floor. "Is that a tattoo on your arm?"

"Yes," he said, rolling up the sleeve. "Koi, for good luck."

"Wow, that's beautiful. Did it hurt?"

"Everybody asks that. Yes, it hurt."

Somewhat stung by his curt tone, Eleanor sat back and took a sip of her drink. "Well," she said, "it does look like it was worth it."

There was a brief silence, and then a knock on the door. "Come on in, Dave," said Eleanor, spotting him as he waved at her through the screen. Charlie hopped down off her lap and went to see if this new person was the kind who'd open a screen door for a cat. "Don't let the cat out."

"Wouldn't think of it," said Dave, reaching down to try to pet Charlie, who rewarded him with a smack on the hand, fortunately without much in the way of claw extension, then flounced off in the direction of the bed-room. "OK, be that way about it, cat. Hi," he said, extending the hand toward Rick. "You must be Rick, and I'm Dave Van Meer."

Rick shook the hand. "I figured. Nice to meet you. Want some soda or a beer?"

"Just some water, thanks." Dave sat down on the couch next to Eleanor. Rick went to get the water. Ruth carried two bowls of chips to the table. Rick returned with another plastic cup for Dave, and Ruth went back into the kitchen for the bowls of chip dip. "I can see you guys must have worked in that kitchen together a lot," said Dave, watching the choreography with interest.

"Not this kitchen so much, but our parents' kitchen wasn't much bigger," said Ruth. "We don't even notice what we're doing, after all this time."

Rick leaned back in his chair, stretched out his legs and took a deep swallow. "So, Dave, you're the big time property manager now?"

"Um... I don't know whether it's big time or not, but yes."

"Good thing Talbott didn't finish buying up half the town, I'd say."

"Rick," said his sister, giving him the fish eye from the dining area.

"Just making conversation."

"Rick."

"Right. So Dave, where'd you go to school?"

"*Rick!*"

"It's OK, Ruth," said Dave. "Penn State, why?"

"Just making conversation. Like I said. I went to Iowa State and couldn't figure out anything that interested me enough to major in. Gave it up and joined the Navy. Did you figure out a major?"

"Architecture."

"Really?" said Eleanor.

"Learn something new every day," said Dave, with a grin.

"So what did you design, truck stops?"

Ruth crossed her arms and scowled at her incorrigible brother, who wasn't looking at her. She let out an exasperated hiss. But Dave didn't appear to be bothered by the query. "If I did," he said, mildly, "they definitely wouldn't be such dreary, smelly concrete slabs. Maybe I should look into that."

Footsteps sounded on the landing, and Adam opened the screen door, carrying a box from the bakery. "Hi everyone!" He took the box into the kitchen, kissed Ruth on the cheek as she stirred a frying pan full of taco filling, and quickly moved to a chair in the living room to get out of Ruth's way. "It's good to see you again, Rick." He held out a hand.

"Sure. Excuse me." Rick ignored the hand, put his beer bottle carefully down on the floor and got up to go to the bathroom. Ruth came out of the kitchen long enough to exchange looks with Adam, who shrugged. No one spoke.

Dave shifted in his seat and looked quizzically at Eleanor, who took his hand and squeezed it gently. "I'll tell you later," she said softly. "It's complicated." Dave raised an eyebrow but said nothing.

Ruth carried bowls of taco ingredients to the table, returned to the kitchen, and took warmed tortillas out of the microwave. "OK, gang, dig in," she said, setting the tortillas on a plate at the end of the counter. "The salad's over there, there's soda and beer in the cooler, and there's plenty more in the fridge for anyone who wants it."

They settled themselves around the table. Ruth was closest to the kitchen, with Adam on her left. Dave sat down next to Adam, and Eleanor sat next to Dave. Rick returned from the bathroom and made a beeline for the refrigerator. Popping the top off his bottle of beer, he claimed the last remaining chair, on the other side of Ruth. The next few minutes were taken up with taco construction and consumption.

Conversation was intermittent, as everyone tried not to talk with their mouths full. Dave asked Adam about the prospects for Da Bears this season. "I'm actually a Packers fan, but don't tell anyone," laughed Adam.

"Ooooh, heresy," said Ruth.

"My lips are sealed," said Dave.

"Really? Can I have the rest of that taco, then?" said Rick.

"Not that sealed." They all laughed. Rick got up for another bottle of beer.

Everything seemed casual enough, but there was still an undercurrent of tension that Dave couldn't quite understand. He wished he'd talked with Eleanor about the gathering ahead of time, but there had seemed no reason to do so. Rick got up to go to the bathroom again. Ruth looked after him, her expression unreadable. She exchanged glances with Adam and went back to her salad. Dave looked at Eleanor, one eyebrow raised. She shook her head.

Rick returned to the table and polished off the rest of his beer. "So, what's in the bakery box, Adam?"

"Rick, let us finish the meal before you go digging into the dessert," said Ruth.

"I wasn't digging, I was just asking."

"I know what you were just doing," Ruth snapped. "Maybe you'd better make that your last beer for a while." She wiped her mouth with a napkin. "Sorry. I asked Adam to pick up some of those Mexican wedding cookies. I thought they'd go well with the meal."

Rick's eyebrows went up. "Wedding cookies?"

"Rick, please."

"Fine! Save me some when you're done." He got another bottle of beer and flung himself into a chair in the living room.

The others were silent, not looking at each other, picking at their food. Nobody seemed to have much appetite any more. Finally Adam rose. "Let me at least clear the table, Ruthie. I think I remember your system for loading the dishwasher."

Ruth did her best to smile. "I think I can let you handle that, but you don't have to do it right away. Let's have dessert first."

He laid a hand briefly on top of her head and went to get the bakery box. They all started passing dishes to Ruth's end of the table and Adam ferried them into the kitchen. Everyone took a few of the powdered-sugar-coated treats out of their box, and then Adam and Ruth exchanged a look. Ruth took the box of cookies and a napkin over to her brother. Rick took a handful out of the box with a muttered word of thanks, but refused to meet his sister's eye. She laid a hand on his shoulder, briefly, and then returned the box to the kitchen.

No one knew what to do next. Ruth made the decision. "Why don't we all go sit in the living room. There's more air circulation there and the chairs are a lot better." Eleanor and Dave moved back to the couch, wiping powdered sugar off their fingers. Adam got a glass of water from the kitchen and sat on the last remaining cushion on the couch. Ruth took the last remaining chair. Everyone looked around. Rick got up and went into the bathroom again. Ruth turned to Eleanor. "How's the latest quilt project coming?"

"I've got the top put together and the hand quilting about half done."

"Oh, that's good. You'll have it finished before it gets chilly again."

"Looks that way. I'll actually put this one on the bed."

"Whatever happened to that really elaborate one you made last year?"

"The Winding Ways? It's in my trunk, but I've decided I'm going to hang it on the bedroom wall as soon as I put a proper hanger on it." She grinned. "I should at least have it out for people to admire, I think. I can't believe how long it took to put it together. I should be bragging about it, not hiding it."

"No kidding," said Ruth. "It was gorgeous. Never saw anything like it. Hang that sucker up, woman!"

Eleanor laughed. "You got it. Come over next week and it'll be on the wall."

Rick returned from the bathroom and popped his last remaining cookie in his mouth.

"I don't think I ever asked you what quilt pattern you're doing this time," said Ruth.

Eleanor smiled. "You probably won't believe this, but it's called Dutchman's Puzzle."

"Oh, that's funny. Did you pick it before or after you met Dave?"

"Before, believe it or not. I had the top almost finished by the time Dave got here. I've been wondering ever since if it was fate or coincidence." She snuggled closer to Dave and patted his hand. Dave smiled and snuggled back.

Rick coughed out a few cookie crumbs. "Excuse me." He went to the kitchen for a drink of water, then plopped back in his chair again and set the cup on the floor, close at hand.

"What are the twins up to these days?" asked Adam.

"Terrorizing the fifth grade, mostly. I hope I can find enough activities to keep them busy this summer. I've been thinking of maybe sending them to summer school."

"Aren't they going to the computer camp?" asked Ruth, surprised.

"That would only be for two weeks, but it doesn't look like I'll be able to afford it. I feel terrible about that."

"I'd be..." Adam began.

"What the hell do you mean, can't afford it!" Rick jumped to his feet, red-faced with fury. "What the fuck did you do with all that goddamn money?"

Ruth was on her feet as well, reaching for her brother's arm. He shook her off. Dave moved forward to the edge of the couch. Adam, who'd been the target of Rick's temper years before, was absolutely still.

Eleanor, speechless, pressed back against the couch cushions. "What... what money?" she managed to gasp out.

"I sent you a checkbook! I've been putting money in that goddamn account all this time, and clearly I should have been asking you what the hell you were doing with it!"

"I never..." Eleanor began.

"Don't you fucking tell me you never!"

"Rick! What's *wrong* with you!" Ruth was getting frightened. She hadn't seen her brother rage like this since... she didn't want to think about the last time. She looked at Adam, who hadn't moved, his eyes fixed on Rick.

"What's wrong with *me?* Ask your goddamn friend there where she's been blowing my money instead of spending it on my children!"

"Your..." Ruth looked from her brother to Eleanor.

"His children," whispered Eleanor. She cleared her throat. "But I never saw a checkbook. You have to believe me, Rick. I never did."

"Yeah, tell me another one. You better account for every last fucking dime before I leave town. I want to know where it went!" He moved toward the couch and both the other men immediately jumped to their feet. "I'm just getting my fucking shoes. Back off, you two." He picked up shoes and socks from the small pile of his belongings beside the couch, whirled, and was out the door.

Adam and Dave stood still. When Rick's footsteps faded away, Adam sat down hard, shaking his head. Dave began to rock back and forth. After a moment, he raised his hands as if he were going to put them over his ears, then let them drop to his sides. Eleanor reached out to take his hand, but Dave had already started walking toward the door.

"Dave, don't chase him," said Ruth.

"I... I'm not chasing him," said Dave, in an odd, choked voice. "I'm..." He turned unsteadily back toward the others. "I'm..." He sounded like he'd run up a flight of stairs.

"Dave?" Eleanor's voice was just as strained.

"I can't do this," he said. And he turned around, went swiftly to the door and was gone.

Chapter 15
The Way We Were, The Way We Are

I nside the apartment, there was dead silence, the three remaining occupants forming a frozen tableau. Then Eleanor sank wearily back into the couch cushions, head bowed. Ruth immediately went to sit beside her and put her arms around her friend. After a moment, Eleanor let herself be held, and laid her head on Ruth's shoulder.

"Do you... do you want me to leave, too?" Adam asked, uncertainly.

Eleanor sighed, eyes closed. "Do what you want." From Ruth's expression, however, Adam realized that she wanted him to stay. He sat down on the edge of the chair Ruth had vacated and leaned forward, elbows on knees. He could not remember ever having felt this helpless before.

"El, do you want to talk about it?" said Ruth, gently stroking a strand of hair off her friend's face.

"No. But I suppose I'd better." She sighed again. "Could I have a glass of water, please?"

Adam jumped up and went to get it. Eleanor sat up, patting Ruth gently on the leg as Ruth let her go. She drank half the contents of the glass, sighed again and set it down carefully on the arm of the couch. "You have to believe me," she said, "what happened wasn't a one-night stand."

There was a moment of silence, which Ruth broke by saying, firmly, "Of course it wasn't."

Eleanor finished the water and gestured to Adam with the glass, which he refilled and returned. She took another sip and then set it down. "It was when I was living in Coralville," she began. "I didn't have a lot of friends there, so when someone from one of my classes invited me to a party one Saturday afternoon I thought it was a chance to have at least a little social life for a change. Of course, when I got there, the place was packed with people I didn't know, talking about things that didn't include me. I was just about to get my coat and leave when I heard someone call my name."

⌗⌗⌗

Rick pushed his way through the crowd. "What are you doing here?"

She laughed. "Same to you!"

"I got dragged here by a friend of a friend. I'm not sure where he got to."

"With me it was someone from one of my classes, ditto."

"Guess that means we're the only true friends in this nuthouse."

She laughed again. "These poor strangers don't know what they're missing. My gosh, Rick, it's been years."

"It's not the years, honey, it's the mileage," he said solemnly. She gave him a quizzical look. "Indiana Jones. My all time favorite movie line."

She did a creditable imitation of Kate Capshaw scree-ching *"Indyyyyyyyyyyyyyyyyyyyyy!"* There was so much noise in the room that only a few people turned to look.

"Wrong movie. You're supposed to say you always knew I'd come walking back through your door."

"Oh, right. So where's Salah?"

"Back in the snake pit, sitting on his asp."

She groaned and smacked him on the arm. He laughed. "Hey, Marian Ravenwood, what say we blow this popsicle stand and go get something to eat?"

Eleanor looked at the sad collection of half-eaten munchies and dirty plates, and the dregs of neon pink punch in the bowl on the buffet table across the room. "Oh yes. Fire up the Jeep."

They took Eleanor's car, since Rick had ridden to the party with his friend-of-friend. After weighing a few options, they decided to try a family-owned Greek restaurant that Eleanor had heard about. Neither of them knew anything about Greek food, but all of a sudden it seemed like the perfect day for a new culinary adventure. Rick told the waiter they wanted to learn all about the food, and to bring them the best of everything. The chef, delighted with the opportunity, came out to describe the dishes himself, and gave them wine to go with their meal, on the house.

Two hours later, glowing with wine, food and fel-lowship, they walked out into a brisk winter night. "Want to go see a movie, or something?" Rick asked, turning up his collar and wrapping his scarf more firmly around his neck.

"Nothing good playing this weekend." She thought about it for a minute. "I have some decent videos at my place, though."

They looked at each other. He held out a hand. She took it. And then, without conscious thought, they were kissing. Passionately.

⊠⊠⊠

"We never did watch a video," Eleanor said, "but it wasn't what you think."

"El, I don't think anything. Really." Ruth smiled at her friend and made a "go on" gesture.

Eleanor drank the rest of the water and set the glass on the floor. She thought for a moment. "Well... we talked for a long time. We'd never done that before, not really talked. Up till then, to me Rick was just your brother and to him I was just your friend." She sat for a moment, looking at nothing in particular. Then she took a deep breath, let it out, and continued. "It got late, and he had said earlier that he planned to drive back to Lyric that night. But it was pretty clear by that time that neither one of us wanted him to go. He did offer to sleep on the couch."

Another pause. "I better go to the bathroom before I go on with this. Too much water." She tried to smile. Ruth and Adam both got up when she did, but she didn't appear to notice. The light through the windows had begun to fade with the day. Ruth turned on the radio, softly, and one of the living room lights. Adam stretched, then got himself settled more comfortably in his chair. Ruth sat back down on the couch. They looked at each other, but there was nothing to say.

Eleanor returned, picked up the water glass and took it to the kitchen. "OK if I make coffee, Ruthie?"

"I'll do that. You take it easy."

"I need the distraction, just for a little bit. Talking about this after all these years..." She let the sentence trail off.

"Of course," said Ruth, sitting back down in silence.

When the coffee maker was going, Eleanor returned to her seat. Ruth patted her shoulder, gently. "Well," Eleanor said, "he stayed the night. Not on the couch. And that was the only time we didn't use protection, because I was sure that since it was only two days after my period it would be safe. You know, I found out there's a word for people who take that kind of chance. Parents." She managed a smile. "The problem was, we hadn't even established a real relationship when we got that news."

She shifted a bit, got comfortable again. "You and Rick didn't talk about what was happening with your parents, so I had no idea how he felt about what they were doing and how angry he was in those days. So when I told him I was pregnant I really wasn't prepared for his reaction. I didn't understand any of it at the time, and I don't really remember a lot about it—just a blast of sound and fury. He wasn't ready to be a father, I do remember that—that was crystal clear. Well, I wasn't ready to be a mother, either, but there it was, and we both had to deal with it the best we could. He didn't ask me to have an abortion, I'll give him that. Not that I would have anyway. He just said he couldn't handle it and he was going to have to walk away so he wouldn't treat his children like your parents treated you."

"I'm still not ready to talk about a lot of what happened with our parents, even now," said Ruth. "They fought all the time and accused each other of terrible things, and they were so focused on hurting each other that they didn't seem to care whether Rick and I heard them or not. And then of course they tried to drag all the dirty laundry through the courts. I thank my lucky stars that I'd left town by the time that was going on." She sighed.

"He was the oldest," she continued, "and I didn't realize it at the time, but he always felt like he had to be the responsible one because our parents never were. He felt he needed to take care of me, and he did. I guess that sense of responsibility made it harder for him to cope and to forgive them for all that crap. I had no idea he was so overwhelmed by it all that one more responsibility drove him away. He never said anything about any of this." A tear trickled down her cheek and she brushed it away with the back of her hand. Nobody spoke for a minute.

"So what choice did I have?" said Eleanor, finally. "I made it through school and then I came home, of course. I was so afraid my parents would hit the roof, but I couldn't think of anything else to do."

"Not your parents," said Ruth. "They wouldn't."

"No, of course they didn't. I don't know why I had thought they would. They just held out their arms and we hugged each other and cried, and that was that. They told me that they'd listen any time I was ready to talk. But I didn't want to talk. It was easier not to. I probably still wouldn't want to if this hadn't happened today."

Adam got up and went into the bathroom, wiping his face with the back of one hand. Ruth hugged her friend. After a moment, Eleanor hugged back. "Well," she said, "when I found out I was having twins I called Rick and told him. All he could do was tell me again that he wasn't ready to be a father no matter how many babies were on the way. What could I do? It wasn't too long after that that he joined the Navy and left to see the world. And I had the twins and did my level best to be a good mom and to erase Rick from my life."

"You've definitely been a good mom," said Ruth. "Those two have turned out great."

"I think so too. Even when they're driving me crazy." Eleanor managed a smile.

"If it's not being too nosy," said Adam, returning to his seat, "what did you tell them about their father?"

"That was... that was a challenge. I didn't want to lie to them, but what part of the truth could I tell? I just made sure they always knew that their father loved them very much, but he was an explorer, traveling around the world, and couldn't come see them just yet. And that I'd let them know when I heard that he was going to come home. They've been pretty good about accepting that. But as for this checkbook Rick says he sent... well, I might have thrown the package out unopened if it arrived soon after the twins did. I just don't remember."

She struggled to her feet and went to the kitchen to pour coffee, then brought back three cups, spoons, and the cream and sugar on a tray. After Adam and Ruth accepted their cups, Eleanor sat back down with hers. She sipped the coffee and thought for a moment. "You know, when he walked through the office door that day, I thought it meant he'd really come back—that he was ready to meet the twins, at the very least. I shouldn't have gotten my hopes up. That was stupid. He's been in town for how long, now, and up till tonight that was the only time we talked. Why did he come back, if he didn't want to see me or get to know his children?"

"I don't know," said Ruth. "I've seen him almost every day and I still don't know. I wish he'd felt he could talk with me. I always thought we were closer than that. I guess not. We'll have to find a way to fix this, if he doesn't just take off straight for the base again."

"I wish I did know where that checkbook got to. If I'd had any idea he'd been paying child support all this time, it would... it would have made a difference. And not just the money."

"Speaking of which," said Adam, "I was going to say that I'll pay for the computer camp. I don't want you to worry about that. When is the deadline and what do I have to do?"

"Adam..."

"Don't say I can't," he quickly cut in. "Look, I didn't even know they existed till last year, and tonight I found out I'm practically their uncle. I need to make up for lost time. Call it all the birthday presents I wasn't around to give them. Call it a Christmas present. Call it whatever you like, but I'm paying for the camp and that's that. And I'll tell you what, I'll pay for you to take a vacation anyplace you want, while the twins are away. I'll pay for Dave to go with you." He sighed.

"I learned only a short time ago that I'd spent too damn much of my life chasing money and not enough time appreciating the riches I already had. And I don't mean just what was in my bank accounts. Let me do this, please?"

Eleanor's shoulders sagged. She got up and went to the window and looked out at the golden sunset light in the square. "All right," she said, finally. "And thank you, Adam. I've got the applications at home and they'll need a check for the deposit."

"I'll come over tomorrow and get them, if that's OK. You don't have to let the twins know I'm doing this, if you'd rather not."

She turned to face him. "I will most certainly tell them, and they'll be so delighted you'll never be able to get away from them." She managed a wavery smile. "You don't know what you're getting into."

"I'll learn." He held out his arms. "Care to hug on it?"

"I.... yes," she said.

⊠⊠⊠

As the light faded in his living room, Dave sat huddled in the corner of his couch, arms wrapped around himself. He hadn't had a panic attack since he'd been back in Lyric and his prescription had long since run out. He was on his own. What was he supposed to do now? He loved Eleanor so much, and this was just the hell of a way to realize that, wasn't it? He couldn't even begin to think straight. His lips quivered and he pressed a fist against his mouth.

Was this the sign it was time for him to move on again? Oh God, he wished he knew.

Finally the panic ebbed away, but in its aftermath, unable to stop himself, he started to cry. He curled tightly on his side and sobbed out all the anguish of all the years he thought he'd left behind. It seemed to take an eternity to let it all out. In the end, utterly spent, he lay on his back, eyes closed, trying to get his breathing under control again.

With one long shuddering breath, he forced himself upright and stood up. He wobbled to the bathroom and washed his face and hands in cool water, making sure he never looked at the mirror. He didn't want to see the man who'd look back. When he felt steady, he made his way to the bedroom, and there, without turning on the lights, he threw his clothes in a heap on the floor and crawled wearily into his bed. The phone rang, and in trying to find the switch that turned off the bell he pushed it off the nightstand onto the floor. He left it there. Quickly, he pulled a pillow over his head, thrashed around once or twice, and finally drifted off to sleep.

⊠ ⊠ ⊠

Rick was running, running, into the dark. He knew he'd have to go back. He'd just run a little farther, that's all. When he got tired he'd go back. He'd go back. He'd go back.

Chapter 16
Cross Purposes

E leanor sat numbly at her kitchen table, staring off into space, unable to think what she needed to do next. It had taken considerable effort to concentrate enough to get the car home and safely into the driveway. It was a good thing she'd put soup in the slow cooker that morning, otherwise they'd all be eating cold cereal for supper tonight. She sighed and tried to focus, because somehow she was going to have to act as though nothing had happened when the twins got home. She sighed again, telling herself firmly that she was just going to have to darn well pull herself together now. The house was getting dark, and she'd need to turn the lights on so her mother would know she'd gotten home. But even that seemed like more than she could deal with.

She had no sense of the passage of time, no idea how long she'd been sitting there, or how long it would take her to get up on her feet. She should call Dave, but she couldn't make herself dial the phone. She thought she felt feverish, but whether that was real or imaginary... could she even lift a hand to feel her forehead? No. Her arms were made of lead. The whole world crushed down on her. *I can't cry*, she thought. *The twins will notice.* But if she didn't cry, how could she cope?

I've been through worse than this and I've survived. I've done it before. I'll do it again. But what about Rick? And Dave?

No telling how much time passed before she finally pushed herself to her feet and found that yes, she could stand, she could walk, she could turn on the lights and go in the bathroom and wash her face and hands in cool water, and make it back into the kitchen to stir the soup and take the loaf of homemade bread out of the pantry to slice for supper. She turned on the lights in the living room and took out the dishes and silverware for supper.

The twins and the dog came through the back door like triple whirlwinds a few minutes later. "Hi Mom! How was the party? We made brownies with Granny but we ate them all before we could bring any home and Granny said she didn't know how we managed it." They put their shoes on the rack in the mud room and Andrew went to get food for the dog. Rachel washed her hands at the kitchen sink, then ran into the living room, only to come back seconds later. "Where's Dave? Isn't he eating with us tonight?"

"Oh... Dave wasn't feeling very well, and he left the party early, so he won't be here tonight. I might take some soup over to him later."

"If you do can we go too?"

"The last thing a man who isn't feeling well wants to hear is your level of noise." She did her best to smile.

"Mom? Aren't you feeling well either?" Rachel looked up at her in real concern.

"I'm fine. Just tired." She considered what to say. "Ruth's brother... um, well, he turned out to be in a bad mood at the party so it was not as much fun as I thought it would be, that's all."

"Ruth's never in a bad mood," said Andrew.

"Well, you're not the same as your sister, and Rick's not the same as Ruth," said his mother.

That made perfect sense to the twins. But they still got the table set in record time, without the usual fussing, trying to cheer their mom up. Over supper they talked about making brownies with their grandmother and how they'd tried to show her how to play a video game. "I think Granny thought she couldn't do it, but she learned really fast," said Andrew. "She says she just keeps the game there for us to play with, but you know what, I bet she practices when we're not there."

Rachel giggled. "I bet she does. Mom, you should sneak over there and try to catch her. That'd be really funny."

Eleanor smiled. "Yeah, I bet it would. Maybe I'll try that sometime."

"Do you play video games with Dave when we're not here?"

"No, I hear enough noise from that thing when you guys are playing with it. Besides, you know how bad I am at video games."

"Yeah," said Rachel, "I could beat you when I was a baby." She giggled again.

"Exactly," said Eleanor. "It's bad enough you guys have been aces all your lives and I've never won a game. I don't want Dave finding out that I'm..." She stopped to draw a quick breath, and coughed.

"Mom? What's wrong?"

"Nothing. I think I must have put too much pepper in the soup. Don't worry. Anyway, I don't want anyone else to know I'm a total video game loser, that's all."

"Yeah," said Andrew, "I wouldn't want anyone to know that either."

"Two people laughing at me is enough," said Eleanor, and the twins wholeheartedly agreed.

After supper, Eleanor shooed Andrew and Rachel into the living room and told them to pick a movie to watch. The usual squabbling ensued, stopped only by a parental threat to do the choosing. Compromise reached, and with a promise of extended bedtime if they behaved, they settled in. Eleanor went back to the kitchen to put supper away.

Without really thinking about it, she found herself getting a Tupperware container from the pantry. Finding it staring at her from the counter, she moved almost mechanically to fill it with soup, then slice bread and wrap it in paper towels. And then she went just as mechanically to get her purse.

"Kids, I am going to run some soup over to Dave's place. I won't be gone long, so I better not find you guys horsing around when I get back."

Brief sounds of acknowledgement came from the twins over the movie's soundtrack. Eleanor went out the back door and got into the car before she could chicken out.

But Dave's apartment was dark. She knocked on the door and called out that she was there, but there was no sound, no light, no sign of occupation. She waited, knocked and called again, then wearily turned around and drove home. The twins appeared not to have moved. She picked up the phone, dialed his number, and got a busy signal.

And every other time she tried that night, the buzz-buzz-buzz sound was the same.

⌘ ⌘ ⌘

Cross Purposes

Ruth and Adam sat together on the couch for a long time after Eleanor's departure, snuggling quietly. There seemed little else that they could do, or could even think about doing. After a while, Adam suggested that they go to the coffee shop for supper, but when the food came, neither had much appetite. They made a halfhearted effort to eat, and then walked back to Ruth's apartment in silence and settled in their places on the couch. When the cranky old courthouse clock started wheezing and clanking and finally bonged nine times, Adam stretched and sat up. "Do you want me to stay here tonight?"

"I really do, but..."

"But all in all it would be easier if I weren't here when Rick comes back."

"Yes. I think so. I don't know. I don't understand what set him off this afternoon, but I just... I just realized he's been restless for a while. Maybe he and I can talk, but it won't work with anyone else around."

"Yeah, I understand. I hate leaving you alone tonight, though."

"He's my brother. We've looked out for each other for so long that we're more in tune with each other than most siblings are, I think. We need to talk this out, and we will, I'll see to that. Well, more likely he'll talk and I'll listen. But maybe after that we can deal with the rest of it."

"The long lost father of the twins."

Ruth was silent for a moment. "Pretty amazing, isn't it? I kind of understand why they didn't want anyone to know. I think. But still..."

"Yeah. We both know about keeping family secrets from the rest of the world."

Ruth sighed. "Yes." After a moment she frowned. "Do the twins even look like him? Isn't it funny, all of a sudden I can't remember what they look like."

185

"I haven't seen them enough to know. But if there were a resemblance, surely someone would have noticed?"

"Enough gossiping old biddies in this town... yeah, if anyone had noticed, someone would have said so."

Ruth got up and went into the bedroom, returning a moment later with a small double frame holding that year's school photos. She sat back down on the couch and the two of them studied the pictures for a while.

"No," said Adam, finally, "not much of a resemblance. They don't look a lot like Eleanor, either, I'd say. But Rachel's definitely got Rick's eyes."

"I wonder what happened to all the pictures of Rick as a boy. My parents weren't real careful with things like that."

They sat in silence for a while, looking at the photos. The courthouse clock bonked out the half-hour. Ruth said, quietly, "And what about Dave? They were so happy. What will he do now?" They looked at each other, wordlessly. For that question, it seemed there was no answer.

A few minutes later Adam stood up, stretched, held out his hands. Ruth got up and slid into his arms. They held each other for a moment, then kissed, gently, and Adam let her go. "Shall I call you in the morning?"

"No, I'll call you when I know what's going on."

"Fair enough. I hope you two can work things out."

"We'll have to. There's just no other choice."

She left one lamp lit in the living room when she went to bed. Rick had not returned. Ruth lay, staring up at the ceiling, for a long time, but finally her eyes closed and she slept.

⌗ ⌗ ⌗

Cross Purposes

Rick had never noticed how feeble the old streetlights around the square were before. Leafy shadows were the only things that moved as he dragged his feet slowly along the deserted, silent street. He finally reached the northwest corner of the square and looked up. He could see through the apartment's side windows that Ruth had left a light on in the living room. Was she waiting for him? Should he just curl up on a park bench in the square and try to sleep till morning? No, that was the coward's way out. And besides, he'd freeze, and if the cops came along they'd think he was just another drunk. Or something. The warmth he'd generated on his run to nowhere had long since faded away. He was going to have to go back and face whatever awaited.

But still, while he summoned up the determination to do that, he stood at the bottom of the stairs, trying to will his feet to move. He had precious little energy left and he ached all over. Finally he gritted his teeth, grabbed the railing, and pulled himself upward. But only Charlie was there to greet him at the door, and when the cat saw who it was, he skittered quickly away. Rick was surprised to find that his feelings were hurt. Had he even wiped out his relationship with that stupid cat?

He shut the door as quietly as he could and stood listening for a moment. Ruth's bedroom door was slightly open, but he couldn't hear her breathing from this distance. She had to be there, though, because she'd left the front door unlocked for him—his keys were still where he'd left them on a side table. He lowered himself wearily onto the couch to unlace his shoes and peel off his socks. There was a huge blister on the back of his right heel. He'd have to do something about that before he went to sleep.

Charlie was still watching him warily from underneath the table, tail twitching slightly. Rick sighed. Maybe he'd at least stand a chance of making things up with the

187

cat. He poured food into the dish as quietly as he could and got out of the way. The cat, still suspicious, stayed where he was until Rick sat down in the living room again, and then walked into the kitchen with a dignified wave of his plumy tail. Well, that was a start, anyway.

"I wish the rest of it was that easy, cat," Rick whispered.

He got ready for bed as quietly as he could, daring only to run water long enough to wash his face and hands, and flush the toilet. Ruth had some aspirin in the medicine cabinet, so he swallowed three of those, and rubbed some witch hazel over the blister. Thank goodness it hadn't popped. He found a suitable bandage in the cupboard and applied it. And that, he realized, was about all he could manage before he just flat-out fell over. He got the cot unfolded in record time, spread out his sleeping bag, and managed to get himself into the bag face downward. For just the briefest moment before exhaustion overtook him, he thought about turning out the light.

He had not moved by the time Ruth tiptoed out of her bedroom and found him in the morning.

Chapter 17
Triple Play

S unday morning, Eleanor covered up her own lack of energy by letting the twins make pancakes from a mix. This turned out to be a great idea for all concerned. With only a little parental advice about using the electric griddle, the pancakes turned out fine—so much so, in fact, that the twins were all for making another batch the minute they finished eating the first one. Eleanor diverted them with a box of hot chocolate mix and some marshmallows and slipped into her bedroom to call her mother.

"Mom? Would you mind taking the twins this afternoon? I was going to drop them off at the movies, but there's nothing playing this weekend that they can watch."

"Of course I wouldn't mind. Is something wrong?"

Eleanor sighed. "Yes."

"Are you sick? Did something happen?"

"I can't talk about it right now—it's not something they need to hear about—but we'll have to talk about it when I've had some time to think."

"Of course, whenever you want. Is there anything I can do for you now?"

"No, not right now. I'll be all right. Thanks, Mom. I think if I just have some time to sit here and work on the quilt for a while it will help."

"Why don't you send them over now? We'll find something to do."

"They need to clean up after pancakes and hot chocolate."

"That sounds ominous. Were they messy eaters this morning?"

"Eaters, no. Cooks, yes."

"Oh boy. Well, send them over in an hour, then." Both women laughed.

"Thanks again, Mom."

When the twin whirlwinds were safely across the street, Eleanor pulled away the old, threadbare sheet she used as a dust cover on the quilting frame. The blue and green calico pinwheels stood out cheerfully against their cream muslin background. She put on her thimbles, picked up her needle and began putting in small, careful stitches, hoping to just let her mind drift for a bit.

But after she'd worked her way around two triangles it became clear that she wasn't going to be able to relax. The name of the pattern kept going through her head with the rhythm of the stitches. *Dutchman's Puzzle. Dutchman's Puzzle.* Finally she poked the needle carefully into the fabric and picked up the phone.

But Dave's number was still busy. It must just be off the hook, she told herself. That's all it is. She hung up, tried to stitch some more, felt a knot building up between her shoulder blades and pushed herself away from the frame. Back went the dust cover. She paced back and forth in the kitchen, unable to decide what she might want to eat for lunch. Then she pushed the redial button on the phone. Still busy. Should she just go over there and see if he would talk?

She got as far as picking up her purse and the car keys, but then she sat down again. No, that wouldn't do. She couldn't just barge in unannounced and insist that they talk. She drummed her fingers on the kitchen counter for a moment or two, and then went to get her address book.

Adam answered on the second ring. "Eleanor? Are you all right?"

"No, but that's not why I'm calling you."

"Can I help?"

"As a matter of fact, you can. Dave's line's been busy since last night and I'm getting worried. He and I really need to talk. He didn't answer the door when I went over there last night to try to bring him some dinner, either."

"I wonder if his phone is off the hook?"

"I'm sure that's all it is, but could you possibly go check on him? I'm thinking that might be better than if I went."

"Of course I will. I'll ask the phone company, and if they say the phone's off the hook I'll go over there and see what's up."

"Thank you so much, Adam."

"Is there anything else you need?"

"Just for this whole mess to get sorted out. I have no idea what to do next."

"I wish I could wave a magic wand and fix it." He sighed. "Well, at least I can check on Dave for you and if he's in there I'll ask if I can do anything for him. If he doesn't want that, I'll ask him to call me when he feels up to it. That might be easier for him to start with."

"I hope that works, one way or the other."

They said their goodbyes and she hung up the phone. Then she went back to look at the quilt frame. She'd gotten as far as grasping the dust cover when she said "Who am I trying to kid?" and let the sheet slide back into place. What else could she do? She paced, trying to think. In the end, she flipped through her small collection of not-for-the-kids DVDs—and surprised herself by laughing when she saw the cover of "Dave." Yes, that would do it. She put the movie in the player, picked up the remote control and settled in on the couch.

⊠⊠⊠

Dave woke, feeling disconnected in time and space. His whole body ached, and he'd kicked the covers into a tangled mess. The bottom sheet had ended up in a wad at the foot of the bed, and he'd rolled over with part of the top sheet beneath him and couldn't get his arms free. He rolled back and forth, finally got himself loose, and then lay back, exhausted.

Eventually he sat up, swung his feet to the floor and wearily put his head in his hands. The clock said 8:35 and the sun was streaming through the south-facing bedroom window. He made himself stand up and walk to the bathroom, where he avoided looking anywhere in the direction of the mirror as he got himself cleaned up. He knew his face was a mess. He didn't need to see it. He trudged back into the bedroom, threw all the covers on the floor and lay down on the bed on his back.

The phone was still on the floor where he'd pushed it. Should he put the receiver back? Why? Who would call? Who would he call? Eleanor must surely be talking with Rick, if she talked with anyone. He scrubbed tears off his face, roughly. What was the point? He put his right arm over his eyes to blot out the light.

An hour later he woke and found that the arm had not only gone to sleep, but had done it so thoroughly that it felt like a warm rubber appendage attached to his shoulder. He couldn't make the muscles move at all. He used the other hand to pull the rubber arm away and laid it down beside him on the mattress. This was something he'd never experienced before and he felt just a twinge of fear. Soon enough, though, the familiar pins-and-needles sensation started up with a vengeance, and then he was able to wiggle his fingers. He let out a sigh of relief. By the time the arm seemed functional again his stomach was growling. It was almost 11 am.

This time he made it all the way into the shower. The warm water helped with the aches. He did the best he could with his razor under the streaming water, so he wouldn't have to go near the mirror. Who'd be looking at him today, anyway? He dried himself off and tossed the towel over the shower curtain rod. Clean underwear, a t-shirt, and a pair of lightweight sweat pants seemed appropriate for the day. He threw the bed covers in the laundry hamper, but doing laundry seemed like more than he could deal with at the moment.

In the kitchen, he stared at the contents of the refrigerator, unable to make any kind of decision. Eggs? Bacon? What? Cooking seemed like way too much work. In the end, he got a box of cold cereal from the cupboard and a carton of milk from the fridge.

He'd just scraped the last bit of soggy cereal out of the bowl and was getting up to take it to the sink when he heard someone coming up the steps. He froze, then dropped the bowl on the table and hurried through the doorway into the living room so whoever it was couldn't see him through the windows. There he stopped, rocking back and forth. *Go away*, he thought, fiercely. He didn't want to deal with anyone right now. He wanted to be left alone.

Knock, knock, knock. Pause. *Knock, knock, knock.* "Dave? Dave, are you in there? It's Adam. I've been trying to call you. The operator said your phone's off the hook and I need to know if you're all right!"

For one wild moment he was tempted to respond with *"Dave's not here!"* But what came out was "Go away!"

"Dave, please. I just need to know you're all right."

"I'm fine."

"Would you please put the phone back on the hook, then? People are worried about you."

"Maybe later."

"All right. Would you call me when you feel up to it, please?"

"I'll think about it." He almost said *go away* again, but this was his boss he was shooing off his porch.

After a moment Dave heard footsteps going down the stairs, followed by the sound of Adam's car pulling out of the parking space. When he was sure Adam was gone, he went back to the kitchen and put his bowl in the sink. That seemed like all he could handle. He trudged into the living room and threw himself on the couch. After a moment he picked up the remote control. Adam paid for every damn channel the cable company put out. Surely somewhere out there was something he could watch so he didn't have to think.

⊠⊠⊠

When Rick finally awoke, he rolled over to see his sister sitting at the kitchen table, reading the Sunday paper and sipping coffee. "Um... hi," he said, unable to come up with anything more complicated than that.

"Hi. What time did you get in?"

194

"I don't know. Late. Early. I'm sorry about last night." He sat up, still achy but no more than he'd expected.

"Why don't you go take a shower or whatever you need to do this morning and I'll make some breakfast and then we can talk?"

He sighed. "Home is where you go and they have to take you in, right? I don't know if I'll ever be ready to talk about this, Ruthie, not really. But I've made such a mess of things I need someone to help me figure out how to fix it, and it looks like you're the one who gets to help sweep up the pieces."

"You know I've always been willing to do that, big brother."

He smiled. "Yes, I do know. You've put up with an awful lot."

She smiled back. "Good thing you can't disown your siblings, right?"

"I bet you've considered it a time or two."

"Go take your shower. I'm hungry. I didn't want to make too much noise in the kitchen while you were sleeping."

"You could probably have come through here with a Zamboni and a marching band and I wouldn't have heard a thing." The cot was just a tad too low to get up from gracefully, but he did the best he could.

Half an hour later, clean, hair toweled dry, wearing a t-shirt and shorts, he sat down at the table and amazed himself with the speed at which he made a mushroom omelet and three strips of bacon disappear. His sister, only halfway through her omelet, raised an eyebrow. "You learn to eat fast in the Navy," he said, putting three slices of bread into the toaster. "I'll hit the store and replace all this, don't worry."

"What, me worry?" She laughed. "It sounds like you're feeling a little better."

"Physically, yeah."

She scooped up the last of her omelet and then got up to take the empty plate to the kitchen. "Want coffee?"

"Give me the biggest mug you got."

Ruth carried her mug to the living room and curled up in the closest chair with her feet tucked under her. After a moment, her brother returned to the chair in which he'd sat the night before. He set his mug on the floor and stretched.

"So," said Ruth, "tell me what happened."

"I assumed Eleanor already told you."

"She did. But that was her side of it. I want to hear yours."

"All right." He took a sip of coffee and looked at the mug, thinking. "You know, I don't remember who invited me to the party. It was someplace in Iowa City. I have no idea where. At the time it seemed like a good idea. I hadn't done much partying in a really long time. But when I got there, it was a big room packed full of people I didn't know, and it was too hot and too many people were smoking. I'd decided it was a waste of time and was getting ready to leave when all of a sudden I saw Eleanor. I couldn't believe it—hadn't seen her since I left home. I went over to say hi, and we started talking, and it turned out she didn't know anybody either, so we left and got something to eat. Can't remember where that was, either."

"Greek food, she said."

"Oh yeah! That's right! The chef came out and told us what everything was. Best meal I'd had in a long time." He stopped. "I don't think I've eaten Greek food from that day to this, though." His shoulders sagged. He took another sip of coffee. "Well, she invited me back to her place. I went there intending just to talk. We both did. I guess you know that's not how it worked out. Neither of us had intended it to go that far, but she was sure it was a safe time of the month and I guess we both convinced ourselves it was true."

He got up, walked to the front window, looked out at the square. Ruth sat quietly, waiting. After a minute or two he said "We were plenty careful after that. But it only takes once."

There was a long silence. Rick turned away from the window and looked at his sister, helplessly. "I was a total dick to run out on her like I did. I should have stayed and been a father to my children. But that was just too soon after Mom and Dad..." He choked. "That doesn't excuse it. But that's what I told myself at the time. I'd be a lousy father. We'd end up hating each other and cheating on each other and hurting the twins and..."

Ruth got up and put her arms around him and held on tight. He pressed his cheek against the top of her head. After a moment he let out a shaky sigh. Ruth stepped back and looked up at her brother's weary face. Then she ran her fingers lightly over the tattoo on his arm. "Those aren't just for good luck, are they?" she said, softly.

"Oh, they are for good luck. That part's true. But you're right. I never forgot that I had a son and a daughter. This was as close as I could come to claiming them. Till now." He rubbed his hand over the tattoo, looking out the window. "She was right not to tell anyone what an asshole she'd slept with. She deserved so much better. And all I could think to do was run away. But you have to believe me, Ruthie, I did open up that bank account and I've been having money deducted from every paycheck ever since. I never looked at the statements the bank sent me. I've been shredding them without even opening up the envelopes. I didn't care how she spent the money. I just wanted her and the kids to know I was doing the best I could to support them."

Ruth patted her brother on the arm. "Come on, let's sit back down and talk. It'll be easier." Rick threw himself across the couch, and Ruth settled back into her chair. "She said she didn't remember anything like that, but if the package arrived right after the twins were born she might have just thrown it out. The twins were born almost a month early and all three of them took quite a while to recover. She had a real hard time for the first few months."

"Taking care of newborn twins... I can't even imagine. I didn't try to imagine. That's part of my problem. Knowing that I had two children was one thing, and being more than just half their DNA was something else again."

Ruth hesitated, then said "She said that when you walked into the office she thought it meant you'd come back."

He was silent for a long time. Finally he picked up his mug, drank the last of the lukewarm coffee and leaned back. "I don't know what I meant to do by coming back here. I took the longest route possible and almost turned back more than once. But I guess I must have wanted to be here more than I wanted to chicken out and run away again."

"So what will you do now?"

"You think I know? I've totally fucked this up in so many ways. And she's got Dave now, and they looked so happy, and I can't stand it if I killed that last night. I can't be a full time part of her life right now, I've got to go back soon. And I have no idea how the twins will react. What on earth did she tell them about their father?"

"I think she told them that you were exploring the world and you'd come see them when you could. You'll have to ask her about that."

"Yeah. Be pretty bad if Dad can't get the story straight. I'm so scared, Ruthie," he blurted out.

She uncurled herself from the chair and held out her arms. He got up and hugged her, trying not to cry. After what seemed like a very long time he let go. "You were an aunt and didn't even know it," he said, with a small quiver in his voice.

"Yeah, how could you do that to me?" She gave a somewhat uneven laugh.

"What do I do now?" He pulled his t-shirt out of his waistband and wiped his eyes with it.

"Call her. Talk. Work things out. It's the only way."

"I will. But I'll have to work up the nerve first. I might not manage it today."

"I understand. But I'm going to keep after you till you do, you know."

"Yeah, Sis, I know."

She took the coffee cups to the kitchen. "Why don't you see if you can find a ball game to watch, and when they get to half time or the seventh inning stretch or whatever, we can go get some lunch."

"Leave it to my sister to have no clue what season it is," he said, grinning.

"It's open season on brothers who bug their sisters too much!"

"You're the best, Ruthie," he said, quietly.

"So are you," she replied, "and you need to start believing it."

"Yeah. That's the hard part, isn't it?" He picked up the remote control and turned on the TV.

Chapter 18
...Can't Trust That Day

Monday dawned bright, sunny, and warm—except under the small dark clouds floating over three weary people's heads.

Eleanor managed to get through breakfast and send the twins off to school without—she thought—their being aware that anything was amiss. She waved to them from the sidewalk, then went back inside to think. After letting Phydeaux out the back door and opening the gate so he could run into the fenced part of the back yard, she made herself a second cup of coffee and sat at the table, eyes focused on nothing in particular. The coffee slowly cooled, untouched.

Rick... well, she'd tried so hard not to think about him at all for so many years, and it was more than she could manage, to sort out what to do now. After shutting him firmly out of her mind for so long, only to be con-fronted by a furious stranger—what next? Would he just vanish again after all that? Could anyone persuade him to meet his children before he left? He might already be gone. Maybe she should call Ruth. But what could she say? "Did

201

your brother take off again? If he didn't, will you tell him to talk with me?"

She jumped when the phone rang. Heart pounding, she hurried to pick it up. It was Linda. "Eleanor, are you all right?"

"I'm... oh my gosh." The clock read 9:15 am. "Linda, I'm so sorry. I..." Oh lordy, now what? Should she hurry in to work? Would she be in any shape to deal with the office today? If she focused on the job it might take her mind off the weekend's crises. But she might make even worse mistakes if she couldn't concentrate. "I... No, I'm not feeling very well today, actually. And I overslept. Would you mind if I didn't come in?"

"Mind? Good Lord, lady, you've taken what, one day off in all this time? You stay right there and get better! Is there anything we can do for you? Bring you over some chicken soup from the deli or something?"

She smiled. "No, I've got plenty of soup here. But thank you anyway. I'm sure I'll be OK by tomorrow."

"If we can help, you call right away, OK?"

"Thanks, Linda, I will."

She hung up the phone and looked at the clock again. Well, no good trying to call Ruth, she'd be at work in the store by now. She picked up her coffee cup, took a sip, grimaced and poured the tepid liquid down the drain. To hell with Rick—what she wanted more than anything was to talk with Dave.

⌗ ⌗ ⌗

When Peter walked through the back door of the Caldwell & Talbott offices a little before 9 am, he found the office already occupied by someone he'd never seen before. "Um... hello?"

202

The man got up from behind Dave's desk and held out his hand. "Hi, you must be Peter. I'm Adam Talbott. Dave wasn't feeling well this morning, so since I'm in town for a few days I thought I'd open up the office for him and see what's what."

"Oh, you're the big boss," said Peter, shaking hands, and then he quickly shut his mouth. *Uh oh.* He needn't have worried. Adam laughed.

"Not so big. I'm just taller than Dave, that's all. So, is the new computer working out OK for you?"

"It's great. I thought Dave and I were going to run the cable through the basement today, for the network connection. I thought wired would be more secure than wireless."

Adam blinked, then smiled. "I don't think anyone's close enough to steal your bandwidth here, but sure, it's still a good idea to take precautions. Wired is fine."

"Taping all that cable to the floor is just an accident waiting to happen." Peter waved at a length of duct tape that secured the wires from one side of the office to the other. "I probably need to find a better place to put the router and switch, too," he said, pointing to the components on the floor next to Dave's desk.

"Yeah, no kidding. How about I go dig through our storage place and see if I can come up with a table or a set of shelves or something. Do you have the tools to run the cable?"

"Dave put all that stuff in the closet in the back, I think. I know he went and got extra cat 5 cable and a long drill bit."

"OK, then, you and I can get the wires run, at least. We can just leave the answering machine on the phone for now. First things first."

Must be nice, being the boss, thought Peter, but he said nothing.

⊠ ⊠ ⊠

Dave had already been awake for nearly an hour when his alarm jolted him at 7 am. He'd been lying in bed, looking at the ceiling. A couple of times he'd turned to look at the phone—still on the floor, still off the hook. He grabbed the clock, turned off the alarm and went back to staring at the ceiling.

What he wanted more than anything else was to talk with Eleanor. But after he'd panicked instead of staying with her in the crisis... He'd had his chance to stand by her and he'd failed. And if he loved her, he'd want what was best—for her to have a chance to get a fresh start with the father of her children. If that was what she wanted. He didn't know what she wanted. He'd run away without giving her a chance to tell him. He let his eyes close.

When he woke, it was five after nine. *"Shit!"* Just what he needed, to be late for work when Adam was in town. He was pretty sure Adam would understand what was going on, but he hadn't intended to put that to the test just yet. He picked up the clock, fully intending to fling it across the room. But then he reconsidered. If he smashed the clock he'd just have to go get another one so he could get out of bed on time tomorrow. Wearily, he got to his feet and straightened out the covers on the bed and put his nightshirt in the hamper. No matter how he might feel about it now, it would be better to come back to the room if it didn't look like a bar fight had gone through it.

He raced through a shower, toweled himself dry, and then took a deep breath and faced himself in the mirror. He'd missed several places when he'd shaved the day before, and the circles under his eyes would be enough to make a lady panda swoon. He shook his head and sighed. Well, at least he could look at himself long enough to get all the whiskers dealt with today.

Should he just go down without breakfast? No, that would get him off to an even worse start, and he was late already. The cereal remaining in the box was just enough to fill the bowl, and there was about a glass and a half worth of orange juice left in the pitcher. He drank the juice, refilled his glass with the last of it, and then filled the pitcher with water and left it in the sink. He'd make extra strong coffee down in the office to help give him at least some energy to face the day. At 9:30 he walked out on the landing and looked around at the world without really seeing it. *Well, Dave, one foot in front of the other, let's go. No. Wait.* He went back inside and picked up his phone and put the handset back on the cradle.

To his surprise, the back door was unlocked and it sounded like there were people talking in the office. Peter didn't have keys, so what was going on? He walked in to see Adam hunched on the floor beside Peter's desk, shining an LED flashlight at the floor. "Yeah, that's it, right here," said Adam, and then he reached out and grabbed the wire and pulled it through. Dave just stood where he was and stared. Adam pulled several feet of wire through the floor and then stood up. He jumped when he saw Dave. "Oh, hi! I wasn't sure you'd feel up to being here today, so I figured I'd help out."

"Yeah, right," said Dave, walking over to his desk.

"The computer's not hooked up at the moment. As soon as we get all the wires in place I'll plug everything in again. Want some coffee?"

"I'll get my own."

"Fine," said Adam, voice neutral, as he pulled the wire around to the back of Peter's computer and clicked it into place. "Suit yourself. The answering machine's still on, but nobody's called yet, so take your time."

Dave sat down at his desk with his mug of coffee and tried to ignore the conversation between Adam and Peter about the computer setup. Peter had already figured out how to copy the company database and other files, and most of the rest was gibberish to Dave. He shuffled the papers on his desk, stacked them neatly and set them aside. Then he flipped through his calendar and saw nothing other than routine calls for estimates on repair work, and one prospective tenant who was going to come in that morning to sign paperwork for a credit check.

The lock on the front door had gotten sticky again—he'd written himself a note to call the handyman and get that fixed today—just one more annoyance he didn't need. He shifted in his chair, waiting for the other two men to get finished with the wires and just shut the fuck up. There was no busywork to do without the computer.

After what seemed like at least two geological ages, Adam and Peter got the computers up and running. Adam promised to go look for something suitable to set the other equipment on. He told Dave he'd be taking the truck for a while. Dave had nothing to say about that. Peter looked over at Dave and apparently decided that today would be a good day to do all kinds of things he didn't have to confer with the boss about. He pulled up the company software and started doing some data entry.

Little by little, Dave managed to get into the rhythm of the day, and forced his mind to focus only on business, but he found he couldn't sit for long. He paced, he went back and forth to the bathroom, and he made another pot of coffee that he didn't really want, just so he had a reason to get up and refill his cup from time to time. Even if the previous refill sat on his desk, minus a sip or two, and got cold. He talked with the tenant and the handyman, and by the time Peter left at lunchtime he was just beginning to think he was dealing with everything normally.

He was checking his email, something he still hadn't gotten used to, when Adam walked in from the back, carrying a small bookshelf. Startled, Dave knocked his empty coffee mug off the corner of the desk. It spun across the floor, miraculously unbroken, and came to rest near his wastebasket. Face blazing red, he bent down to pick it up. As he did that, Adam put his burden down on the other side of the desk, moved the electronics off the floor and onto a shelf, and then sat down in one of the visitors' chairs and said nothing. Waiting. Dave marched the cup over to the counter in the back and caught himself before he slammed it down. He took a deep breath, set the cup down gently, and turned back to face his employer, struggling to un-grit his teeth.

"*Now* what!" He couldn't keep from sounding hostile. Even if it got him fired, he couldn't make himself be civil.

But Adam clearly wasn't ruffled. "Dave, I wasn't sure you'd want to come to the office today, and I don't mind finishing out the day if you want to take time off. But more than that, I just wanted to make sure you were all right. I told you that when I stopped by yesterday. That's all."

"Of course I'm..." He took another deep breath, let it out slowly. Then he walked to his chair and sat down. Adam said nothing. "No, I'm not all right. But it's really none of your business."

"Look, we don't know each other very well and I'm probably stepping over the line here, but..." Adam stopped. "I'll just go ahead and ask it and if you want to take a swing at me for it, I'll deal with that. Have you thought about talking with Eleanor?"

"Do you think I'm an idiot? Of course I've fucking thought about it! Back off, Adam."

"OK, OK. I'm sorry. It's none of my business." He cleared his throat. "Ordinarily I'd let it go at that and I would back off. But this cuts pretty close to home with me. Last year I found out what happens when people who care about each other don't talk. And I nearly lost Ruth for good."

"So now you think you're Dear Abby?"

Adam was silent. "You're right. I'll just butt the hell out right now. But can I ask you to keep in mind that Rick has to go back before too long, and you'll still be here?"

Dave slapped a hand on his desk. "You think so, do you? I'm a traveling man. That's what I do."

"Is that what you want?"

"Go away, Adam. You've poked into my life too damn much already."

Adam sighed and got to his feet. "Yeah, I guess so. Nobody died and made me God. All right, then, let's leave it that I'm your employer and I don't want to lose one of the best people I've ever hired, and I'm not just saying that."

"Go the fuck away. Lock the door on your way out. I'm closing up for the day, what do you think about that?"

"I think it's a good idea." He turned the sign on the front door to read CLOSED, pulled down the shade and went out.

⊠⊠⊠

"What do you plan to do today?" Ruth asked Rick over breakfast.

"Hell if I know. Work in the shop for a while. Figure something out. See if I can be the big tough sailor who actually, oh, I don't know, talks to the mother of his twins."

"Maybe you should stop by the office and offer to take her out to lunch."

"Oh Christ no, that wouldn't work. It'd just upset her day. And there's no way we could figure this out in a lunch hour. Hell, it'd probably take me that long just to say hello."

"Yeah, you have a point. Will you please promise me to call her tonight, though?"

He sighed, got up and took his dishes to the kitchen. "I'll try, Ruthie, that's all I can promise."

Ruth got up and hugged her brother. "Well, at least that's a start."

As Ruth and Chet went about the business of opening up the store for the day, Rick got settled at the back table and put the flash drive in the virus-ridden computer. There was something about this virus that didn't quite add up, and he was determined to find out what. If the tools he'd brought with him on the flash drive weren't enough, he knew a few off-the-beaten-path web-sites where he could get more, and there were people he could call. One way or the other, he'd get to the bottom of it. At least he could do one good thing in this town before he turned tail and headed out again.

Ruth looked over at her brother from time to time, but he was focused on the computer, absently running his fingers over the koi tattoo. Well, she thought, maybe solving the puzzle of the virus would give him a breather before he had to solve the puzzle of his life. All she could do was hope.

Chapter 19
Revelations

May

It's generally accepted that inertia means that bodies in motion tend to stay in motion, and bodies at rest tend to stay at rest, unless acted upon by some outside force. The three people who most needed to talk with each other kept going the way they were going—or resting the way they were resting, depending upon how one looked at it—and no one's inertia was disturbed. At least for the first part of the week.

After Monday, Dave began to get his feet back under him, metaphorically speaking, and actually managed to get some work done in the office, both with and without his new assistant. Peter proved particularly adept at explaining things so Dave felt he could almost understand, but after seeing how much information there was in the company database, he became more concerned that without the computer he'd be completely lost. Peter assured him that there were plenty of safeguards in place and they weren't likely to get any malware, but still, Dave had concerns. "Can you print me out a list of the tenants' information that I can keep in a file drawer somewhere?"

"Oh sure, that's not a problem," Peter said, sounding supremely confident. "How much of this information do you think you'll need printed out?"

"You can choose?"

"Of course. I just tell it what fields you want. It's easy."

"Easy for YOU to say," said Dave, darkly. He got up to take a look at Peter's screen, which was turned away from him by the angle of the desk. Peter made a quick gesture with his left hand on the keyboard and showed Dave the database screen.

"I think just tenant's name, address, who's living there, the owners, the rent and any repairs we've made in the last year should be plenty. If I'd been running the place longer that stuff would have all been on paper from the get-go."

"Easy peasy, don't worry." Peter started clicking things, Dave went back to his file folders, and pretty soon the laser printer started to spit pages into the tray.

"You must think I'm a complete idiot when it comes to computers," said Dave.

"Not at all. We all had to start somewhere. You just got a later start than I did," Peter assured him.

"Well, that's one way of looking at it." Dave laughed, but he had to admit he felt a little better about his lack of skills.

Eleanor was back at work on Tuesday, and brushed off her employers' concerns about her "illness." "I think it was just one of those 24-hour bugs," she said. "I'll be fine."

"You look tired, though," said Linda, with real concern.

"I am, but I'll take it easy in here today and I'm sure I'll be fine."

"Oh, OK, in that case, why don't you do this research for me? A couple hours clicking on stuff on the internet should be relaxing enough." She handed over a list of properties out in the county that had recently been listed, and another, shorter list of places she'd heard via the grapevine might be coming on the market soon so Eleanor could find comparable properties. And Linda was right, it was just the kind of busywork Eleanor needed to keep her mind off her worries.

For most of the morning, she poked around various real-estate-related web sites, gathering whatever she thought might be useful to help with future sales. Ron was out with a client looking for farm properties in the northwest corner of the county, and after an hour Linda went to pick up a new client who was coming to work at the community college and needed just the right place for her family—about as sure a sale as anyone could hope for, which was always good news for the office. Eleanor turned on the radio after Linda left, and worked till lunchtime. By the time she got back to work after lunch, she was feeling like some kind of equilibrium had returned, and she told herself quite firmly that she was going to call Dave. Soon.

Rick went out for an hour late Tuesday afternoon and returned with a motorcycle helmet. "I guessed at the size, but they told me I can bring this back if it doesn't fit," he told Ruth.

"Let me get this straight. You want me to ride on that... thing with you?"

"Thing! You are dissing a fine, fine Harley, I'll have you know! Come on, let's go!"

"Not now, I'm busy!"

"What are you, chicken?"

Chet laughed from across the room. "You're playing with fire there, boy."

Ruth glared at Chet. "I know how this guy drives. He left some pretty good tracks on someone's lawn, once upon a time."

"Do tell!" said Brad.

"Uh uh," said Rick, firmly. "That was then, this is now, and besides, Ruthie, if you're on the back of the motorcycle you can scream at me if I do something you don't like."

"That'll be the day," she scowled. But she allowed her brother to talk her into trying on the helmet, which did fit.

"Come on," said Rick. "Go put your boots and your denim jacket on and we'll blow this popsicle stand for a while. These guys can handle the phone calls."

"Yeah!" said Brad, and Chet clapped.

"That's it, you guys are all fired," said Ruth, but then she laughed and went upstairs to change. Rick gave the other two a thumbs-up as he went out the back door.

And so they continued, in self-imposed inertia—until Thursday, when the outside force nudged everything off the rails.

⊠ ⊠ ⊠

Thursday morning, the phone at Electronic Wizardry went crazy again and it didn't take long to figure out that another virus was on the loose. The first five callers got the standard answer: We'll get ahold of the virus software people and you can get an update when they figure it out. The sixth caller, however...

"Hi, Mrs. Ward, what's the problem?"

"Oh Ruth, I'm so sorry to bother you, but I think my computer has got that virus thing."

"Really? I thought Ron had that all set up safely for you."

"Well... yes, he did, but the twins were here last weekend and they may have changed something."

Ruth tapped her foot on the floor. She had a pretty good idea that Eleanor's mother was nowhere near as unaware as her grandchildren were counting on her to be. "Uh oh. Did they tell you they changed something?"

"No, but they did a lot of whispering and when I came in to check on them I saw that they'd made themselves a CD, which I don't think they've done on my computer before. I haven't even turned it on since Sunday, but today I wanted to send an email and all I have is... well, it looks like stars."

From behind her, Ruth heard "Get away from the door, cat, I mean it," followed by a meow from Charlie, who had decided to abandon his usual perch on the Victrola in the front window in favor of sitting on the table in the back so he could keep an eye on Rick all day. When Rick was out, Charlie did guard duty at the back door. Rick zipped through the screen door and scooped up the cat, who bumped noses with him in delight. *Ah HAH*, Ruth thought, looking at her brother.

"You know what? I'm going to have Rick stop by in a few minutes and take a look at that. I bet he can figure out whether they did something and I know he can get your computer working again."

"You're sure? I hate to interrupt his day when all I want is to send an email."

"He's been trying to figure out how to put a stop to these virus attacks, and he'll be delighted to get his hands on a computer that's just gotten infected." She turned to see that Rick was watching her from the table in the back, and he nodded. "He's just told me he'll be happy to help, so don't worry about taking him away from here."

"Oh, thank you! You don't know how much I appreciate this, Ruth."

"Rick is on his way right now. Hang in there, you'll get your computer back soon." She put down the phone and turned back to her brother.

Rick, who had already set Charlie on the table, picked up a small plastic tool box and his flash drive. "OK, so where exactly am I supposed to go?"

"Eleanor's mom's place."

"WHAT! No way. NO way. No WAY." He sat back down in his chair and crossed his arms defiantly across his chest.

"Way. I told her you were coming and she didn't tell me to put you in a crate headed for Mars instead, so you get your sorry ass over there and fix her computer."

"God, Ruthie! I can't do this. She'll kill me."

"You're a big tough sailor, Mrs. Ward's about five feet tall, and if she took a swing at you with a frying pan I'm sure you could get out of the way fast enough. You're going to have to take my word for it that she sounded really happy to hear you were on your way. You're going."

Rick sat still, breathing hard. Ruth gave him an industrial strength glare, which he returned with interest. Chet piped up with "Want me to come with you for protection, boy? She's not gonna smack an old geezer."

"Oh, very funny. Well, damn the two of you. All right. I'm going. But you better be ready to call the paramedics."

Walking up the steps to Mrs. Ward's door almost took more courage than he could muster. But he managed it, got a hand up and knocked. And nearly fell down the stairs again when Paula—who was indeed about five feet tall, white haired, dressed in beige slacks and a blue sweater, with a face that was a close match to her daughter's—greeted him with a wide smile and every evidence of relief, not rage. She ushered him into the bedroom she'd turned into an office and offered to get him coffee or something to eat or anything else he needed. He'd gotten all his fight-or-flight reflexes fired up for nothing. He asked for coffee just so she'd leave the room and let him sit down without her seeing how shaky he was.

She set the coffee mug down on a coaster. "I don't let the twins eat or drink in here, but I know I don't need to worry about you," she said, smiling.

"I'll do my best not to betray your trust, Mrs. Ward," he said, managing to smile back.

She laughed. "Thank you, I appreciate that. I'll leave you to your work now, but when you get it fixed I'd love to hear what was wrong with it." She went back into the living room and picked up a magazine.

Inertia took over again, for a minute or two. Rick stared at the screen without blinking. Stars, yes, it was definitely stars, but this time it looked like a constellation moving across the screen. Orion, that's what it was. *What the...*

He had to get behind the computer to get at the USB port to insert his flash drive, but once that was done, he could reboot using his specialized tools. And after that he got so absorbed in the job at hand that the perceived threat of being beaned with a skillet or smacked with a rolling pin faded away. The second time he rebooted, the constellation faded out after thirty seconds and a message appeared on the screen.

EVEN THE POOREST PHARAOH BELIEVES HE RULES AMONG THE STARS.

And then the computer restarted itself and the infection appeared to be gone. He wrote down the message and started a complete virus scan just to be sure, then sat back, wondering what on earth that was all about. Well, nothing much to do till the scan was finished. He drank what was left of the coffee and got up to take the mug back to the kitchen.

Paula looked up from her magazine. "Do you have any idea what happened?"

"Well, you were right, you had a virus, but I think I've got it fixed. I'm running an antivirus scan just to be sure. Did you do anything unusual with the computer in the last few days?"

"Here, why don't you come sit down, it's easier for me to talk when I don't have to look up at you."

"Oh, of course. I'm sorry." He sat on a comfortably squashy chair facing her. "Did the computer do anything unusual before you turned it on this morning?"

"I haven't actually had it on since Sunday. But the twins were using it, and they made a CD. I've never seen them do that before."

"Do they use your computer a lot?"

She laughed. "I think Eleanor's a bit too strict for their liking. She has pretty firm limits on how much time they can spend on it. The twins and I have an agreement that if they help me out around here, I let them use my computer and I don't tell their mother how long they play. I guess that's what grandmothers are good for."

"I guess so. Wish my grandmother had had a computer. And that we'd had that kind of agreement."

"Have you always liked doing this kind of thing? Computers, I mean?"

"I... well, yes, I have."

"The twins are so excited about going to computer camp. It's about all they've talked about lately. But if they were responsible for this virus thing I'm not so sure they ought to be turned loose on a computer camp."

"Are they... are they definitely going, then?"

"I assumed they were, from the way they were talking. They've read the brochures backwards and forwards and they've got their agenda all planned out. I pity the counselors, I really do."

"I wish I knew them better." He leaned back in the chair. "I wish I hadn't been gone so long."

Paula looked at him, frowning slightly. "Were you in Eleanor's class in high school? I can't remember."

"A year ahead."

"Oh. No wonder I couldn't place you at first. Have you just moved back to Lyric?"

My God. Doesn't she know? What do I do now? "No, I'm on leave from the Navy. I have to go back soon. But I..." He had to say it. "I need to meet the twins before I go."

"Oh, to find out if they did this? That's a very good idea. You haven't met them yet?"

He was silent for a moment. "No. Not ever. There's something wrong with me, isn't there?"

"I'm afraid I don't understand, Rick." She was frowning at him again. "What do you mean?"

He looked at her, helpless, not knowing what to say or do next.

"Are you all right?" she said. "Can I get you something?" With genuine concern in her voice.

"I... Mrs. Ward, I just... Oh God, I can't beat around the bush any more. Didn't Eleanor ever tell you that I'm the twins' father?"

Her face went absolutely white and she sat back in her chair, hand pressed to her heart. What had he done? He got up and took a hesitant step toward her. She waved him back. Needing to do something, anything, he ran to the kitchen and returned with a glass of cool water. She took it from him and sipped, gratefully. He hovered, anxiously. Finally she set the glass down on the table and looked at him. "I think... I think maybe you better sit down again. We need to talk."

He sat. "I'm so sorry. I knew how close you and Eleanor were and it never in a million years would have occurred to me that she wouldn't tell you. Have I hurt you? Will you be all right?"

"After all this time... and you're going back, you say? You're not going to stay?"

"I... I have to go back, I'm still on active duty. But before I go I want to meet my children. I just don't know if that will hurt them more than it helps, and I'm so afraid I've gone so far that Eleanor will never forgive me." He put his head in his hands. The next words were almost a sob. "Can you help me, please?"

Paula got up, knelt on the floor beside him and put a gentle hand on his shoulder. He flinched, then settled back and looked at her with anguished, tear-filled eyes. She got a tissue out of the box on the table beside him and handed it to him, wordlessly. Wordlessly, he accepted it. After a moment she stood up again. "I'm too old to be on the floor for long," she said, with what was almost a laugh. "Well. Under those circumstances, you were very brave to come over here, I must say."

"Yes," he said. "I was afraid you'd shoot me when I knocked on the door."

"You got lucky. I sold all the guns after my husband died." She chuckled, then looked at him with no trace of humor in her eyes. "Why did you go off and abandon Eleanor? Why did you leave her here all alone?"

"Because I was an idiot and scared to death and too damn full of myself to know how to act like a man."

"That's honest, at least."

"Yes. Now. I wasn't, back then. Do you think I can possibly make it up to them?"

"You know who has the answer to that, Rick."

He sighed. "Yes. What I don't know is whether I've already burned my bridges."

"I can't tell you that either."

"I know."

Silence filled the room. Suddenly there was a chime from the computer, which both of them had forgotten. Grateful for a chance to move, to think about something else, Rick went back to look at it, and Paula silently followed. The computer appeared to be working normally. "Let me just check a few things here," he said, typing rapidly. "Oh, I see, someone turned the firewall off, and I can guess who." He clicked the mouse. "Oh, and the antivirus software, too. I really need to talk with those kids. There, it's all back on, and you shouldn't have any more trouble."

"Thank you, Rick." She thought for a moment. "You know, the virus could be a blessing in disguise."

"How so?"

"You said it yourself, you have to talk with the twins. I will call Eleanor at the office and ask her to bring them here for supper because it looks like they messed up my computer and we need to discuss it."

"I... yes. That's a good beginning. And I'll just have to wait and see if I can tell them the rest."

"Why don't you go do what you need to fortify yourself and come back around five? Should I let Eleanor know you'll be here?"

He thought about it. "Yes, but just tell her I want to talk with the twins about what they did to your computer. That's the truth. There's no way of knowing if we'll be able to deal with anything else."

"All right. Do I owe you anything for the house call?"

He was genuinely surprised. "You think I could charge you for nearly giving you a heart attack? Surely you jest."

"Put it on my tab, then, and don't call me Shirley."

He blinked for a moment, then burst out laughing. Maybe this was going to be all right.

Chapter 20
Repair Work

It was two very subdued fifth graders who slunk into their grandmother's house that afternoon, shooed firmly across the porch by their mother, who followed right behind to cut off any possibility of retreat. Their grandmother silently pointed to the couch. They sat, trying not to look guilty, and waited while their mother sat in the chair next to someone they'd never seen before. He looked up at her for just a moment and it seemed as though he was trying to smile. Their mom didn't smile back. There was a painful silence. Finally Paula said "Kids, this is Rick, Ruth's brother, who I know you haven't met before. He came over here to fix my computer today and found out why it wasn't working. He wants to talk with you."

They looked warily at the big man sitting beside their mother, who looked back at them with what appeared to be great interest. He had very short light brown hair and green eyes, and he was wearing a World of Warcraft shirt. The shirt part was promising, but he wasn't smiling. "I found a virus on your grandmother's computer today," he began, "and after I got it fixed I discovered that someone had left it unprotected. Do you two know anything about that?"

The twins looked at each other, at the floor, anyplace but at this stranger asking embarrassing questions. Finally Rachel said in a very small voice, "We heard about this cool game at school."

"Oh?" said Rick, in a casual tone of voice. "Let me guess, a game that you download, not one that you buy, and you didn't think your mom would let you download it."

Andrew risked a glance at his mother. "Yeah. Mom's had the parental controls on our computer since we were babies. She doesn't let us download anything unless we ask her first, and we have to log out and let her log in to do it."

"Your mother is very wise," said Rick. "That's why her computer didn't get a virus and your grandmother's did."

"But we're not babies any more," said Rachel, indignantly. "We've been using computers all our lives and this is the very first time anything bad happened."

"Do you suppose that's because you knew what you were doing, or because your mom had the parental controls?"

Rachel hung her head. "I don't know," she said, softly.

"So," said Rick, leaning back in his chair, "tell me about this game."

The twins shuffled their feet and shifted around on the couch. "This is going to take all night and we'll never get our supper," said their grandmother, "so I suggest you guys start talking and get it over with."

"It was a first-person shooter," said Andrew. "Something all the kids at school were talking about. But we'd never seen it." He glared at his mother. "She doesn't let us play that kind of game, not on the computer and not on the Nintendo. It's not fair. We're not babies."

"And all your friends are out there killing aliens and you're just doing Disney stuff?" said Rick, whose mouth was twitching suspiciously. Eleanor gave him the kind of glare the kids had seen all too often as they got older. Rick quickly held up a hand. Eleanor clearly wasn't happy about it, but she didn't say anything.

"Yeah," sighed Andrew, after the grownups settled down. "We're the only ones."

"Somehow, I doubt that's true," said Rick, "but I can definitely see where it'd look like all the other kids are getting to do all the cool stuff and your mom's being strict for no reason. Let me ask you this—did you ever ask your friends what their parents let them do?"

"They'd lie about it," said Rachel. "Who wants to admit they're still restricted?"

Rick nodded. "Well, there you go. Things haven't changed much since I was in school. So, what did you do to your grandmother's computer so you could download this oh-so-cool game?"

The twins glared at each other and there was a moment of visual combat. "It was your idea," said Andrew.

"You didn't stop me," said Rachel.

"It's still your fault," said Andrew.

"Is not," said Rachel, at which point their mother put her foot down. Literally.

Eleanor stomped on the floor and said "Either you two quit bickering and get on with this or neither I nor your grandmother will let you touch a computer ever again, and that's a promise. Rachel, tell Rick what you suggested. Andrew, don't be acting so smug. No doubt you would have suggested it first if she hadn't beaten you to it." This was so patently true that both twins wilted.

"Granny's computer wouldn't let us download the game," Rachel said, "so I thought we could turn off the firewall and see if that changed anything. It still didn't work, so I..." she gulped. "I turned off the antivirus. And then it downloaded the game. I burned it on a CD for us but then Granny walked in and I forgot to put everything back the way it was."

"Mmm-hmm. And then what?"

"Nothing. The CD is still in my room."

"I think you'd better hand it over to your mother as soon as you get home," said Rick. The twins sighed together, then nodded, conceding defeat. "I doubt you could have installed it on your mom's computer anyway, not if your access is restricted."

"We could have..." Rachel began. Her brother elbowed her and gave her a look. She scowled at him, but said nothing more.

"Played it over here? No, you really couldn't have," said Rick. "Trust me. But I'm still going to suggest that your grandmother put in a new extra strong password just in case. OK, so now we know what happened, what are you going to do to make up for it?"

"Not download games again?" said Andrew, hopefully.

"Somehow, I don't think that's quite enough. Why don't you tell me, and your grandmother—what would be the proper penalty for this?"

"Um..." he said, looking to his sister for support, "grounded from the computer for a week?"

Rick looked at Eleanor, and then at Paula. "What do you ladies think of that?"

"*Two* weeks," said the ladies in unison. The beginnings of indignant noises from the twins were cut off cold by an industrial strength glare from their mother.

Another paired sigh. "All right," said Rachel, sounding like the world was coming to an end. Andrew made an indeterminate noise.

"That settles that," said Paula. "Now, why don't you two go play in the back yard while I finish making supper. You need to start figuring out how to play without a mouse in your hand."

"All right," said Andrew, whose mournful tone matched his sister's, and the twins dutifully got up and went out.

When she heard the door close behind them, Paula turned to Eleanor and said without preamble "Rick told me. I know you had your reasons, but..." Her voice trailed off. Eleanor looked at the floor. No one said anything.

Finally Eleanor gathered courage, straightened up and looked her mother in the eye. "I don't really know why I didn't talk about it, Mom. I think because I was so overwhelmed, and I had no idea if I'd ever see Rick again. And then I just got in the habit of not talking. Can you possibly understand?"

"Of course..."

Rick cut in, reaching a hand out toward Eleanor, who did not take it. "I don't think there are words in the world for me to use to tell you how sorry I am. Not only for the past but for blowing up and running away again the other night. All I can do is hope you'll forgive me." Tears welled up in his eyes. "I've been such a bad father, thinking that giving you money was enough to make it OK, and I didn't even do that right. I don't know what's wrong with me." He hung his head, and the hand drooped down by his side. No one could think of anything to say. The silence stretched out until Paula finally rose and told the others she was going to see to supper in the kitchen.

Rick shifted in his chair to watch Paula go. Then, shifting again, he looked at Eleanor for just a moment. He turned away, unable to meet her eyes. Finally he said, quietly, "Would you... Do you think it's time to tell the kids about me?" Something occurred to him. He turned back to face her. "I don't even know what you've told them about their father. I mean, Ruth took a guess at it when I asked her, but she didn't think she knew the whole story."

"Nothing bad, don't worry." Eleanor smiled. "They haven't asked many questions, so I didn't have to make up stories. I just told them you were exploring the world and someday you'd come home to meet them. I thought... I hoped... that might be true."

"Do they... did you tell them we weren't married?"

"Of course. But that didn't bother them. Quite a few of their friends have parents who are divorced or single."

"Ah." He sat back and his shoulders relaxed for the first time since the twins had walked through the door. "Should we call them back in and tell them now?"

She considered that. "No. Let's let everyone eat dinner first, just chit-chat about whatever, and that'll help them relax around you a bit and maybe figure out that you're not going to take them out behind the woodshed."

He managed a shaky laugh. "I don't think your mom actually has a woodshed. But yeah, that's a good idea. I... they're amazing kids, Eleanor. I can't take any credit for that."

"Well, they sure didn't get the computer stuff from me."

"After all this, I wonder if that's a good thing or a bad thing."

Repair Work

⊠ ⊠ ⊠

Over supper, the twins asked Rick questions about being in the Navy and working on a submarine, which both of them thought was the most amazing, exotic occupation ever. He tried to tell them stories that would live up to their expectations. Rachel asked him what his job title was. "Screen door inspector," he said with an absolutely straight face. The kids did not understand why their grandmother burst out laughing.

"Think about it," she said. "A screen door on a submarine?" And then the twins burst out laughing too.

"It's only an old joke if you've heard it before," said Eleanor, joining in the laughter.

By the end of the meal everyone had relaxed, and the twins were eager to win back their grandmother's goodwill so they jumped right up and offered to load the dishwasher. As they rattled dishes and clanked silverware, the adults went back in the living room and sat down. No one spoke. Rick's heart was pounding as though he'd just run a race. He waited silently for... his children.

Kitchen tidied, the twins returned to the living room to find the adults looking at each other, saying nothing. "Why don't you two sit down for a minute," said Paula. "I think..." she looked from face to face. Eleanor looked at Rick and nodded. "I think Rick has something he wants to tell you."

They sat. "About the virus?" said Rachel. "We know that was our fault."

"No, not about the virus. About..." His throat closed. The twins looked at him, puzzled. He took a deep breath. "Um, kids, it makes perfect sense that you guys are so good with computers. Because... because I'm your father."

There was a moment of dead silence.

"WHAT?" said Andrew. Brother and sister looked at Eleanor for confirmation.

"Yes," she said. "He is."

"I'm sorry I stayed away so long," said Rick. "I..."

"Didn't you... didn't you want us?" Rachel sounded as though she was about to cry.

"Oh, Rachel, is that what you thought? I'm so sorry. I don't know how I can possibly make that better." He paused, trying to think of what to say next, then looked his daughter in the eye and said, firmly, "I want you to know right now and for all time that of *course* I wanted you. How could I not want my own children? But I didn't know how to be a father, and I was too afraid I'd mess things up. So I did something unforgivably stupid. I got scared and ran away."

"That doesn't make any sense," said Andrew, angrily.

"I know it doesn't. It was a terrible thing to do and I'm sorry. I don't know what else I can say."

Andrew stood up. "And you sat there and got us grounded! Somebody ought to ground YOU for the rest of your life!"

"Andrew," said his mother, in a warning tone.

"No, Andrew is right," said Rick. "I should definitely be grounded for life for doing something that bad."

"After Rick figures out where that computer virus came from I'll ground him," said Paula, breaking the tension. "Would that be OK with you, Andrew?"

Andrew glared at his father. Rachel was still slumped on the couch, head down. "You... you're a *poopyhead*," said Andrew, using the worst word he felt he could get away with. Rachel punched him on the leg as a warning.

"Absolutely, I'm a poopyhead," his father agreed, quite sincerely. "And a lot of worse names that your mom would wash both our mouths out with soap for saying." His son's mouth twitched a bit at that. His daughter hid a smile behind a hand.

Something occurred to Rachel. "Wait—Mom can't have a husband and a boyfriend," she said. "You can't... Mom has a boyfriend now, so you can't be our dad."

Rick sighed. "You'd think so, wouldn't you? But actually it doesn't have to work that way. I don't know if I can explain this well enough so anyone can understand, including me. I love your mom, Rachel, and I love you guys too. That will never change. But..." he ran a hand through his hair. "It takes more than just loving someone to be married to them. A lot more. And your mom and I never had time to figure out if we should get married or not. I was stupid and I got scared and ran away, and that caused more problems than I could have possibly imagined. I know better now, but I can't change what I did and it'd take a long time for me to make up for that. I'm in the Navy, and I have to go back soon. So I couldn't come back here for good till I get out, and that's almost two years from now. And then we'd have to be together long enough to decide whether we wanted to get married, and that'd take even longer. Heck, I wouldn't even expect you guys to like me for a long time. And if it turned out that your mom and I didn't want to get married after all that, then we'd both have to start all over again." He took a deep breath. "I'm not anyone's husband, and your mom has a great boyfriend. I've met him, and I want you to know I didn't come here to break that up. Being your father doesn't change the boyfriend part."

"That makes no sense," said Rachel.

Rick looked at Eleanor, helpless.

"Rachel," she said, "you know people don't have to be married to have children together. It's better if they are, but sometimes it doesn't work out that way. You always knew your father and I weren't married. It might be that everything would finally be OK if we did get married, but like your dad says, it takes a lot more than that. I was really mad at him for a really long time."

"And I deserved that," said Rick, looking Eleanor in the eye.

"But he is your father," she said to the twins, "and now you know a little more about him. Maybe we can agree to take it one day at a time from here. But don't start making wedding plans, OK?"

Rachel shook her head. After a moment, she spoke up again. Her voice quivered a little. "But if you didn't come back to marry Mom, why did you come? Did you get done exploring the world and come back to see us like Mom said you would?"

"I'm not quite done exploring the world yet, but yes, I did come back to see you. I was too dumb to realize that when I first got here, which *really* doesn't make sense. But that's why it took me so long to come over and meet you or even let you know I was here. I was dumb."

Everyone sat in silence for a while. Finally Eleanor rose. "Kids, it's getting close to bedtime and I know this has been a lot for you to deal with today. Let's go home now, and if there are other questions you want to ask Rick, I'm sure he'll answer them another day."

"Yes," said Rick. "Make a list of everything you want to ask me and I promise I'll answer. I need to make up for a lot of lost time."

The twins looked at each other and grinned. Clearly, they were in sync about something. "No problem," said Andrew, and the two of them scurried out the door.

As Eleanor followed them, Rick called to her. "Would you do something for me too, El?"

"Maybe. What?"

"Call Dave. I meant what I said."

She stood for a moment, then nodded and went out.

Chapter 21
Patchwork

The twins were restless. Eleanor couldn't blame them. She felt the same way. After the years of silence, to have Rick confess honestly to being scared and stupid and every bit as bad as his son said he was... she had no idea how to deal with that. She made herself a cup of coffee, just to have something to do. The twins looked around the door from the living room where they'd been halfheartedly pretending to find a video to watch. "Mom?" said Andrew.

She set her cup on the table. "Yes?"

"Why didn't you tell us about Rick before?"

"Yeah," said Rachel. "Didn't you think we were old enough?"

"You two come sit down and we'll talk, OK? Would you like some chocolate milk while I drink my coffee?" This suggestion was greeted with enthusiasm, and some of the restless energy was burned up getting glasses, and finding the syrup, and bickering about how much syrup and milk to pour into each glass. Finally they settled in at the table, sipped at the milk and looked at her, expectantly.

"I guess in the beginning I didn't tell anyone about Rick because I was so mad at him. But—can you guys understand this? It was also because I loved him and I didn't want anyone else in town to know that he'd done something so bad, running away from such good kids. Does that make any sense?"

The twins thought it over. "Everybody else in town would have been mad at him too," said Rachel.

"Well, they shoulda been," said Andrew. "He deserved it."

"I know you're upset with him right now, Andrew, and I understand why, but think about it. If everyone in town was mad at him, you can bet a lot of people would tell him so. You know how people talk sometimes, grownups and kids alike. And if he knew everyone in town was mad at him, do you think he would ever have come back?"

"And you wanted him to come back?"

"Of course I did. More than anything else I wanted him to know what great kids he had."

"Oh," said Rachel. "You didn't tell us about him because you didn't want us to be mad at him too."

"Well, I *am* mad at him," said Andrew, firmly. "He's a poopyhead and he tattled on us."

"Andrew," said his mother, "he didn't tattle on you. If anyone tattled it was Granny. I know this is hard to deal with, but you need to try. He did come back and he came back to see you, weren't you listening?"

"Well, he shoulda come sooner!" Andrew's eyes welled up. "He shoulda, Mom. I don't want a bad dad like that."

"He shoulda, no doubt about that. But what's done is done, and I bet if you give him a chance now, he'll do his best to make up for lost time." Eleanor held out her arms and Andrew ran to her, followed by his sister. Eleanor hugged them both tightly. No one spoke for a long time. Finally Eleanor felt her son relax. She relaxed as well.

"Both of you, I know this is one of the hardest things you've ever had to face. But we're going to work things out, OK? Just keep in mind that you have two parents who love you very much. And Rick will be doing his very best to make up for being a bad dad."

Andrew considered that for a moment and then wriggled free. "I love you too, Mom," he said, kissing her on the cheek. "Can I take the chocolate milk into my room?"

She laughed. "Taking advantage of me, are you?"

"Well... maybe a little." He grinned. "Can I?"

"Just this once, but if that stuff ends up anywhere but in your tummy..."

"I'm already grounded."

"I'll think of something else." She gave him a mock frown.

"Me too?" said Rachel with an equally big grin.

"I'm being double teamed! All right, but at least shut your doors so Phydeaux doesn't get any ideas!"

Rachel kissed her too and the two of them took off, with the chocolate milk. Eleanor didn't watch them. If they spilled on the way she didn't want to know.

⌗⌗⌗

The house was finally quiet, and she sat at the quilt frame, needle going up and down. Slowly the tensions of the day faded away. She lost track of time. Another block was finished, and another, and all of a sudden the clock chimed ten. She put her needle and thimbles away and flicked the cover over the quilt frame. Should she turn on the news? She sat in her favorite chair and picked up the remote control from the basket next to her, without looking at it—only to find that it was the cordless phone that she held in her hand. She looked at it for a long time.

She got up, fully intending to put the phone back in its cradle in the kitchen, and got halfway there. And then she made a quick turn, sat down at the table in the darkened room and dialed. It was late, but if she put this off any longer she might not be able to do it, and then it really would be too late.

Her mother answered on the third ring. "Mom? I know it's close to bedtime, but could you possibly come over for a while?"

"Of course I can. What's happened?"

"I... I need to talk with Dave. I need to go over there and I don't know how long it will take.

"I'll be right there. Is there anything else I can do?"

"Not right now, but thanks, Mom."

Dave was lying on his back in his bedroom, which was illuminated only by the penumbra of a streetlight in the alley. He heard the footsteps coming up the stairs. Who-ever it was stood on the landing for what seemed like a long time before they knocked. He turned to face the wall. Who the fuck would be at his doorstep at this time of night? If he made no sound they'd go away.

"Dave?" It was Eleanor's voice. "Dave, I really need to talk with you. I... things aren't the way you think they are. I don't know how to make it right if we can't talk. Please let me in."

He squeezed his eyes tight shut. Clenched his fists. Drew his knees up. And then all of a sudden he was off the bed and heading for the door.

When he opened it, Eleanor stood on the landing with her arms wrapped around herself. "Can I please come in?"

"I...sure." He stepped back to let her pass. "Sorry there's no lights on. I was in bed."

"Let's go in the living room and sit down, OK? Please?"

He led the way, turning on a lamp by the couch, blinking in the sudden brightness. Eleanor sat in a chair, and after a moment Dave pushed himself into a corner of the couch.

Eleanor set her purse on the floor. The room was quiet for a moment. Then she took a deep breath. "The kids met Rick tonight."

"And he's going to be their dad and you're telling me goodbye."

"Of course not..."

"It's all right, I understand. As soon as Adam can hire someone..."

"You're getting it all wrong. Will you listen to me for just a moment, please?"

"Yes," he said. He turned away from her and used the back of his hand to wipe his eyes.

Another silence. Finally she said, "Rick is their father, but... I think if you'll stay you could... be their dad."

In a choked voice he said "You don't mean that."

"What makes you think you're an expert on what I mean or don't mean?"

He sat silently for a moment. "You're right. I just... I can't get between Rick and his children."

"Did anyone ask you to?"

"No. I... I'm sorry. I don't understand any of this. Excuse me a sec." He got up and went into the bathroom to get the tissue box, pulled out a handful and blew his nose. He flung the wadded tissue in the general direction of the wastebasket, then made his way back to sit down. "I don't understand."

"The kids told Rick that I already had a boyfriend so he couldn't be their dad."

"They... They what? What did Rick say?"

"What it boils down to is that he said they were right."

Dave had no words. Finally he choked out "He's going to leave them... you... all over again?"

Eleanor sighed and rubbed her eyes. "He's not abandoning us again, if that's what you mean, but he can't stay here much longer, his leave is almost up. And we've got too many years to deal with in such a short time, and neither he nor I have any clue if we'd ever be able to put everything behind us. What he said was, 'your mom has a great boyfriend and I didn't come here to break that up. Being your father doesn't change the boyfriend part.'"

"I... I don't know what to say."

"I didn't know what to say either. I still don't. Except that I don't want you to leave."

Dave sighed, leaned back and looked at the ceiling. And then he turned toward her and for the first time in his life it all began to spill out. "That's what I've been doing for years, El, leaving whenever things got tough. And now when I finally thought I'd found someplace I wanted to stay, all of a sudden it looked like I had no choice but to leave. These past few days... God, it's been like staring down a black hole, thinking I'd have to pack up and go. I..." His voice faded out.

"Have you really done that all your life?"

"Well... not all my life, but enough of it."

"I'm glad you haven't packed your bags yet. I do want you to stay."

He choked. "No one's ever said that before."

"I don't believe that. Maybe you just didn't hear them." He could see tear tracks on her face.

240

He thought about it. "No one said it because I didn't give anyone the chance."

"What happened? Talk to me."

He sighed. "That's hard. I've never had anyone say that to me either."

"Please try. I'll listen."

"I... remember I told you I'd studied architecture? That was true. I wanted to be an architect ever since I was in grade school. I started doing research on it when I was in junior high and I knew exactly what I needed to do and where I wanted to go. My dad was a firefighter, and he got killed in a building collapse when I was in the fifth grade and his insurance was barely enough to keep my mom and me going. I knew from the get-go that it was all up to me. I worked every summer and saved my money. Never had time for a social life like the other guys. When I got old enough for college I busted my butt and got scholarships and grants and worked to pay my own way through. Same deal, all work and no play, which is why I've never been any good just shooting the breeze like everyone else. I never learned how."

He stretched his legs out for a moment, trying to relax. "My mom died of lung cancer my sophomore year, and her insurance came to enough for me to finish school, so I had a little more time to make friends. Not that I really did. My senior year, I met... well, her name doesn't matter. She was in one of my classes, and invited me out for coffee, and..." He stopped and cleared his throat. "It was my first real relationship, can you believe that? A senior in college out on my very first date. I didn't have the instincts or the social skills... I must have been crazy. But she loved me. Or I thought she loved me, she was so patient while I learned all the stuff the other guys knew since junior high. She said she..." His voice trailed off.

He sat quietly, remembering. After a moment he went on. "Her parents were rich, but I didn't know that. Not at the beginning. She was their only child. We... we got engaged. Started planning the wedding for the summer after graduation. It was just going to be the two of us and some friends. She said she wasn't going to tell her parents till after it was over, and I told her I thought that was a terrible idea. I guess I should have kept my mouth shut."

"I'm in favor of honesty," Eleanor said.

"Maybe so. After all this time I still don't know what I could have done differently." He cleared his throat again. "So her parents came to visit for a weekend and we met. I did my best. They did a real good job of pretending they approved. I had no clue that I wasn't what they'd had in mind for their precious daughter. Like I said, no social instincts. Her father made a big deal out of my studying to be an architect, said he'd commission me to draw up plans for an addition to their summer house. I told him I'd be happy to as soon as I'd passed the board exams and gotten my license. Think about it, he said, I'll send you photographs of the house and you can use those to get an idea of what you'd like to do. I fell for that," he said, bitterly.

"After that, it was all about the plans for the summer house. He never let up. Just do the drawings, he said, and I'll get them vetted by a friend of ours, and he named a big muckety-muck architect that everyone had heard of. Vetted. I've always remembered that. Vetted." He clenched his fists. "So I graduated with honors, and I felt so good about that that I did his drawings. And he hired a contractor and went ahead with the addition without telling me or his daughter. And I don't know whether whoever 'vetted' the drawings was responsible, or whether he hired someone to sabotage it, or what, but the deck collapsed while a crew of caterers was on it setting up for a big party, and three people ended up in the hospital, and we were all lucky nobody got killed. And when the investigation started he claimed he had no idea I wasn't licensed and he never would have gone ahead if he'd known."

"Oh, Dave..." She gave a small sob and pressed a hand to her mouth.

"She believed her dad, of course. Gave me back the ring and told me to go away and never come back. Her dad said that was the best thing he'd heard in ages, and if I was gone by the end of the week he wouldn't press charges and he'd take care of the rest of it, but he'd better not hear of me trying to be an architect anywhere else or he'd ruin me. What choice did I have?" He sighed again, opening his hands. "I've been traveling ever since then. Never knew when to stop. I started having panic attacks when someone wanted me to be sociable. I don't know if you noticed I was fighting one off the first time you took me to Ruth's. And that's what happened the other night. I had to get out. It wasn't you, it was me. But then I didn't know how to go back."

"I wish... I wish we'd had a chance to talk about this before now. I should have taken my mom up on that weekend offer." She rubbed her face with her sleeve.

He ventured a shaky laugh. "I kinda doubt it would have come up in the course of conversation, El."

She thought about that, smiling for the first time. "Yeah, now that you mention it, I guess you're right."

"What... what do we do now?"

"I think the three of us need to get together and talk, and nobody gets to run away, period. We have to figure things out. No matter how hard that might be for any of us. I think we can do that. We have to."

"We have to," he echoed. "Yes."

243

"You know, it was my mom who got this whole thing started, even though she didn't know it at the time. Her computer got one of those viruses because the twins switched off the protection to download a game. And Ruth sent Rick over to fix it, and the more I think about it the more I think she knew exactly what she was doing."

"Your mom didn't know? About Rick, I mean."

"Nobody knew. I never told anyone. Not even my mom."

He was silent for a moment. "Is your mom going to be OK?"

"I think she handled it better than anyone. Which means I'm sure she'll be delighted to take the twins off our hands while we talk this all out."

He considered that. "Just have the kids move over there for a week, then?"

She laughed. "It might take that long. But let's hope not. I'll ask her tomorrow. And in the meantime, you'd better show up for Friday supper just like always."

"Just like always. I... I'll be there. I... I love you, El."

She wiped tears off her face with the back of her hand. "I love you too, Dave. And I should have said that long before now."

They rose and clung to each other with all their might.

Chapter 22
Connections

"D ave! Dave's here! Are you OK, Dave? Did you hear we got grounded? Did you know Mom's making tacos? Did..."

Friday night was already off to a great start. "Kids, you are acting like a two person stampede. Give Dave a chance to get halfway through the door, why don't you?" But Eleanor was laughing. Dave set a bottle of sparkling apple juice on the table and kept right on going to pull Eleanor into his arms and kiss her, which both embarrassed and delighted the twins, who whooped and applauded. Eleanor, who'd been stirring taco filling, held the spoon well away from the back of Dave's shirt. A small blop of seasoned hamburger fell on the floor and the dog made a move on it and departed at top speed.

"You guys finish up whatever your mom told you to do," Dave said, still holding Eleanor, "and then we'll go in the living room and you can tell me all about getting grounded while she gets supper ready. You must have really outdone yourselves this time."

"It's not the baddest thing we've... uh oh," said Andrew, slapping a hand across his mouth.

"Oh really? Do tell," said his mom, setting down her cooking spoon and crossing her arms.

"Nothing! Really! We're done! Come on, Dave!" He grabbed Dave's hand and towed him, laughing, into the living room. Rachel grabbed Dave's other hand and followed. Eleanor shook her head and went back to work on supper.

As they ate, the twins talked about school, and their friends, and the prospects of computer camp. Apparently, they'd actually gained a bit of status among their friends for having messed up their grandmother's computer in the attempt to get the forbidden game, and went on in some detail about it, which annoyed Eleanor. "You're just lucky Rick was able to fix it," she said. "If you'd messed it up permanently, I would have made you do chores for Granny every day for a year to work off the cost of a new one." Dead silence. The twins looked at their plates and picked at the last of their tacos. Guessing the real issue at hand, Eleanor continued, "Yes, Dave knows about your father. It's OK."

The twins looked at Dave. They didn't have to say anything; the question was plain enough to see. "That's right," he said, firmly. "Your mom and I and your dad will work things out. For a while you'll just have to make sure you keep three people from finding reasons to ground you, OK?"

Rachel snorted. "Grownups can always find reasons," she said.

"Yeah," said Andrew. "Always."

"Somehow I think you guys have something to do with that too," said Dave, trying not to grin, which set off a flurry of oh-so-sincerely-indignant denials from the twins. But in the end, they burst out laughing too.

After supper, the twins started squabbling again about which video they were going to watch, until Dave settled the matter by saying he'd pick one that he hadn't seen, and they could tell him about it while they all watched. That got some raised eyebrows from all concerned, but eventually Dave sat on the couch with his arm around Eleanor, listening to an animated commentary on "Aladdin," to which, to be honest, he was not paying close attention. Still, he was enjoying being back together with everyone so much that he was genuinely sorry when the movie came to an end and it was Andrew and Rachel's bedtime.

The twins headed for their rooms, but found all kinds of reasons they absolutely positively had to come back out in the living room. But every time they did, all they saw was their mom and her boyfriend snuggled on the couch watching another video.

⠿⠿⠿

Just before lunchtime on Monday, Dave was looking at the calendar on his computer and talking across the office with Peter about the week's schedule, when Adam walked in the front door carrying a bag from a large electronics store. Peter made a quick gesture with his left hand on the keyboard. "Hi guys," Adam said. "I've got your new phones here. Peter, now you can have your own phone on your desk." Adam set the bag down on Dave's desk and took out a box containing a cordless phone system with two handsets, and another box containing two headsets and phone cables. It took only a few minutes to get the old phone disconnected and the new system in place.

"Cordless phones?" said Peter, frowning. "You sure those are secure?"

Adam rubbed his chin. "Well, apart from the fact that I don't know what kind of major secrets anyone could get from us if they listened in, yes, the communications between the handset and the base station are encrypted. I don't think you have anything to worry about."

"If you say so," said Peter, sounding unconvinced. He pulled the power cord for his phone's charger under his desk to plug it in.

"Those phones will take about an hour to charge up completely," said Adam, "so I'm not sure what will happen when people call. I need to figure out how to record all the greetings. We can have more than one on this model."

"Oh, so we can say 'leave a message,' or 'call back in an hour,' or 'not in this lifetime, pal'?" laughed Dave.

"Not a bad idea, that," said Adam with a straight face, and then he laughed. "Give me a minute to read the directions here, unless one of you guys wants to be the phone voice?" Getting no takers, he plopped down in one of the chairs.

Dave looked at the phone, which seemed to have an awful lot of buttons. "I want those directions when you're done, Adam. This thing looks like the cockpit of a 747."

Adam waved a hand. "It's easier than it looks. I think the most time consuming thing will be programming in the speed dial. Be thinking of which numbers you need for that. The electrician, the exterminator, the handyman, whatever."

"The pizza place," said Peter, looking at his handset with interest.

"Maybe in the secondary list," said Adam, going back to his reading.

Peter put the handset back in its charger. "Well, guys, that's it for me for the day." He clicked his mouse a few more times, looked at the screen for a moment and then turned off his monitor. "You can teach me all about the phone tomorrow, Dave." Peter's computer whirred and then shut down.

"You've got a lot more confidence in me than you should have," said Dave, darkly.

After Peter had left, Adam said "Dave, is your computer password protected?"

"No, I didn't know how to do that. Peter's got most of this stuff on his computer too."

"He doesn't have Quickbooks, does he?"

"No, I didn't see that he'd need that, and I wouldn't know where to find the disks anyway. He was never in here alone," he hastened to add.

"That's good. I was just wondering what he was doing over there."

"Inspection schedules, I thought."

"You didn't see what he did when I walked in?"

"No."

"Oh, you probably don't know about that. Here, watch this." He opened up the company database and Firefox on Dave's computer. "Look here," he said, pressing alt-tab quickly with his left hand. "That switches from one program to another. He switched pretty quickly, but I saw what he did. Makes me wonder what's on that computer these days. I bet he cleared his browser cache before he shut down."

"Oh, I've seen him do that left-hand thing lots of times, but I had no idea it meant anything. The rest of what you said might as well have been in Chinese." Dave sighed. "Damn, I've got a lot to learn about computers."

"Well, it's probably nothing. But if he keeps doing it, would you send me an email or call me when he's not here and let me know? Now, let's password your computer. It's my fault that wasn't done from the get-go."

❌ ❌ ❌

Ruth was cleaning the counter in the front of the store when Eleanor walked in. "Whoa! Abandoning your desk in the middle of the day? What will the neighbors think!"

Eleanor laughed and held out a small white case with a blank grey screen. "Fat chance. Ron's trying to set up his old music player with a speaker system so we can listen to something besides the radio during the day, and he's let this thing sit in a drawer so long the battery won't charge any more. So he asked me to bring it over here to have you put in a new battery. And I wanted to stop by anyway—the kids gave me their list of questions for Rick, and I can't wait to see how he answers some of them."

"Oh really? This sounds good. Let's see."

At that point, Rick pushed his way through the curtain. "I heard that. It's *my* list. Gimme." He held out a hand, and with a mock show of horror, Eleanor pulled a folded piece of notebook paper, showing definite signs of hard use, out of her purse and handed it over. Rick stuffed it inside his shirt, crossed his arms dramatically, and stalked off into the back.

"Bet we won't see him for the rest of the day," said Ruth.

"I'll make you a copy after the kids get done with it," Eleanor whispered.

"I HEARD THAT!" came from the back.

"YOU DID NOT!" said both women, in unison, and then they burst out laughing.

Eleanor winked at Ruth, and gestured to confirm she'd make a copy. But what she said was "Any further word on the virus hunt?"

"Rick made some calls yesterday and sent some emails, but it's really too soon to hear back. He knows people back on the base who know a lot about security. I guess we're all just waiting for something to happen one way or the other. I hope what Rick told his friends will give them the answer."

The door bell jingled as Brad walked in. "Sorry, ladies, I would have snuck in through the back door as usual, but that cat has his butt parked right by it. I didn't feel like tangling with him today, so I came around front."

The "ladies" looked at him. His hair hadn't been combed and he had dark circles under his eyes. He looked like he hadn't shaved in a couple of days and his glasses were smudged. Charlie had never liked Brad. And since the cat had abandoned the front window to stay with Rick in the back, his attitude toward Brad had turned into positive aversion. Brad approached Charlie at considerable peril these days.

"Are you feeling all right, Brad? Would you like to take the day off?"

"Oh, I'm fine. I just stayed up way too late playing video games. I can't use that as an excuse to get off work or I'd never show up again."

"Ah," said Ruth, raising an eyebrow, "the games come first, is that it?" Brad looked sheepish, ducked his head and headed into the back. "Speaking of which, El, how's the Great Twin Grounding working out?"

"There were a lot of thunderclouds around the house for a while, but I doubt I'll ever have to do it again. Well, not because of computer hanky-panky, at any rate. I told them they'd better get an attitude adjustment or I'd just give the computer to the junk store. They knew that was a pretty pathetic threat. So I told them their dad would come over and put some super Navy security on the computer and all they'd be able to do is visit the Sesame Street web site for the next five years. That, they believed."

"I bet. So they're... they're doing OK with suddenly having a real live father?"

"They're getting used to it. I gather they're getting plenty of mileage out of it at school. Some of their friends' parents were classmates of Rick's, so they're hearing good things about him. That helps."

Ruth turned to look toward the back of the store, but either Rick hadn't heard this exchange, or he declined comment. "That's good," she said with a smile. "Maybe Rick can get together with some of his old classmates before he has to go back, kind of join the Dad Club."

"I'm going to ask him to take the kids shopping for their computer camp supplies before he leaves. That might help break the ice, too."

"Tell him to get their school clothes while he's at it, make himself useful for a change."

"Let's not push our luck," said Eleanor, but she was smiling too. "Well, I gotta get back to the salt mines."

"I'll probably have to order a battery for the player."

"Take your time. I've heard Ron's music collection."

⊠⊠⊠

Questions for Dad by Rachel and Andrew
1. How old are you?
2. Where do you live? Can we come visit you sometime?

3. Do you just have the motorcycle, or do you have a car too?

4. What's your favorite movie?

5. Did you help Mom pick out our names?

6. Will you give us an allowance?

7. What music do you like best?

8. When do you get vacations from the Navy?

9. "Do you have a gun" was scribbled out and "Do you know how to fly a jet?" was written in.

10. Rachel is allergic to penicillin. Is that because of you?

11. Do you play video games?

12. If you move back here, whose house will you live in?

13. (Whatever had been here had been firmly scribbled out.)

Rick sat at the table in the back of the store and considered. Then he folded the paper again and went to the file cabinet in the front of the shop to get the bag of cat food. Charlie, suitably distracted, abandoned his post by the door at warp speed, and Rick was then able to slip quietly outside and go upstairs away from the danger of snoopy sisters. Digging a pen out of a drawer in the kitchen, he began to write.

Answers for Rachel and Andrew, by Dad
(It feels weird, but good, to call myself Dad!)
1. I'm 33.

2. I live in Norfolk, Virginia, when I'm not on the submarine. I don't know if you can come visit, that would be strictly up to your mother and whether I am available when you've got time off school. We can talk about it.

3. Right now, I just have the motorcycle. It's easier to store when I'm out at sea.

4. My favorite movie is "Raiders of the Lost Ark."

5. No, I didn't help pick out your names, but I think your mom picked really good ones.

6. Talk with your mom. I will only give allowances with her approval, period. If she says no, that's that, and I'll be checking with her. I know that much about being a dad!

7. I like all kinds of music as long as it's not screechy, sour, or boring.

8. I get vacations (we call it "leave") every year. But I won't be getting as much time off next year as I did this year, because I kept not taking my leave till my commanding officer said enough was enough and made me take all of it, all at once. He was right. I'm going to tell him that as soon as I get back.

9. No, I don't know how to fly a jet, or any other kind of plane for that matter.

10. I don't think Rachel's allergy is my fault (I am not allergic to penicillin and neither is Ruth) but I am allergic to poison ivy, so who knows?

11. I play video games sometimes, but usually I don't have the time. I bet you guys could kick my butt.

12. If I move back here, which sounds like a really good idea, I will get my own place. And you two will always be welcome there.

He looked over his answers, and then added "But don't expect more privileges at my house than you get at home!" to the last one. Then he found an envelope and sealed the paper inside it. No sense letting the whole world read it before the kids did.

Chapter 23
Pong and Ping

Rick had left a deliberately unprotected computer running in the back of the shop. Monday morning, he turned on its monitor and found what appeared to be a Pong game in progress. The "ball" was flashing what appeared to be a pattern, but it was doing it too quickly for him to make out what the pattern might be.

"Pong?" said Chet in disbelief. "*Pong?* Even I heard 'a that one. What the hell do those guys think they're doing?"

"I have no idea, Chet, but you know what? One of my best friends from Great Lakes works for the FBI in Des Moines, in their cybercrime unit. I'm going to take this hard drive and hand-deliver it him right now. This has gone beyond what we or Horemheb or anyone else should have to mess with." He held the power button on the computer till it shut off and went to get a screwdriver from Ruth's tool rack.

Ruth sighed. "I'm so tempted not to even turn the phones on today. My God, enough is enough."

"No kidding," said Chet. "Every dumbass in town will be down our neck again. They just don't freakin' learn." He put his lunch bag and thermos bottle in the far reaches of the back of his bench and sat down, but didn't start working. He swiveled around on his stool to face Ruth. "If I can figure these damn things out, why the hell can't they?"

Rick slid the side panels off the computer and chuckled. "Because you're a different kind of dumbass, Chet."

Chet threw a small cardboard box in Rick's direction and missed. "Smart enough to know whose butt to kick in this shop, sonny," he said, gruffly.

"That's why I'm leaving town, to get out of your way!" Rick pulled off cables, removed some screws and slid the hard drive out. "Hey, come to think of it, we need to each have our own login on the store computer, with passwords. I know that will be kind of a pain till we get used to it, but that way I can keep my data separate if I have to work on security stuff on that computer. Actually..." he thought for a moment. "I'll buy a laptop as long as I'm out. You can have it after I'm done with it, Ruth. But we should set passwords anyway."

"Are you sure that's necessary?" his sister asked, frowning.

"No, I'm not sure, but it can't hurt. Once someone figures out who's behind the virus, we can put the computer back the way it was, if you want."

"You think they'll catch that jackass before you go back?" Chet sounded extremely dubious about that prospect.

"No clue. But the FBI has all kinds of tools I don't have, so who knows?"

"Just one damn thing after the other with these fool computers," groused Chet.

"Oh?" said Ruth, in mock surprise. "And just whose idea was the computer repair business, I wonder?"

"Fixin' 'em is one thing, usin' 'em is something else again." Chet huffed off back to his bench.

"You need to come set your password," Rick told him.

"Been ages since I looked at anything on the internet and I let Ruth mess with all that other stuff. I'll get to it later. I got real work to do."

"Suit yourself." The "you cranky old coot" was implied. Rick grinned. Since Chet wasn't looking her way, so did Ruth. And then she quickly sat down to set up her password.

"I probably won't be back by the time Brad comes in, so I'll write down what he needs to do," said Rick, slipping the hard drive into an Electronic Wizardry bag. "Although I doubt he'll need the directions. Just make sure he sets up his own password before he goes home today, please. I've created an account for him with Wizard as the temporary password, and he can change that to whatever he wants." He thought for a moment. "And if *anyone* asks where I am, just tell them I'm out running errands. Make up something plausible if you have to. I don't have reason to suspect anyone, but I'm beginning to think we can't be too careful." He wrote briefly on a sheet of paper, then took the hard drive out the back door, flipping open his cell phone as he went.

Sure enough, the store's phone rang less than a minute later, and Ruth and Chet went back into "We told you so" mode for the rest of the day. Brad came in, was given instructions, and dealt with his password without comment. "What's up with this computer?" he asked, pointing to the one Rick had left in pieces on the table.

"Oh, Rick went to get some kind of part a customer wanted installed," said Ruth, improvising swiftly. "I was on the phone so I didn't catch what he was doing."

Brad frowned as he looked inside the computer's carcass. "He took the hard drive out."

"Well, maybe the customer wanted a bigger hard drive. I don't really know. Could you answer the phone while I go to the bathroom, please? I haven't had a chance to turn around all morning."

⊠ ⊠ ⊠

By the end of the day, Ruth was exhausted. She dragged herself and the cat upstairs and found her brother sitting at the dining room table with the new laptop. Its packaging was strewn around him on the floor. Charlie, who loved nothing better than chewing plastic, made a beeline for the box and the wrappings, and Rick got up quickly to head him off before he chowed down. Charlie hissed in righteous indignation, but by that time Ruth had gotten some fresh food poured for him and he stalked off, with an "I'll get even with you guys for this, just you wait and see" tone of tail.

"I don't suppose," said Rick, "that your boyfriend the landlord would mind too much if I ran some ethernet cable up here? The wireless signal from downstairs is for crap. They don't build floors like this any more."

"I don't suppose my boyfriend the landlord would mind a bit, so have at it, if you don't think you'll make the whole floor fall down while you're drilling in it. I never had any need to do that before."

"Clearly, you needed me to drag you into the internet age," Rick laughed. "I'll be sure to bookmark a bunch of really good web sites for you before I hand over the laptop."

"Oh boy, I can hardly wait," said Ruth, with a noticeable lack of enthusiasm.

"I can hear how happy you are about that already. I bought a wireless relay. I just need to find someplace reasonably cat-resistant to put it." He started picking up the packaging and folding it into less cat-attracting configurations. "OK, not much more I can do here till the battery charges and I get a connection run. Does Chet have a really long drill bit in the shop?"

"Not in the shop, I don't think, but he's got tools up the ying-yang at home. Why don't you call and ask him?"

"I'll let him eat his supper first. I don't need this stuff Right Now This Minute. Hey, how about I treat you to supper out tonight?"

"You had me at 'treat.' Lead on, Macduff."

⊠⊠⊠

Rick's cell phone rang Tuesday morning just as he was finishing his breakfast. "Hello? Oh, hi, Jack. No, I'm just eating breakfast... no, just my sister, why?"

There was a long pause.

"Really? Jesus. You think they did it?" He listened. "Oh, yeah, that makes a lot more sense. No, I don't know anyone there personally, I don't think, but my sister does." He listened again. "OK, I'll see what we can do on this end. Yeah, I've got the shop computer protected and I bought a laptop after I saw you yesterday. We're cool. Thanks. I'll email you later today." He flipped the phone shut.

Ruth had stopped in the middle of pouring herself a bowl of cereal. She set the box on the table and looked at her brother. "What's going on?"

"Ruthie, you're friends with Amy Kim, right?"

"Yes. Why?"

"My buddy Jack says the bouncing Pong ball is actually flashing the Mintaka logo off and on."

"You think they…"

"No, that's just the point. Jack doesn't think they would do that to themselves, and neither do I. It's a good bet someone is out to get them. Could you put me in touch with Amy, privately? I don't want to go barging into the office and raising people's hackles, but I think it'd be a good idea to talk with her about this."

"I haven't even seen her downtown for weeks." She looked at the clock. "I might be able to catch her at home before she leaves for work." She went to the phone and dialed. After four rings, Amy's answering machine picked up. "Amy? This is Ruth. Could you call me sometime… Oh, hi! I'm glad I caught you. My brother's got some important news about the viruses and wondered if he could talk with you… no, this is different, I think you and the company will want to hear it, I really do." She listened for a moment. "OK, I'll put Rick on the phone." She turned to her brother. "Amy has to leave for work in just a few minutes, so make it quick."

"Thanks a million, Ruthie." He took the phone. "Hi Amy, I don't know if you remember me… oh, yeah, that's right… well, listen, we're on your side with this one, believe me. I just got a call from a friend of mine at the FBI and he says it looks as though someone's got it in for Mintaka and that's where the viruses are coming from. Do you know of anyone…" He listened. "OK, that's all right. Could you very quietly ask around? Would that be possible? To my way of thinking it'd have to be someone who's after someone pretty high up the food chain… yeah. If you find anything out, could you call me here at Ruth's? Leave a message on her home machine if you like… yeah, I know, it could take some time, but I think it's worth a shot. Thanks so much, Amy, I'll let you get to work."

He put down the phone and looked at it for a moment, then took a deep breath and let it out slowly. "I think we need to keep acting like we don't know anything, at least while Jack and Amy are asking around. I hope it won't take too long to figure it out. The patch from Horemheb should be in the shop email this morning."

"Oh, I forgot—Brad asked why you took the hard drive out of that computer yesterday. I told him you might be putting in a bigger one for a customer."

"Oh? He didn't remember that the computer was abandoned?"

"I... you know, I have no idea. You'd probably better put another hard drive in it. I did tell Brad I hadn't heard you clearly because I was on the phone. You don't think he's..."

"No, I don't think anything. I'm just taking Jack's advice to make sure everything seems normal in the shop and keep my eyes open. I'll put another hard drive in that computer and have it up and running before Brad gets to work this afternoon, and if he asks about it I'll tell him it's my test platform and I needed more drive space. Which is the truth, actually."

"OK, good. You handle it. Now let me eat my cereal so I can face the phone calls and the crazies."

"You'll need more fortification than just cereal for that, Ruthie."

"You said it. Unfortunately, cereal's what I've got."

⊠⊠⊠

Hi, Adam (Dave wrote in an email). Just a quick note because I've got to run do a move-out inspection this morning. Now that you've mentioned it, I've kept an eye on Peter. He does the alt-tab on the keyboard every time I come back to the office, and sometimes he just sits looking at his screen and clicking the mouse when he thinks I'm busy. Yesterday, he pulled one of those flash drive things out quickly before he left for home. Don't know if it means anything but I'm letting you know. Hope all's well in the big city.

⊠ ⊠ ⊠

The antivirus updates from Horemheb and the other companies had come through at lightning speed, and the shop was getting more or less back to normal when the phone rang Wednesday morning. After greeting Ruth affectionately and catching up on a bit of the news, Adam asked to speak to Rick. Ruth raised her eyebrows, but said nothing as she handed her brother the phone.

"Hey, Adam, what's up? ... Really? ... Oh, that's not a problem, but the best ones are kind of pricey... Sure, I'll do that, and I'll let you know." He put the phone down and shook his head. "Verrrrrrrrrrry interesting. Adam wants me to go over to the office and install a keylogger on Peter's computer."

"What the sam hill is that?" said Chet, putting down his soldering iron with a clatter.

"It'll let Adam see exactly what Peter's typing on his computer, all day long, and what web sites he goes to."

"Really! Y'think that guy's the virus twerp?"

"I have no idea, but apparently he's doing something suspicious enough that Adam thinks this would be a good idea. Ruth, he says he left you a credit card for major expenses?"

"Sure, it's in the safe. Wouldn't it be weird if it turned out Peter was the one?"

"Well, let's not start suspecting him of anything just yet." Rick thought of something and started to laugh. "Who knows, he might just be looking at dating sites on the company connection. Let me call Dave and figure out when's the best time to get the software installed. Oh, wait—Ruth, do you happen to know when Peter's likely to be there? I don't want to call if he might be listening in."

"No, but you could call Eleanor and ask her."

"Now why didn't I think of that?" He smiled. "Go unlock the credit card so I can do the boss man's bidding."

In short order, it was established that Peter worked in the mornings and left at noon. "Hey, maybe you and me and Ruth and Dave could get together this weekend?" Rick asked Eleanor. "It's been a long week for everyone, whaddya say?" He listened for a moment, then laughed. "OK, I will, and now we both need to get back to work." He stood up and moved so he could see the big Mickey Mouse watch on the wall near Ruth's bench that served as the shop's clock. Not quite safe to call Dave. "Eleanor said I should talk with you about this weekend. What have you two been doing behind my back?"

"Who, us?" Ruth batted her eyelashes. "What on earth could we do behind your back?"

"I wouldn't put anything past the pair of you," said Rick, giving her a mock scowl.

"Oh, get to work and we'll discuss the weekend later. Go on." His sister laughed and turned back to her bench.

Chapter 24
Life's a Picnic

A *picnic?*" said Rick, as Ruth said goodbye to Eleanor after supper and put down the phone. "You have *got* to be kidding me."

"A picnic. At the lake, away from everybody's phones and computers and distractions, and out in the open where there aren't many things to throw." She tried to look serious, but he knew her too well.

"Aw, Ruthie. I had a hard enough time asking Eleanor and Dave to get together without having to add in sunburn and ants. Come on. Besides, Eleanor might decide to drown me in the lake."

"Go buy some sunscreen and bug repellent and an inner tube," she said. "We're going. Right after we close the shop on Saturday. Eleanor's mom suggested it and she's providing the food, so it's a done deal, ants or no ants."

"Paula had better be a damn good cook, that's all I can say," said Rick, darkly.

"She is. Get a move on if you need all that stuff," said his sister unsympathetically.

❈ ❈ ❈

"I think I remember the last time I went on a picnic," said Dave, smiling, as Eleanor hung up the phone.

Rachel piped up. "Oh, we went on a school picnic last year and Andrew spilled grape juice all down his shirt and someone pushed one of our friends' heads under the water fountain, and I got a real bad sunburn on the top of my head because I forgot my hat. It was great."

Dave's eyebrows shot up. "Well then, I'll obviously have to go buy a purple shirt, just in case," he said with a straight face. The twins giggled. "Or maybe I should go buy Andrew a purple shirt and you a purple hat?" That set off a major burst of laughter.

"Just as long as it's not a purple plastic purse," said Rachel.

Dave had no idea what she was talking about, and said so. "It's a book," Andrew explained. "*Lilly's Purple Plastic Purse*. The lady next door gave it to Rachel last year. It's for little kids. She just had no clue. So Rachel had to thank her for it and act like it was something she wanted, and keep it for a while till she could give it away to her friend Anna's little sister."

"That was a tactful way to handle it," said Dave. Rachel smiled.

"You don't have to go shopping just yet, though," said Eleanor to the twins. "This picnic is for grownups only."

"What! No fair! You didn't say that! We get to go!" came the indignant chorus, but Eleanor held up a hand.

"No, this is for the grownups to talk. You're going to the library with Granny, and if you don't get too mouthy about it she'll check out some videos for you to watch."

"That's NOT the same as a picnic," said Rachel, darkly. Her brother agreed in the same tone of voice.

"I didn't say it was," their mother replied, in firmly parental tones. "But neither did I say you were going with us, so that's the way it is. And I'll tell you something else right now—it's too nice an evening to look at rainclouds in the house. If you guys want to pout you can go do it in your rooms. If you want to behave, you can pick out a video to watch before bedtime. That's the choice."

"I'm tired of our videos," said Andrew, and caught a warning look from his mother.

"You know what?" said Dave, quickly, "We all happen to be in luck, because I went and checked one of my favorite videos out of the library this afternoon. *Mary Poppins*. You have not lived until you've heard Dick van Dyke mangle a Cockney accent."

"What's a Cockney accent?" Rachel asked.

"It's... um, it's the way Michael Caine talks."

"Who's Michael Caine?" the twins chorused in unison.

"He's... uh... well, you know what, I can't think of any movies he's been in that you guys are old enough to watch." That made everyone laugh.

"He was Scrooge in that Muppet Christmas Carol show, but I don't remember whether he used his real accent in that or not," Eleanor added. "Maybe we should see if we can rent that tomorrow."

"Aw, Mom," said Andrew, "it's not time for Christmas junk."

"It is time to find out what a real Cockney accent sounds like, since you're about to hear a terrible fake one in a great movie," said Dave, and that settled it.

⌗⌗⌗

When Dave showed up at Eleanor's house shortly before noon on Saturday, the twins had already left. "I can't believe this is the same place," he said. "It's too quiet."

"You wouldn't be saying that if you'd gotten here an hour ago," said Eleanor, who had spent the morning in full-tilt Mom Mode, out-stubborning the two-person stampede. "I was ready to shove the two of them in a bag and ship them off to Uzbekistan, one way. Heaven help me when they get to be teenagers." She offered Dave some coffee and he accepted. A large, well-stuffed plastic shopping bag with sturdy handles and a small insulated cooler sat on the table.

"Is that our lunch?" he asked.

"Most of it. I have a salad in the fridge, and Ruth and Rick are bringing the drinks and dessert. We're supposed to meet them by the lake sometime after 12:30 so they have time to close up the shop."

"Did they kill the virus again?"

"Apparently so. Ruth said that at least people have finally gotten the idea that they need protection and if they don't listen, they get hit, so it didn't take as long this time around. I wish someone would figure this thing out and put a stop to it. But Mintaka's not exactly a world class player, so it's not attracting much attention."

"Is it Mintaka's fault, do you think?"

"I really have no idea, but when it first happened Ruth said Rick thought they might have been involved, somehow."

"That doesn't make much sense, though, sabotaging their own customers."

"Yeah, I think that's why nobody's taking the idea too seriously. Oh well, as long as the twins don't get ideas again, we shouldn't have to worry much about it ourselves."

"Those kids are amazing, El."

"Too amazing for their own good, sometimes." She smiled. "But yeah, they are."

⊠⊠⊠

Rick had left the shop in mid-morning to stake out one of the prime picnic tables, since Ruth, Chet, and Brad seemed to be holding down the fort OK, and the virus seemed tamed for now. The spot he chose was in a small grove of trees. A battered cast-iron grill on a pedestal stood nearby. Not knowing what Paula was providing for lunch, he'd swung by the store to pick up a bag of charcoal and some lighter fluid, just in case. His plan had been to wait till Dave and Eleanor showed up, and then go back for Ruth. But Ruth had pointed out the difficulties involved in trying to carry their contributions on the back of a Harley, so the plan had been amended.

A participant to be named later would take someone's four-wheeled vehicle back into town to pick Ruth and the rest of the edibles up, while someone else remained to hold their claim to the prime picnic spot. Rick caught himself hoping he wouldn't be left alone with Dave. But he'd just have to deal with it if it happened. After facing the kids, their grandmother and their mother, and living to tell the tale, getting past one last hurdle couldn't be too hard... could it?

Not that being left alone with Eleanor would be all that much easier, though. Maybe he should volunteer to drive back for his sister right away before they figured out what he was up to. As if he could get away with that. He laughed, and sat down to wait. *Que será, será.*

The warmth of the day and the soft breeze had made him drowsy by the time Dave and Eleanor approached the table from the parking lot. He blinked and got to his feet, unsure how best to greet them. What he really wanted, he realized, was to hug Eleanor, hold her tight in simple thanks for being willing to let him back into her life, in whatever way they could work out together. And so, gathering courage, he stepped out from the picnic table bench and approached them. He held out his arms to Eleanor, silently, while he looked at Dave. Who looked back at him, then at Eleanor, smiled and silently nodded. Holding Eleanor, Rick tried, wordlessly, to convey his gratitude and his hopes. And it seemed she understood, because she clung tightly for a moment, then smiled at him when they let go. And then she stepped back beside Dave, which was as it should be.

"When we made plans," Rick said, leading the way back to the table, "we all forgot about the transportation. Ruthie wasn't about to carry a case of soda and a bakery box on the back of the Harley. Could one of you go back and get her, please?"

Dave and Eleanor looked at each other for a moment, considering. Then Dave said "I'll go. You guys need some time to talk." He held out his hand for the keys, kissed Eleanor on the cheek and left.

Eleanor and Rick sat down on opposite sides of the picnic table. Neither knew where to begin. Finally Rick said "Is Dave really going to be OK with this?"

"Eventually. We've talked. I think more than anything he just wants to know what you want to do. He doesn't want to step on anyone's toes."

"Do the kids like him?"

"Oh yes. They think they've got him wrapped around their little fingers already. Little do they know."

"That's good." He sat silent for a moment. "Did they... did they say anything more about me?"

"Some. You know, I'm sure they had a father in their imaginations for most of their lives and nobody in the world could measure up."

He sighed. "No, I don't suppose so. Do you think they'll forgive me? Eventually?"

"I'm sure they will. Andrew's quit calling you names already, so that's a start."

He tried to smile. "One step at a time."

There was a long silence. Rick finally said, working to get the words out, "What I need to ask even more is if you'll forgive me. It's taken me a long time to realize that that matters more to me than anything."

"I... yes." It might be a tired old cliché, but at that moment she felt as though the weight of years had lifted from her shoulders. A weight she had carried so long that it had been second nature. "I do forgive you, Rick. And you should forgive yourself, someday if you can't manage it now."

A tear trickled down his cheek and he brushed it away with the back of one hand and reached out to take her hand with the other. "This is the first time since I left you that I think that might actually be possible."

"That's good. Now, we go on from here, all right?"

"Yes, we go on from here." He was silent for a while. Then he said "Would you find out what supplies they need for the computer camp and let me know? I'll buy whatever they need. Maybe they'd let me take them shopping before I go back."

"No better way to start getting back in their good graces. In fact, I was going to suggest just that." She smiled. "Good work... Dad."

By the time the others returned, Rick had gotten the charcoal going and Eleanor had set out the plastic plates and cutlery her mother had provided. When they opened up the plastic containers Paula had sent, they discovered that lunch was going to be Paula's special barbecue-seasoned burgers, and there was a bowl of potato salad along with the green salad Eleanor had brought. "A real feast," said Rick. "Navy chow will never taste the same."

"I thought the best chow was on the submarines," said Dave. "They have to bribe you guys to deliberately sink yourselves somehow."

"A fresh charcoal-grilled burger is about as likely as a screen door," Rick laughed.

The four of them made short work of the burgers. "I wish your mom would give up this recipe," said Ruth. "This is one of my all-time favorites, and she's guarding that spice mix like it's the map to the Lost Ark.

"Maybe now I've given up a big secret she'll be willing to give one up too," said Eleanor, thoughtfully. "Otherwise, I guess we have to put in a call to Indiana Jones. You up for that, Rick?"

"A lot depends on whether Indy can sweet-talk Paula, I'd say."

"I'm betting Paula will kick his butt." Everyone laughed.

They sat silently, feeling as though the issues among them didn't really need more discussion, at least not that day.

After a peaceful few minutes, the wind picked up and Eleanor started gathering up the items that might be blown away. Making conversation, Dave asked Rick about the latest virus.

Rick thought about that for a moment. "When I was looking at Mrs. Ward's computer the last time around, I used some specialized tools and saw a weird message on the screen, something about a pharaoh and the stars. I've got it written down. I think that might be a clue, if anyone can figure it out."

"Stars?" said Dave. "Really? Is it possible that Mintaka is involved, somehow?"

"I don't think so. It wouldn't make much sense for them to sabotage themselves, but there's definitely something going on that might involve them peripherally. Don't tell anyone I said that, though, because I'm betting it's part of the solution and I don't want it to get around before I figure it all out." He tipped up his nearly empty plastic cup and an ice cube dislodged itself from the bottom and bopped him on the nose. Spluttering, laughing, he put the cup down and wiped his face. "What the hell kind of name is Mintaka, anyway? Some Indian tribe?"

"No," said Dave. "It's one of the stars in Orion's belt."

"Orion?" said Eleanor. "That's funny. Orion was a big deal to the ancient Egyptians. What was the message about the pharaoh?"

"I may not have it exactly right, but it was something like 'even the poorest pharaoh thinks he rules the stars.' Something close to that."

"Interesting. And Horemheb was a very minor pharaoh who didn't last long. He wasn't even royal, he was a general who married into the family. Usurped the throne after King Tut died." She looked around, seeing the others' puzzled expressions. "What, don't you guys follow Zahi Hawass? I don't believe it, that guy is all over the TV. I knew those National Geographic specials would be worth it someday."

"Za who?" said Rick, trying and failing to look clueless. "OK, don't hit me, I know who he is." He thought for a

275

moment. "A minor pharaoh... huh. I didn't know that about Horemheb before. Look, this is another thing you shouldn't mention, OK? One of the guys I was buddies with at Great Lakes works for the FBI now. I gave him a hard drive with the Pong virus on it and he's been looking into it. Those guys have way better tools than I do. If you all will excuse me, I want to call him right now and tell him about this."

"We are the mighty virus killer team!" said Dave, with a big grin.

"Yeah baby!" Rick raised his empty cup in salute. "Rue de day, suckas. We gonna *git* you." He got up and walked down by the lake away from the picnic grounds and flipped open his phone.

The wind swirled and blew Ruth's empty plate off the table. "I think that's a signal," she said, getting up to chase after it. She noticed for the first time that the sky was beginning to cloud over. "We should move somewhere else before the rain starts. You guys want to stop by my place for a while?"

"No, you guys come to my house," said Eleanor. "I want to show you the quilt."

They shuttled the debris to the trash, and when Rick returned he pushed what remained of the charcoal carefully to the back of the grill with the spatula Paula had packed for the burgers and doused it with water from the lake, as Eleanor put the rest of the utensils and leftovers in her mother's big plastic bag. And then they all stood for a moment, smiling, in silent understanding. Yes, all kinds of things were going to be all right.

⊠⊠⊠

Ruth and Rick sat on the couch. Phydeaux, wagging madly, followed Dave toward a chair, but Eleanor put a stop to that. "No, you stay right where you are."

"Who, me?" Dave asked, stopping dead in the center of the room. Phydeaux turned his head from side to side, clearly confused. Dave reached down to pat him.

"You. Stay right there. You're my model."

"The things we do for love," Dave said, trying and failing to sound world-weary. "Go on, dog, *you* get to sit over there." Phydeaux sat down where he was, by Dave's feet. Dave patted him again. "OK, have it your way, you dumb dog, but I bet you'll wish you'd moved." The dog's tail thumped the floor.

"Quit fussing," called Eleanor from the bedroom.

"I'm not fussing!"

"Yes you are. Just stand there, it'll be over before you know it."

"I don't like the sound of that," said Dave, as Eleanor returned to the room with the quilt bundled up in her arms.

"Hush. Hold your arms out."

Dave complied, and Eleanor draped him with the quilt. He held one edge of it up over his head with both hands so most of it was on view to the rest of the room. "I can't see a darn thing from back here. It's all white!"

"Oh, like you didn't look at it when we were pinning it. Quit fussing. I'll show it to you in just a minute."

"Wow, El," said Ruth. "That's gorgeous." The quilt had pinwheel shapes of dark blue flowered calico, and echoing triangles of lighter blue, with cream colored fabric around them. The border was made of thin stripes of plain dark blue fabric surrounding ribbons of the two calico colors.

277

"Hold it up just a little higher please, Dave? I want them to see the bottom border."

"This is as high as it goes."

"Just stand still then." Eleanor picked up the bottom of the quilt and Ruth and Rick leaned forward to see "Dutchman's Puzzle," the date, and Eleanor's initials embroidered in red on one of the dark blue stripes.

"It's perfect, El," said Rick. "You'll have to show me some of your other quilts sometime. You're an artist."

Eleanor blushed. "I don't know about that. It's just cut-up fabric."

"Right. It's sewing it back together where the art comes in."

"Can I put this down now? My arms are getting tired," Dave said, as plaintively as he could manage, from behind the quilt.

"I suppose. I just thought one Dutchman's puzzle deserved another."

Dave emerged from behind the quilt and folded it neatly, admiring the colored side as he did. "I'm no puzzle. You got me pretty well figured out."

Thunder rumbled outside.

"Yipe," said Ruth, "we better scoot before it starts pouring or we'll be here all night."

Eleanor went to the window to look across the street. Paula's car was in her driveway. "I better call Mom and get her to send the kids back. Would you guys like to borrow my car?"

"Or I can run you home and you can come get the Harley in the morning," Dave suggested.

Rick took a quick look out the window. "Hasn't started raining yet. We should try to make it home before it starts because the bike's rain cover is at Ruth's place. Thanks, El, and you were a great model, Dave."

"I keep discovering new talents every day," said Dave, setting the quilt bundle on the couch and following Ruth and Rick through the kitchen as Eleanor picked up the phone. "You sure you don't want to stay here till the storm blows over or let me take you home? I'm sure we could find some kind of cover for the Harley."

"No, thanks, we'll make it OK if we hurry. See you later!"

As Ruth put on her helmet in the driveway, she said "I had to bite my tongue to keep from asking Eleanor how that quilt looked on the bed. I was afraid she'd take it the wrong way."

Rick laughed. "Oh? Heaven forbid, little sister. We can't be making naughty suggestions to our friends."

⊠⊠⊠

The computer-camp shopping trip was somewhat less than successful, at least as far as the twins were concerned. Eleanor handed Rick the official list of supplies and the car keys, and Rachel and Andrew spent most of the trip squabbling with their father about what items the camp had obviously forgotten to include, but which they nevertheless considered essential. "I told you, the camp will provide you with all that," said Rick, trying to keep the level of exasperation down below explosion level, after the fourth or fifth suggestion that they make a trip out of town to a big store that sold laptop computers and software.

"Yeah," said Andrew, "but we'll have to share the camp stuff. We'll learn better if we bring our own."

Rick scowled at his son for a moment. He'd always sworn he'd never use any of those irritating parental phrases from his childhood, but enough was enough. Time to go for the gold. "Do you guys have any idea how much one laptop computer costs, let alone two?"

"You can put it on a credit card, can't you?" said Andrew, hopefully.

His father blinked. "Is that the way your mom does it?"

Both twins looked down. "No," said Rachel, in a very subdued tone of voice.

"Well, then?" Rick tried to sound Parental.

"How were we supposed to know you weren't different?" Andrew demanded.

"Now you know. Let's get a move on. We still need to go buy you some underwear."

Rick walked off quickly, so he could claim he hadn't heard what was being muttered behind him.

When they got home, laden with bags full of boring new clothes and shoes, some new duffel bags and the new backpacks that had been Rick's only concession to endless pestering, Dave and Eleanor were sitting in lawn chairs in the back yard, drinking iced coffee. "Go put that stuff away," said Eleanor, correctly interpreting the twins' expressions, "*neatly*, and then we'll cook some burgers on the grill. I got Granny's secret recipe while you were shopping."

"Whoa! What did you do?"

"Don't shout, Rachel! I just had to ask her the right way, that's all. Go put the stuff away now. You guys can help set the picnic table when you're done." When her children were safely inside, she asked Rick "How did it go?"

"About what you'd expect from kids who got clothes and not computers."

"That bad, huh?" She laughed. "Well, the three of you seem to have survived it."

"Oh man," said Rick, "talk about a parental baptism by fire!"

Dave made a great show of looking Rick over for scorch marks. "I think you'll live."

"Only if I get a couple extra burgers. Get a move on, El."

"I'll barbecue your butt if you don't watch your step."

"Ha. I think the twins got it halfway there already."

"Go on," said Eleanor. "I bet you loved it."

Rick laughed, and lowered his voice conspiratorially. "Don't tell them this, but I wouldn't have missed it for the world."

"You're on your way to dad-hood, then."

"Yeah," said Rick, with a contented smile. "Yeah."

Chapter 25
Winding Ways

June

R ick set the box on the post office counter. "Good
morning. I'd like to send this by parcel post."

"Hope it's not a birthday present," said the clerk with a
smile.

"Nah. Just sending myself all the stuff I don't want to
carry with me. It doesn't matter if it takes a month to get
there."

"Such faith you have in us," laughed the clerk, sliding
the box onto the scale.

Rick came out of the post office feeling somewhat off
balance. Now that it was almost time to leave, he wished
more than anything else that he didn't have to. He shook
his head, remembering how scared he'd been about getting here in the first place. No, not scared, exactly. But not
in any hurry to roll into town. At least now he knew for
sure what his decision would be when they came after him
to re-enlist. Nope, going back home to be with my family.
What a nice sound that had.

He parked the Harley behind the store and went
upstairs to put his jacket and helmet away. As he stepped
through the door, he looked around the apartment as

though he'd never seen it before, trying to fix all the details in his mind. The cot and sleeping bag were going to Paula's house after he left, since space was so limited here and Paula often had guests. He'd already started setting up the laptop for Ruth. He checked the time, went to wash his hands and made a quick lunch.

When he got to the shop, Ruth, Chet, and Brad were working, but all of them were relaxed enough to look up from what they were doing and greet him. "All set?" Ruth asked.

"Yeah, got the box sent off and put gas in the bike. I was just thinking how funny it was that I dragged my feet so much on getting here, and now I don't want to go back."

"There's no place like home, there's no place like home..." said Brad, falsetto.

"Damn, I should go find some ruby slippers before I leave town," said Rick with a laugh.

"Be fun tryin' to find 'em in your size," said Chet, turning back around to his bench.

"I'll try the BX when I get back to Norfolk."

"Somehow," said Ruth, "I don't think that'd get past 'don't ask, don't tell.'" Everyone laughed.

"Anything you need me to take care of back here?" said Rick, looking around. "If not, I need to run over and see Dave for about half an hour."

"No more'n the usual crapdoodle an' cat hair," said Chet, poking into the depths of a laser printer.

"You handle that stuff so well, Chet, I'd just be in the way. I'll see you guys later."

As he crossed the square headed toward the Caldwell & Talbott offices, he saw Peter walking along the south side away from him. Good, he'd timed his visit perfectly.

Nevertheless, he ducked into a store doorway and watched to make sure Peter kept going to the corner and then off the square and out of sight. Then he continued to his destination.

"Hi Dave, ready to catch some squirrels?"

Dave raised his eyebrows. "You really think something squirrely is going on?"

"Well, we'll find out, won't we?"

Rick sat down at Peter's computer, inserted his flash drive and pressed the power button. Dave stood behind him and watched with interest. It wasn't the usual screen that came up first. "Special tools," said Rick. "Adam didn't give him admin access, but if he's the virus creator he'd know how to get around that without leaving tracks, and since you saw him pull out a flash drive, he might have."

"That's Martian to me, you understand," said Dave. "I didn't even know what alt-tab was till Adam explained it."

"Well, there's no reason you'd know about what I'm doing right now even if you'd been using computers for a while. This is something not exactly available to just any-one with a credit card... ah HAH!"

"What?" A cryptic list was scrolling slowly down the screen.

"Can you get Adam on the phone? He's going to want to hear about this right away."

⌗ ⌗ ⌗

Despite Rick's protests, Eleanor and the twins had in-sisted on throwing him a going-away party. "You just want to celebrate because you're getting rid of me," he told the twins, who made a great show of agreeing with him and then collapsed in giggles. Nevertheless, he showed up at Eleanor's house at the appointed time late Sunday after-noon to find Eleanor, Paula, the twins, Ruth, Adam, Dave, and Chet waiting for him in the back yard. "Holy smokes, Chet, you're outside in the sunlight, aren't you afraid you'll turn to dust and blow away?"

"You're the one's gonna get a stake through the heart if you don't watch your step, sonny," said Chet, who was wearing a disreputable looking old straw hat and holding a bottle of beer. Rick held up his hands in mock surrender and went to get his own bottle. He was surprised to find that it wasn't the usual American swill but something from a microbrewery he'd never heard of.

"What is this?" he asked the gathering at large.

"Give it a try," said Adam. "I don't touch the stuff myself, but I have it on good authority that it doesn't degrease engines and strip paint."

Rick flipped off the bottle cap and took a sip. He looked at the bottle with new appreciation. Then he took a good long swallow. "Whoa. Yeah, whoever told you this stuff tastes good wasn't kidding. I need to make a note of the name."

"I should let you know that I had to have it shipped in from the brewery in Oregon, you can't just go buy it anywhere."

"Oh," said Rick. "Showing off again, rich guy?" But it was clear he was joking.

"Talk to your sister. She won't let me shower her with diamonds and trips around the world. Hell, she won't even let me take her away to Chicago. So I have to drown everyone else's sorrows in premium beer." He raised a can of ginger ale in a salute. Rick walked over to clink with him. Everyone else raised their drinks as well. "To Rick," said Adam. "Glad we got a fresh start, sorry you're leaving, y'all come back now, hear?"

"Oh, now I get it, you're rich 'cause you're really Jed Clampett!" The adults laughed and the twins looked at each other with matching "who understands grownups" expressions. "Never mind, kids, it was one of those jokes you have to be old enough to understand."

"A dumb joke, then," said Andrew, and quickly scurried to the other side of the yard. Rick made a show of starting after him, but went only as far as one of the lawn chairs, where he sat down to properly sip and appreciate the beer. Once his father was safely sitting down, Andrew edged closer. "Is that a tattoo on your arm?" he asked.

"You bet," said Rick, rolling up his sleeve. "Look, I got twin fishies."

Rachel hurried over and put a careful finger on the brilliantly colored koi. "Really? Was that for us?"

"Really for you."

"Oh, that's cool!" said Rachel.

Andrew came over and looked closely. Then he gave his father a big grin. "Way cool," he said.

"Glad you like it," said his dad.

"Hey, Mom!" Andrew called to Eleanor, "Since Rick has a tattoo for us, I need to get one for him, right?"

Eleanor gave Rick a glare. "Oh, thanks a lot!"

Rick laughed. "Can't do it till you're 18, kiddo, and between now and then we'll have figured out how to talk you out of it."

"That's what *you* think," said Andrew, running off to the other side of the yard.

After a moment, Paula came over and sat down beside Rick.

"You're going to have to be on your toes to keep ahead of those two," she said with a smile.

"I can tell that's the voice of experience speaking."

"I gather it won't be all that long before you'll be back here getting more experience yourself?"

"Oh yeah. I made up my mind, I'm coming back. I thought I had a good life till I realized what I was missing."

"I'm so glad," she said, and patted his hand. "I mean, that you're coming back. How long till you leave the Navy?"

"A little less than two years, but who's counting?" He grinned.

"Oh, I wouldn't be so quick to grin if I were you," said Paula. "That means the twins will be thirteen when you get back, and you'll really be in for it. Torpedo practice will seem like a walk in the park in comparison."

"I don't mess with torpedoes, I'm just a lowly computer mechanic. Maybe I should change my specialty, quick!" He looked over to where the twins were playing keep-away with Phydeaux and a ratty, tooth-marked red Frisbee. "Is thirteen really so bad?"

"It varies from kid to kid, I think, but you'd better be prepared just the same."

"Be prepared for what?" asked Eleanor, coming up to sit on the other side of Rick.

"When he gets back and the twins are having the thirteenies," said her mother.

"Oh lordy. Listen, you'd *better* come back. That's going to take all the grownups we can muster."

"I don't remember being bad at thirteen."

"Ruth?" Eleanor called. "Your brother doesn't remember being bad when he was thirteen."

"He's got a memory loss, then," Ruth called back. "He was a royal pain."

"Was not," said Rick, indignantly, and stuck his tongue out at his sister, who stuck her tongue out in return and went back to talking with Adam, Chet and Dave while Dave prepared the grill.

"Kids," Eleanor called to the twins, "get that Frisbee away from the dog and go wash your hands. We'll be eating soon." She looked over at Dave, who was just beginning to lay burgers on the grill, for confirmation. He nodded. It took a short tug-of-war to separate Phydeaux from the Frisbee, but after that, the twins racketed into the kitchen to do as they'd been told.

Nearly an hour later, Rick put his paper plate down beside his chair on the grass and gave a contented sigh. "The burgers were fantastic as always, Mrs. Ward."

"You can call me Paula, now that you're back in my good graces, and I didn't make the burgers, Eleanor did."

Rick turned to look at Eleanor. "No end to your talents, is there?"

She laughed and brushed that off. "Listen, if it took all these years to pry that recipe out of my own mother, I must not be talented enough."

"Good enough for me," said Rick, seriously, and reached out a hand. After a moment, she smiled and took it. Dave, who was sitting beside Eleanor on the other side, smiled too.

"Ooooo," said Andrew, "look, Rachel, they're getting mushy!" His sister rolled her eyes.

"Mushy? That's not mushy. I'll show you mushy," said Rick, getting up and pulling Eleanor up with him. He gathered her quickly into his arms and kissed her. She tensed for just a moment, then kissed him back with enthusiasm. When they pulled apart, laughing, there was a round of whoops and applause from everyone else in the yard. "Now, come here, you two," he said, pointing at the twins. "It's group hug time!"

Rachel was willing to move forward, but Andrew pulled her back. "No mushy stuff!"

"If you don't come over here on your own, Andrew, I'll chase you down and hug you anyway," said his father, trying hard not to laugh.

"Oh, all *right!*" said his son, dragging himself across the yard as slowly as he thought he could get away with. Rick gathered the twins and their mother into his arms and held on tight, eyes closed in absolute happiness.

⊠⊠⊠

Very early the next morning, Rick packed the last of his belongings into the saddlebags on the Harley and turned to hug his sister.

"You ride carefully, please," said Ruth. "I don't want some dimwit running you off the road between here and there."

"I'm glad you know the problems would be some other guy's fault."

Ruth put her hands on her hips. "Don't make me change my mind about that, biker boy."

"When I come back I'll drive a station wagon, how's that?"

"Make it a minivan and you're on."

"A minivan!" He held up his hands in mock horror. "Noooo! Anything but that! A fate worse than death!"

"Big macho dude," said his sister, shaking her head. "You'd better get going to avoid the major rush hour on the square."

"Yeah, ten cars going the same way, I'd never get through them. Seriously, Ruthie, this has absolutely been the best vacation of my life, and I'll be back as fast as I can manage it. I've got more leave next year and I'll never be reluctant about taking it again."

They hugged each other again, wordlessly. And then he started up the Harley and rode slowly away. Ruth walked around the corner and watched till he was out of sight.

The shop seemed very quiet and empty that morning, even though Chet and Ruth both did their best to carry on normal conversations and get their work done just as always. Both of them kept looking over at the table where Rick had usually sat. Charlie sat patiently by the door, waiting. "He'll be back next summer, Chet," said Ruth. "He promised."

"I know that. I got ears." Chet didn't sound nearly as grumpy as usual, though.

Brad came in after lunchtime and looked around. "There's definitely something missing," he said. "I hate to say it, but I miss Rick already."

"We all do," said Ruth, just as the bell on the front door chimed. She went out front to see who it was.

A tall, auburn-haired man in a dark suit and tie stood at the counter. "Hi," he said. "I wondered if you could fix this MP3 player for me?" But what he held up was his FBI credentials in a leather wallet. He pointed to his name—Jack Herhold—and Ruth's eyes widened.

"Rick's friend?" she mouthed, silently. He nodded. "Uh, sure," she said, "I think we can fix that. What did you do to it?"

"Dropped it on the floor, unfortunately." He pointed to the back and mouthed "Brad?"

Ruth's mouth dropped open. She managed to nod. "I'll, um, I'll have to open it up to see if there's anything inside that can be fixed. Can you leave it here, and I'll, um, call you tomorrow?"

"No problem," he said, slipping through the curtain. Ruth trailed behind.

"Brad DeWitt?" Jack said, as another man in a dark suit stepped into the shop through the back door. Brad jumped to his feet, but one look at the two men and he knew he had no options. He sighed and sat back down.

"I'm Jack Herhold from the FBI, and that's my partner Scott Carmichael. We'd like to have a talk with you. Will you come with us, please?" He took a set of handcuffs off his belt.

"You won't need those," said Brad.

"Sorry, it's procedure," said Jack, and sounded as though he really might be sorry he had to do it. "Scott parked the car right outside the back door, though, so if we move quickly I don't think anyone will see."

"Small mercies," said Brad, and put his hands behind his back.

Epilogue

July

Dear Dad,

How are you? I am fine. I'm sorry I called you names. I am glad I finally got to meet you and hope you'll come back again.

Computer camp was amazing. It gave me lots of new ideas. But I don't get enough time on Mom's computer for the things I want to try and her computer is too slow anyway. Don't you think I need a laptop with a super fast processor and a big hard drive and lots of memory? I don't want to forget all the stuff I learned so I need to practice till next summer because Adam said he'd send us back next year. Don't you agree?

I hope you haven't gone out to sea yet and can write me back.

Love,
Andrew

Dear Andrew,

Nice try. Your mom's in charge of deciding who gets what computer and when, and I already suggested a nice desktop model that will be perfect for doing your homework. (It won't have internet access, the better to lead you not into temptation.) Somehow I don't think computer camp or sixth grade require a gamer model laptop, but I like the way you proposed to get one. We'll have lots to talk about next time I get to Lyric. In the meantime, you'd better be darn sure to stay on your mom's good side, because the computer purchase is going to be 100% her decision. I won't get a say in it at all, so asking me to talk her into changing her mind won't work. I know who's boss!

I go back out to sea in three weeks and we won't be able to communicate while I'm on duty, but that doesn't mean I don't want to hear more about what you're doing. Just keep writing and I promise I'll answer all your mail when I get back.

Love,
Dad

Dear Dad,

I'm glad I finally know who you are. I hope next time you come to visit we can talk more because I will be used to the idea of having a dad I can talk with by then. I hope you don't mind me saying it was weird meeting you for the first time. It was great to get to hug you at the party. I hope we are like you thought we would be. It is weird saying Aunt Ruth, too!

At computer camp we used Photoshop and Dreamweaver and I learned how to do a lot of neat stuff. Mom says they won't run on her computer. Did you see her computer? Is that really true? I didn't think her computer was that bad. Can you talk with her about it?

Well, I can't think of anything more to write. I hope you can write back.

Love,
Rachel

Dear Rachel,

I hope we talk more too when I come back (and I will!) You and your brother are the most amazing kids I ever met, and that's the truth. I wish we'd had more time together after we found each other, but I will try to make up for that in the future.

Photoshop and Dreamweaver are very expensive, and to be honest, they are more than even most adults need for everyday use. Your mom and I talked about the possibility of getting you and Andrew your own computers (but don't get too excited because we also were unanimous that they will not be connected to the internet!) and if your mom gives her permission we can talk about buying other software that will be just as good and a lot less expensive. It is all up to your mom, so not messing around with the computer you've got already would go a long way toward making a case for having your own.

I will be going back out to sea soon and won't be able to communicate for a while, but I hope you'll keep writing and telling me what you're up to. I will answer any letters you send me as soon as I get back.

Love,

Dad

Dear Rick,

The kids are all full of energy after getting back from computer camp, so I suggested that they use some of it to write to you, and I was a mean old Mom and made them use pens and paper to keep them occupied for a while. They've just come to hand over the envelopes, all signed and sealed. They have already been dropping not so subtle hints about this and that computer and software. I'm glad I wrote down your suggestions (and thank you so much for arranging to have the bank send me the debit card... I am still somewhat staggered at the idea that I can actually just go ahead and buy the computers before school starts, although I haven't told the kids or I would never hear the end of it).

As it turns out, you were absolutely right about Horemheb and Mintaka. We haven't got the full story yet, even with every tongue in town wagging about it, but from what I gather from the most reliable sources, apparently there was some kind of ridiculous longstanding grudge between the guy who started Horemheb and the married couple who own Mintaka. Something that's been festering since they were in college together years ago. The Horemheb guy apparently paid a hefty bribe to Mintaka's top tech person to loosen up the security (there may be more to it than that, but the investigators have a ways to go yet) and guess who they got to write the viruses—Brad, Ruth's part-time helper! Oh, come to think of it, that's probably not a surprise, I'm sure Ruth or your FBI buddy (or both) told you all about it. She and Chet about fell off their chairs when the FBI showed up at the store. Brad put that pharaoh message in the virus because he was ticked that they brushed off his demand for more money, like you thought. And I guess you already know that poor Peter was only looking at porn on the office computer. After Adam showed him the keylogger and scared the crap out of him he let him off with a warning. Peter's still working in the office, so I guess he's learned his lesson.

At any rate, it sure knocked the gossip about you and me off the local grapevine's front page, so now I don't have to worry about who's pointing at me behind my back at the grocery store. (I am laughing just thinking about that, and yes, I'm joking.)

Dave said that if I talked with you, to say hi from him. He has been unbelievably busy these days because Adam and his partner (whom I barely know to look at and who doesn't show up around these parts more than once or twice a year) are talking with the town council about building a senior housing complex out near the golf course. There are a ton of permits and reports and who knows what-all to be dealt with before they even begin. Adam's already said that Dave will have final approval on the plans and gave him a raise in advance. It's amazing that Adam finally turned into a human being—of course, Ruth had more to do with that than anyone. You and your sister have a lot to be proud of, probably more than you know.

Instead of taking a vacation while the twins were at camp, we decided to take a trip to Yosemite in the fall. Neither one of us has been there, so it'll be our first big adventure together. Mom's practically pushing us out the door already!

I know I said it before, but I'll say it again—I am glad you came back. And I hope it was just the first of many visits to come.

Love (and I mean that),

Eleanor

Dear El,

Aw shucks folks, I'm speechless.

I read the kids' letters first, and they are both very clever—I can see as a Dad I am going to have to work my butt off to stay ahead of them. I told them that we'd talked about buying computers for them but there would be no internet connection and they'd better darn well keep you happy between now and then or the deal is off. Rachel asked about software and I said I had a few ideas about that, and I'll look into it and let you know what I think would work best for them. You should probably buy two copies of everything so Andrew won't feel left out (and I'm sure both of them will be bugging you for their own web site shortly thereafter, but I know you'll know a million good reasons why not).

Ruth told me a bit about the Mintaka deal. I'm sure eventually my FBI friend will give me the full scoop, once they've sorted it all out. I feel sorry for Brad, who was a nice guy and who got badly used, but it wasn't like he didn't know what he was getting into. Remember my Grandma saying "Lie down with dogs, get up with fleas"? She had a stupid saying for every situation, didn't she?

My very best to Dave, who was long overdue for good things in life. Including you. Yosemite sounds wonderful. I've never been there either, so you'll have to be sure to tell me all about it.

I will be headed out to sea shortly and won't be able to communicate for a while, but please keep writing. We make a good team. Less than two years to go before I come back to Lyric to stay. I can't wait.

Oh, and the next time I send you flowers, I won't be too chicken to say they're from me.

Love (and I mean that too)

Rick

⊠⊠⊠

"Isn't it too warm for that?" said Dave, looking at the bed.

"What, you don't think it's appropriate?" said Eleanor, turning down the covers.

"Still think I'm a puzzle, do you?"

"Let's get under the quilt and figure that out."

Acknowledgements

Authors put some of themselves into every character they write (whether we realize we're doing it or not) but the events in the lives of the citizens of Lyric are fiction. The fact that two of my brothers are named Dave and Rick is just coincidence. Really. Dave Van Meer and Rick Peyton told me their names long before I ever opened up a Scrivener screen and started typing. (And I'm sure my brother John is still waiting for the other shoe to drop.)

Special thanks to my friend Bonnie Allison for pointing out quite firmly that someone in Lyric ought to have a tattoo. She was right!

And thanks to the denizens of CompuServe's Books and Writers Community, who were very helpful indeed with critiques of an early draft—especially my friend Carol K. who wasn't shy about telling me (in so many words) that Dave was a wimp. Dave has a new lease on life as a result. Thanks also to Ron Wodaski, who gave me invaluable advice on the cover design.

Thanks again to my husband Jim and my son Daniel who put up with my sometimes-exasperating lack of connection to the real world while this book was being created, and to my daughter "Blinkie" for wielding her red pen with skill and vigor. Deniz Bevan and Heather Coman are two of the world's most able editors, and I thank them both for catching all the stuff I didn't see.

Like Eleanor, I didn't know that Mariner's Compass was not a beginner's quilt block, and that's where I started, too. I managed it, on the back of a shirt, no less, and I fell in love with the process of quilting. Dutchman's Puzzle is a real quilt block pattern and it's the first one I pieced on a large scale (although unlike Eleanor I never finished the quilt). My encyclopedia of quilt blocks notes that it's also called Dutchman's Wheel or Wild Goose Chase, both of which would work for Dave Van Meer. And there's a variant called Return of the Swallows, which suits Dave as well. You can see a fragment of my Dutchman's Puzzle quilt on the book cover.

And most of all, thanks to the people who run National Novel Writing Month, where this manuscript got its start and during which it finally got through to me that this book's predecessor could be finished after all.

www.ingramcontent.com/pod-product-compliance
Lightning Source LLC
Chambersburg PA
CBHW020227260626
47156CB00002B/579